I0588396

REVIEWS

"Loved it! Very Riveting! Well drawn characters with an intriguing story line. It's a "must read" science fiction masterpiece!"

"This superb science fiction tale takes a look at what people will do to obtain something they want. Here, the best and the worst of humanity are on display. Readers will find themselves pulled into the telling of this tale from the outset. Believable characters, an inventive plot, and a strong sense of place all work together to make this book unputdownable. Short chapters keep the action moving; suspense builds as Michel's business rival, Yan Huen and his for-hire spy, Devlin Archer, try to steal the secrets of the cure and of the mysterious Ouroboros. Science fiction aficionados will find much to appreciate here… don't miss this one. Highly recommended."

"This book was so much fun. From the plot to the smaller scientific ideas surrounding the story, it kept me highly entertained."

"Masterful piece of sci-fi thriller fiction. Brilliant character development, well-paced action, and truly touching emotional moments throughout. One of my favorite fiction reads of the last few years!"

"This was a fun story that kept me guessing what was going to happen next. It had an entertaining, almost spy-thriller type of plot that I could see being adapted for the big screen. I won't ruin the ending, but the neat part is that its proposed solution to all human sickness could actually work, which I wasn't expecting. Fun!"

"A prescient thrill-ride, brimming with futuristic inventions, espionage, and an ending I never saw coming. Great read and a real page-turner - I can see this being made into a movie one day, or at the very least, a blueprint for futurists. Loved it!"

"The world-building is spectacular. Clark does his due diligence with his research to ensure that each technological advancement feels real. Several things implemented in *Hadron's Run* are simply clever, like using "Solar Shades" to halt global warming. As the plot progresses, there is an anticipation of "what's the next big thing," as the reader follows each character through the lottery process. The payoff is exquisite. Not too much, not too little and the antagonist earns the comeuppance in the most satisfactory way."

HADRON'S RUN

BY
WOODY CLARK

© Copyright 2024 Woody Clark

All rights reserved. No part of this book may be reproduced in any form or by any electronic or mechanical means, including information storage and retrieval systems, without written permission from the author, except in the case of a reviewer, who may quote brief passages embodied in critical articles or in a review.

Trademarked names may appear throughout this book. Rather than use a trademark symbol with every occurrence of a trademarked name, names are used in an editorial fashion, with no intention of infringement of the respective owner's trademark.

The information in this book is distributed on an "as is" basis, without warranty. Although every precaution has been taken in the preparation of this work, neither the author nor the publisher shall have any liability to any person or entity with respect to any loss or damage caused or alleged to be caused directly or indirectly by the information contained in this book.

This is a work of fiction. Names, characters, places, and incidents either are the product of the author's imagination or are used fictitiously, and any resemblance to actual persons, living or dead, events, or locales is entirely coincidental.

r25-0618

"Want to change the world? There's nothing to it."

~ Willy Wonka

PROLOGUE

Michel Bouchon, the world's first trillionaire, earned that distinction when his invention, the Everwake pill, became the first medication in history to be ingested by nearly every living person on the planet. Taken once a day, the supplement fully oxygenated the body's bloodstream and in turn, allowed mankind to eliminate its greatest impediment: sleep.

With eight additional waking hours, the human race became more productive than ever before and took innovative leaps at a blistering pace. Because of his ingenuity, the fifty-eight-year-old's creation was labeled a "Game Changer" in human evolution and was subsequently compared to the invention of the wheel.

However, with increased human activity, came the unintended consequence of even faster climate change. Faced with rising ocean levels, depleted farmlands, and civil unrest, Michel set forth to solve the scourge of global warming.

And did.

After years of work and at great expense to his personal fortune, Michel announced the release of the Orbital Solar Shade. A satellite positioned to mirror the Earth's orbit around the sun, the OSS measured the exact distance needed for its 10,000-square-foot sail to cast a fixed shadow onto the Arctic. The almost imperceptible change in temperature created by the shade was the precise amount needed to cool the massive ice sheet and prevent further erosion.

With the planet's temperature stabilized, Michel was labeled a hero, a savior, and to some, The Messiah.

Michel's life soon began to unravel, however, when it was announced that due to his work on the OSS, he had been diagnosed with an aggressive form of cancer. The disease was said to be ravaging his body and, tragically, had left him with little time to live.

For the next several years, Michel was not seen or heard from, and rampant speculation about his fate varied wildly. Conspiracy theories abounded, but most assumed he had succumbed to his illness in quiet isolation. Begrudgingly, the world mourned, and slowly began to accept the fact that the man who had saved the planet had been lost forever.

Until now.

CHAPTER 1

"By the time I finish this sentence, three weeks will have passed."

As Devlin Archer digested what he had just heard, he suddenly realized the futility of every maneuver he had devised. The clandestine drops, false passports, and meticulously chosen safehouses were now worthless.

More importantly, though, so was the money.

He'd never again see the man who had hired him or a dime of the millions he'd been promised.

With his breathing becoming shallow and his pulse quickening, Devlin began to grasp the urgency of his situation. If he didn't escape quickly, he would be trapped in this underground tomb, forced to spend an eternity here with these people.

And most likely, to die with them.

Struggling to formulate a plan, Devlin's mind raced and invariably drifted back to the beginning - the moment when everything had, ironically, been put into *motion*.

CHAPTER 2

Dressed in firefighter's gear, Devlin waited patiently inside the car he'd stolen earlier that morning. Several blocks from Bouchon Industries' headquarters in the heart of Silicon Valley, the underworld's most insidious spy calmly surveyed the employees scurrying through the building's main entrance. Like most structures in the tech capital, the exterior was futuristic in appearance and massive in size. Predominantly glass, the company's façade reflected the sun like a beacon, standing out amongst the equally mammoth buildings surrounding it.

In his early fifties, Devlin Archer lit a cigarette, letting the nicotine steady his nerves. Atop his six-foot frame, he fastidiously maintained his light brown hair recently flecked with gray. Clean-shaven with an aristocratic nose, he exuded unbridled confidence through his steady breathing, contoured jawline, and deeply cleft chin.

Classically handsome, the operative's most striking feature, however, was his piercing light blue eyes. They radiated from his face like a wolf's, commanding attention and submissive obedience. His eyes had been his most valuable tool on countless occasions, opening more doors than his light fingers or legendary hacking skills.

From his vantage point in the parked car, Devlin could clearly make out the "Bouchon Industries" lettering that adorned the roof of the building. His face broke into a sly smile, knowing that the pending diversion would take place atop the twenty-story structure.

He took another puff and peered out the window, gazing towards the fog-filled marine layer. His relief was palpable as he saw that the haze had settled into the Bay Area, just as it typically did this time of year. Pleased with his foresight, he knew that if he couldn't see the drones hidden by the thick mist, neither could anyone else.

Devlin leaned back in the driver's seat, reminiscing about the countless missions like this one he'd undertaken over the previous decades. As with those, every detail of this job had been meticulously planned down to the nano-second. Sure, there had been times when things hadn't gone as smoothly as he would have liked, but that was to be expected when assassinating Sudan's head of state or installing malware into the mainframe of Indonesia's largest biotech firm.

In the end, he'd always found a way to make things work.

Always.

The most significant difference between those jobs and this one, however, was simple: the size of the payday. Blackmailing Fortune 500 company CEOs or instigating regime changes in war-torn countries had always paid handsomely, but for reasons only his employer understood, this commission had taken his compensation to an entirely different level. The speed and urgency with which this assignment had manifested had certainly caught his attention, but not nearly as much as the massive cryptocurrency payments that had flooded his blockchain accounts.

The watch alarm began to beep on his wrist, anchoring Devlin to the present. He quickly regathered his thoughts and focused on the task at hand. Leaning over the passenger's seat next to him, he opened up his laptop and entered a few commands. Concentrating intensely, within moments he saw the message he was waiting for, "Drones Targeting."

Devlin let out a deep breath of relief as a timer on the screen began to countdown from five minutes. Expertly synchronizing his watch to it, he closed the laptop and left it on the passenger's seat.

Exiting the car, Devlin grabbed a five-gallon canister of gasoline from the trunk. He methodically began to pour fuel on top of and inside of the car, careful not to let the cigarette that hung from his mouth get too close. Taking one last drag, he inhaled deeply until the end burned bright, then tossed the butt inside of the car, ensuring he left the door open so that the ensuing fire would have the air it needed.

Devlin slung an oxygen tank over his shoulders, donned his firefighter's helmet, and pulled on his gloves. With an air of calm determination, he strode towards Bouchon Industries' Headquarters, unfazed by the vehicle erupting into flames behind him.

Approaching the front door of the building, Devlin paused for a moment to check his watch. Waiting for the timer to count down from nineteen to eighteen to seventeen, he slowly reached for the door handle and entered the administrative office.

Once inside, Devlin glanced at the enormity of the lobby and the massive crystal chandeliers that hung from the rafters, fifty feet above the entryway. Replete with white leather couches, workers scampered along the lobby's marble floor to elevators lining the walls, their steps echoing in the open space. As expected on a typical workday, the inside of the Bouchon Industries' corporate headquarters was bustling with activity, just as Devlin had planned.

Devlin strode towards the security checkpoint with purpose, where a large security guard rose to greet him.

"Where's the fire?" the security officer asked incredulously.

Devlin looked skyward, pointed, and said, "The roof."

Confused, the security guard looked up and said, "I haven't heard about any fire on the –."

Suddenly, a massive explosion from above rocked the building, and the entire structure began to shake. The interior lighting flickered as the five-ton chandeliers slowly swayed in large arcs from one side of the atrium to the other. Stunned, everyone in the lobby froze and glanced around in nervous bewilderment.

"Get everyone out of here, *now*," Devlin commanded the security guard.

In shock, the guard remained motionless as his mind raced, trying to process what was happening. Without warning, a second violent explosion shook the building. Screams rang out as the swaying chandeliers forcibly collided, dropping massive shards of crystal onto the marble floor below.

The lobby quickly devolved into mayhem as shrieking office workers covered their heads and bolted toward the building's front door.

"I said NOW!" Devlin ordered.

The glare of Devlin's steel blue eyes jolted the security guard back to the moment. He pulled out his walkie-talkie and yelled into it, "We've got a fire on the roof! I repeat, a fire on the roof! Evacuate the building!"

Still confused and unsure how to proceed, the guard turned to Devlin for guidance and pleaded, "Who should I call?"

"Everyone's on their way!" Devlin shouted over the cries of the office workers that jostled past him, "Just get everyone out of here!"

Another detonation concussed the building. After locking his panicked eyes with Devlin for a moment, the security guard quickly spun around and pressed a large red button on the wall behind his desk. Deafening alarms began blaring throughout the entire building while red and white lights flashed along the walls. Within moments, workers streamed out of their offices and swarmed the security check point, trying to exit the building as quickly as they could. Surrounded by a mass of white-collared employees, Devlin pushed through the crowd and became lost in the throng of bodies.

Devlin wove through the pandemonium of frightened office workers and raced up a crowded stairwell. He moved with resolve down a labyrinth of hallways until he reached the office he had mapped out weeks before. Staring intently at its door, he became impatient as the seconds ticked by and countless workers pushed past.

"Come on…" Devlin whispered to himself as he continued to glare.

After a few more moments, the door to the office sprang open, and the rotund man he was waiting for finally waddled through. Rubbernecking wildly, the middle-manager quickly closed his office door and merged in with the rest of the crowd as they scampered towards the nearest exit.

Like a salmon swimming upstream, Devlin made his way toward the man and swiped his dangling key card as he brusquely brushed past. Adroitly palming the key, he continued down the hall until he reached the non-descript door he knew held his immense fortune behind it. With a quick tap, Devlin used the newly acquired key card and opened the door to the high-tech computer room, which housed scores of multi-million-dollar machines that functioned as the building's central nervous system.

Once inside, Devlin closed the door behind him and as anticipated, found the cutting-edge equipment room was bereft of evacuated office workers and security personnel. Filled with servers, cameras and a bank of computers, the secrets these humming machines held were just moments from his fingertips, and Devlin began to tremble with excitement as he sat down in front of a computer workstation.

Disguised in his helmet, mask and gloves, Devlin smirked at the security cameras lining the walls, knowing his face shield kept his identity safeguarded.

Expertly, Devlin inserted a USB encoder into the computer's main drive and immediately began entering a series of commands that lit up the monitor's screen. He ran a number of customized scripts he had coded over the years and his azure eyes gleamed as the screen filled with hundreds of highly encrypted files.

"Bingo," he murmured as a smile spread across his face.

Each dossier was undoubtedly worth a fortune to any one of Michel Bouchon's competitors, and yet Devlin remained focused, reminding himself that his client had paid him to procure only one specific file. Scanning scores of documents, Devlin quickly found what he was looking for and pulled out a large capacity flash drive which he inserted into the computer.

After a few strokes on the keyboard, he clicked on the file labeled *Photosynthesuit*, and the download of what his employer had labeled "the world's most highly sought-after secret" began.

With each agonizing second that passed, Devlin remained transfixed as he anxiously waited for the file to transfer from the computer to his flash drive. Devlin focused intensely, monitoring the transmission of data as it rose from "25%" to "50%."

So engrossed was the spy in his furtive efforts, he was unaware of an innocuous camera that slowly began to rotate towards him.

Finally, the download was complete, and although it had taken less than a minute, to Devlin, the seconds had stretched like hours. He quickly pulled out the flash drive and slipped it securely into his pocket. Walking with purpose back across the computer room, he paused in front of the door to compose himself, taking a deep breath to steady his nerves. He then slowly opened the door, exited the room into the bedlam that still filled the hallway, and casually merged with the mass of frenzied people filing for the exit.

Devlin approached the front door's security checkpoint. Surrounded by scores of office workers, the overwhelmed security guard noticed his tall frame and firefighter's equipment in the panic-stricken crowd and shouted, "Hey! When's the back-up getting here?"

"Any second," Devlin replied over his shoulder, continuing to calmly stroll through the lobby door of the Bouchon Industries' headquarters with the rest of the frantic employees.

In front of her computer in a quiet office, Layah Golden had watched the entire break-in unfold and monitored the actions of the man who was not only stealing her company's most guarded secret, but irrevocably altering the course of her life. As her German shepherds, Hadron and Cern lay at her feet, she picked up her cell phone and sighed deeply.

The tears that filled her eyes obscured her vision, but she kept her focus resolute. Forlornly, Layah whispered into the phone, "Initiate."

CHAPTER 3

Slouched on the end of the examination table in his doctor's office, Charlie Weaver sat in stunned silence as his physician explained the results of his lab work. The determinations from his blood samples and the irrefutable truth the scans revealed had still not registered, and neither had the inevitable.

Barely aware of the man's voice as he detailed his options, Charlie's shock, and the deafening hum of the incandescent lights above, left him overwhelmed, unable to comprehend what he was being told. Muffled phrases like "Quality of life" and "Hospital Resources" were occasionally perceptible, but as he fought the intense ringing inside his head, Charlie soon realized he hadn't heard a word.

Not since the first one: "Parkinson's."

Broad-shouldered with wispy blonde hair and a chiseled jaw, the thirty-five-year-old had always been sure to keep in peak physical condition. Charlie had the physique of a linebacker, having spent countless hours exercising in the gym. He had used his bulk and strength as assets in his career, but now, none of the push-ups or miles on the treadmill mattered. Soon, he'd been told, he would be a shell of himself and most likely, not live to see his next birthday.

The doctor continued to trace x-rays of Charlie's spine with his finger, while Charlie's mind flooded with regrets. Not of the things he'd done, but rather of the things he hadn't *yet* done. The pyramids in Egypt, why hadn't he gone to see them? That 1970 Chevelle he'd always wanted, why had he waited to buy it? But mostly, Charlie thought about the regrets he had with his family. Why hadn't he told his wife and his son that he loved them more often? Why hadn't they spent more time together? What could have possibly been more important than *them*?

Charlie's mind raced from one thought to another until his reverie was abruptly broken by the Doctor who placed a gentle hand on his shoulder, asking, "Do you have anyone to help you get your affairs in order?"

Sighing, Charlie glanced down at his wedding ring, twisted it slowly, and said, "No."

Still in a daze, Charlie approached the front door of his apartment and struggled as he tried to insert the key into the lock. His hand was shaking uncontrollably from the disease coursing through his body. Charlie missed the hole several times before taking a deep breath, focusing, and finally getting the key to engage. With a frustrated huff of relief and a curse at his newly diagnosed malady, he pushed open the door and walked into his dilapidated flat.

Month-old pizza boxes littered the floor. Empty liquor bottles riddled the counter and sat atop over-filled waste baskets. Clean and dirty clothes were strewn about the space, ensconcing the furniture underneath. Charlie flicked on the lights, paying little attention as he stepped over the law enforcement service medals that had spilled onto the floor from half-opened moving boxes. As with most of his old life, these accomplishments no longer held any meaning for Charlie, and he scoffed at how innocent he'd once been to place so much importance in them.

Distracted by the dripping sound from the water leak in his ceiling, Charlie quickly made his way to the near-full crock pot he'd left on the floor. Picking up and then emptying its contents into the kitchen sink overflowing with dirty dishes, Charlie set the pot back down beneath the ceiling's water spot and morosely wondered to himself just how many more times he'd have to manage that chore.

Deflated, Charlie made his way to the one area of his apartment that he had actually taken the time to unpack: his liquor cabinet. He grabbed a handle of whiskey, his fist shaking as he raised the bottle to his lips and took several deep swigs, draining it until it was nearly half empty. Lowering the bottle and letting out a long sigh, his eyes impulsively drifted, as they always did, to the mantle above his television.

The shelf brimmed with mementos of his wife and son; pictures of their wedding day, various vacations, ultra-sounds, and of course, the newspaper clipping he'd spent the last six months trying to erase from his memory. The front-page image burned his eyes as if looking directly into the sun. Yet, no matter how much he may have wanted to, he never could find the strength to avoid direct eye contact with the smiling faces that innocently beamed back at him.

The picture of the two of them had been taken at a friend's wedding, with his wife holding their 8-year-old son on her lap. Her windswept auburn hair had framed her face perfectly, while his son had arched his back to proudly display the polka dot bow tie he'd been asked to wear as the ring-bearer.

He was a striking image of his mother, with the same soft pale skin, gentle demeanor, and natural glow that resonated from his eyes. Even in the black and white photo, a brightness emanated from them both, much like a radiant warmth or a halo's resplendence.

With tears beginning to streak down his face, Charlie's mind drifted back to a life and family that no longer was, and a desire to live that he no longer felt. He once again read the headline that he had memorized months ago and that had haunted his every waking moment, "Mother and Son Killed by Drug-Impaired Driver."

Reflexively, his vision blurred and his jaw clenched.

As it did most nights, Charlie's body began to succumb to numbing depression, and as he tilted the whiskey bottle to take another overly long swig, he wiped away his tears with his trembling hand and quietly whispered to the photo, "I'll see you guys soon."

CHAPTER 4

The gentle nudging of Hadron and Cern's noses, along with their soft whimpers, snapped Layah Golden back to the moment.

The distressed cries of her German shepherds forced her to refocus. She steadied herself, knowing she was now just moments away from delivering the most influential speech in mankind's history.

Although she would have enjoyed a little more time daydreaming about the past, or a future that had been meticulously planned, she was acutely aware that all of that was now a distant memory with a new and treacherous course mere seconds from being launched.

She waited off-camera in the secured studio and straightened her white lab coat. The brightness of the lights forced her eyes to flutter. Reflexively, she rubbed them with the hand that held Michel Bouchon's handwritten letter, whose words she knew would alter the course of human evolution.

"Shhhh," she demurred to her agitated companions at her side, both of whom had identical coloring and matching muscular builds. "Everything will be alright…Michel promised."

Hearing his name jolted the two canines to attention. Their heads now rigidly faced forward and their tails trembled in expectant excitement. Their eyes darted from side to side as their panting became accelerated and their tongues dangled from their mouths. Layah itched behind their ears and felt comforted by the devotion of the two guard dogs, both of whom had been with her from that very first day.

Layah was a diminutive woman in her late sixties, with coiffed, curly gray hair and rectangular glasses that sat delicately atop her upturned nose. Her countless scientific breakthroughs were overshadowed only by her steadfast tenacity and supreme confidence. With eyes that radiated an unparalleled intelligence, the aura of her barely five-foot-tall frame often filled a room before she entered it.

And yet, even with such a cachet of experience and innumerable accomplishments earned, Layah was surprised to feel, for the first time in a long time, her self-assurance beginning to wane. Regardless of the triumphs that filled her resume or the accolades she had achieved in the past, today was undoubtedly different.

Today was more important than any that had come before, as her words would never be more poignant or her actions more consequential. Did she have the fortitude to deliver a message that would echo throughout time?

Ready or not, Layah was committed to at least one certainty: she would make sure that the man who was responsible for this day, would never forget it.

Glancing at the microphone that sat atop the flimsy table where she would address the world, she pictured herself sitting in the plastic folding chair as she read Michel's decree. What would they think? How would they react? Was Michel doing the right thing?

These questions, and a flood of others, overwhelmed Layah. Her mind drifted, but her eyes caught the television that hung from the studio's wall projecting an array of salacious journalists speculating wildly about what she would reveal. They, of course, had no actual facts – yet that trivial detail did little to slow their speculation and misguided views.

Especially those of television's most bombastic news anchor, Art Decker.

In his late forties, Art had the manicured hair of a movie star and the forced smile of a used car salesman. His porcelain veneers gleamed from the camera lights, his voice booming over his fellow on-air personalities. With skin the color and texture of cured cow hide, his overly Botoxed cheeks moved imperceptibly as he addressed the television audience.

It wasn't the man's outrageous "hot takes" or over-the-top grandiosity that most unnerved Layah, but his viscid smugness which oozed through the television screen. Layah fought to withhold her revulsion and the instinctual urge to shut off his image as quickly as she could.

With her skin crawling and the hairs on her arms raised at the sound of his voice, a thought suddenly occurred to Layah, and instantly her nausea dissolved as easily as the hot air the windbag spewed.

Wasn't this gossip peddler the exact person for whom Michel had said they would need? Hadn't their entire plan hinged on it? Might there actually be a use for a man as revolting as Art Decker?

A smile spread across Layah's face as she once again marveled at the genius of Michel Bouchon. His foresight gave her strength, and she approached the lone microphone with renewed resolve, her trepidation having quickly faded.

Speaking before billions would be easy.

Especially now that she had found their mouthpiece.

CHAPTER 5

Charlie was awoken on his couch by the vibrating of his cell phone, the empty whiskey bottle resting beside him. He rolled over and fought back the urge to vomit as he picked up the phone off his floor. Charlie squinted through bloodshot eyes and saw his partner's name illuminated on the screen. He let out a guttural moan.

"Don't I see you enough during the work week, Darryl? Jesus," Charlie pleaded.

Breathlessly from the other end of the line, Darryl implored, "Are you watching Charlie?! It's going to be bigger than the Super Bowl!"

Annoyed that this conversation hadn't already ended, Charlie asked, "What are you talking about, Darryl? It's early."

"Turn on your TV, Charlie," Darryl continued. "There's already more than a billion people tuned in or watching online!"

"Watching what?" Charlie asked.

"Michel Bouchon! There's going to be some sort of announcement from him."

Although aching with the pains of a raging hangover, the enormity of what he'd just heard stunned Charlie, and he fought through his nausea to sit up on his couch.

With his head throbbing, he asked, "Michel Bouchon? Are you sure? I thought that guy was dead."

"So did everyone else. It's on every channel, radio station and online streaming service. It's…just turn on the God damn TV!"

Still in a fog, Charlie reached for his remote and fired up his outdated TV. As the screen slowly brightened, Charlie gingerly rose to his feet and shuffled his way over to the kitchen, where he started pouring water into the coffee maker. Once again, his hand shook uncontrollably, forcing him to clench his fist to steady it.

On his TV he could see that a press conference was about to begin, and although his head pulsated in pain, he turned up the volume to make sure he didn't miss a word.

Half of the screen showed Art Decker moderating a group of other talking heads while on the other half of the TV, a lone microphone sat silently on a nondescript table in front of a plastic folding chair.

Reading off a number at the bottom of the screen, Art smugly reported, "We've now reached 2.7 billion and rising quickly, folks. That's the number of people around the world who have, at this very moment, tuned in for this afternoon's press conference. This has truly become a worldwide event. Simply stunning."

He shuffled papers and spoke to the other contributors, rhetorically asking, "So what do *you* think Michel Bouchon is going to announce? And where has he been? I'd be lying if I didn't admit that as recently as this morning, I'd assumed the man had died years ago!"

Art was then handed a single sheet of paper and, in obvious frustration, threw it in the air and addressed the other journalists, "Jesus Jerry, I think we all know of Michel Bouchon's accomplishments at this point, don't we? The Everwake pill, the Orbital Solar Shade…those are all well documented achievements of the man, and our planet thanks him for his contributions to its continued sustainability. What *I* think is important to remember and is often overlooked though, are some of his less successful ventures."

Sipping his coffee, Charlie slowly poured Irish cream into his cup and groaned, knowing what was about to come. Charlie could sense that even during an event as monumental and historic as this one, pompous attention seekers like Art Decker would somehow make this news story about themselves.

Art continued, "Like his ill-advised forays into nuclear power, copper mining, and plastics. I think we all remember those disasters, don't we?"

Art's fellow panelists grumbled in agreement.

Art continued, "For those living under a rock, might I remind you of the Bouchon nuclear complex which melted down and ultimately caused a massive contamination leak that left hundreds of surrounding miles uninhabitable for centuries. Those five nuclear plants were supposed to create enough clean energy to power half of the continent, but instead resulted in an environmental disaster that dwarfed Chernobyl. Not to mention the enormous copper mines he'd purchased that had reportedly contained only a fraction of the estimated minerals, causing the mines to run dry in less than a year. And who could forget the ill-fated plastics plant that never sold to a single customer. All catastrophic gambles that make today's announcement suspect, don't you think? Who's to say the guy hasn't lost it? I've even heard rumors that the man is now broke!"

"Preposterous," one of the guests quipped.

Rolling his eyes, Art continued, "Obviously. It would be impossible to spend the money he has in a hundred lifetimes, let alone one. But regardless, I know I never would have made those kinds of investments in his position, and perhaps it is *those* projects that will forever define the legacy of Mr. Boucho- "

Art Decker was suddenly cut short as Layah Golden walked into the picture.

Layah confidently sat in front of the lone microphone. An unnatural hush came over Art and his panel while she adjusted herself in her seat, pulled the microphone close to her, and unfurled the sheet of paper she clasped in her hand.

Delicately unwrapping her notes, the crinkling sound of the paper was deafening in the silence, and Charlie smiled, knowing that more than three billion people around the world sat on the edge of their seats, awaiting the next few words that came from her mouth.

Layah lowered the paper, looked directly into the camera, and said with little fanfare or pomp, "Hello, my name is Layah Golden. I am Michel Bouchon's senior scientist and the co-creator of the Ouroboros. Mr. Bouchon has asked that I read his following statement."

Layah then raised the paper, adjusted her glasses, and began reading, "Ladies and gentlemen, as many of you know, I have been stricken with a deadly disease which until recently, had meant a death sentence for myself and all that are similarly impaired. But today, it is my great honor and privilege to announce, that I have discovered a cure."

Layah hesitated as the tension grew, and the entire world held its collective breath.

She continued, "But not just a cure for my disease. A cure for ALL diseases."

Layah paused to let the gravity of her words sink in before continuing. "Yes - *all* diseases. Including HIV, ALS, and even Cancer."

She glanced at the camera as if to punctuate the moment, then returned her attention back to the paper.

"This is truly a remarkable milestone in human history that our team has been able to achieve. Although I would like to cure everyone that is suffering, unfortunately I cannot. For this reason, I announce today that I will be holding a lottery to choose ten recipients of my cure. Once selected, winners will have the opportunity to be cured of whatever disease afflicts them."

Transfixed like almost every other living person on the planet, Charlie did not notice as his hand shook and spilled the contents of his coffee cup into the sink in front of him.

Layah continued, "This means that for the next ten weeks, Layah will choose a weekly winner randomly on live TV. She will also choose three additional alternates during the following three weeks in case any initial winners decide to forgo their spots. Names can be submitted to the lottery by anyone in the world through our website, and there is no limit to the number of times a person can enter.

Lastly, The Chosen can do whatever they want with their winning spot as they are transferable. Ladies and gentlemen, today marks a new era in human evolution that will forever redefine our lives, and our future. Godspeed, and until next week."

Lowering the memo, Layah abruptly stood and walked off the screen as Hadron and Cern followed dutifully behind.

For a moment, Art Decker sat in shock at what he'd just heard, unable to formulate a thought or pithy remark. Once the magnitude of Layah's words began to sink in, however, he quickly became apoplectic.

He stammered, "Is she alluding to a vaccine? Or a pill? She said she was a scientist. Is it possible Bouchon's created some sort of new nanotechnology? What kind of cure-all could she possibly be talking about, and what the hell's an Ouroboros?"

Charlie numbly listened to the panel as they speculated furiously, but his shock quickly wore off as he realized the ridiculousness of what he'd just heard.

A cure for all diseases? That was impossible.

And even if it were, registering for a lottery with billions of other entrants was simply a waste of time. Charlie wasn't quite sure what Michel Bouchon was selling or what his true motivations were, but he appreciated the man's flair for the dramatic.

As Art continued with rhetorical questions to his guests such as, "How is this even possible?" and "Why would only 10 people be cured?" and "Why choose alternates?", he suddenly raised his hand to his ear and listened for a moment.

"Yes, great questions, Jerry. What did Dr. Golden mean when she said that the winning spots were "transferable", and that The Chosen could do anything they wanted with them? Was she implying they could sell them? Is that even moral?"

While the television contingent Art was chairing babbled rabidly back and forth, one of the commentators suddenly raised her voice and asked, "All of that aside Art, do you really think this is something that he could pull off?"

Exasperated, Art threw up his hands in the air and replied, "For Christ's sake, Mary, if anyone can do it, it's Michel Bouchon."

"But you said he was losing it, that you'd heard he was broke and –"

"The hell with what I said. That was before. I'm signing up on that website the second we go to commercial break."

Charlie chuckled at the absurdity of the spectacle unfolding before him and topped off his coffee with more liqueur.

Still on the phone, Darryl asked, "Did you see that, Charlie? That's the most incredible thing I've ever heard of, and that's saying a lot, considering we're talking about Michel Bouchon!"

Charlie laughed and said, "Sure, Darryl. Wake me up when he's found a cure for gullibility."

Surprised, Darryl asked, "After everything he's done, you still don't have faith in Michel Bouchon?"

As Charlie raised his cup of coffee to his mouth, his hand shook uncontrollably, spilling coffee all over his shirt.

Frustrated by his newly diagnosed infirmity, Charlie sighed and replied, "Faith? No."

CHAPTER 6

Yan Huen lounged on a lavish couch in one of the many living rooms aboard his 900-foot mega yacht, awe-struck by what he'd just witnessed on the enormous TV that adorned his wall. The world's second wealthiest man pondered the announcement and couldn't help but marvel at the ingenuity and creativity of his biggest rival. What a spectacle! The stunt had captivated the planet and brought the adversary he spent every waking hour obsessed with even more prestige.

Yan had always craved this kind of adulation, and not for the first time, he found himself envious of the only man on Earth that made him feel that way, Michel Bouchon.

In his early forties with a waistline rivaling his height, Western tabloids had dubbed him "The Buddha of Beijing", while cartoonists around the world had exhaustively mocked his thick-rimmed glasses and severely thinning hair. Although not handsome in the classical sense, Yan's distinctive appearance had never hindered his accomplishments, or the path he had taken on his way to becoming a tycoon.

Yan grew up on the dingy streets of Chongqing and learned at a young age the guile it took not only to survive, but to flourish. The oldest of eight children and the product of an absentee father, Yan had been forced to provide for his family when his mother had been unable. At the age of 12, as most of his peers were attending school, Yan had been left with no other option but to commit his first crime and begin a career path that would eventually lead to untold riches.

With a cheap color copier he had stolen and a bottle of bleach, Yan had entered the world of counterfeiting as a pre-teen, eager to fill his family's financial void left by his father's abandonment. Bleaching the color out of the smaller denomination bills and then reprinting large values on top of those blank notes had been the easy part. Made of the same fiber material, the newly minted currency easily passed for its counterparts, and was accepted by retailers without hesitation.

The challenging aspect of his scheme had been sustaining his discipline, a lesson that had served him well until today. Overprinting and flooding the market was an intoxicating way to make quick money, but Yan's innate cunning had guided him to slowly introduce the bills into circulation. Smaller amounts produced attracted less attention, and as a consequence, he had maintained his ploy unimpeded.

Throughout the following decades, Yan had progressed from counterfeiting to money laundering to real estate. With each step, his empire had grown exponentially, as his business decisions often required a "nuanced" sense of morality. Virtues like "playing by the rules" and "taking the high road" had held many of his ambitious competitors back, and Yan had found those sorts of barriers to be the excuses of weaker men. Success, he believed, took exceptional fortitude, and a willingness to do whatever was necessary to win.

By the time he had made his first billion, there were few laws Yan hadn't yet broken, and only one grandiose goal that remained in his sights: Becoming the World's wealthiest man.

Creating a generic version of Michel Bouchon's Everwake pill had been Yan's ticket to overtaking the man he was haunted by, and although his rival had tried to stop him by suing for patent infringement, Yan's attorneys and the less than stringent laws of China, had left him untouchable. With impunity, Yan had blatantly stolen the formula of Michel's greatest invention and, as a result, banked the billions that flowed in a seemingly never-ending cascade.

To be sure, competing with Michel had forced Yan to cut corners on quality control and materials from the outset. For some users, these shortcuts had resulted in life-long comas and occasionally even death. Yan had, over the years, overlooked these outliers – they were simply collateral damage in his cost-benefit analysis. And although his method of conducting business was seen by some of his contemporaries as distasteful, the *masses* had undoubtedly benefited from his knock-off - or at least, that was what he had told himself when he was alone.

In the end however, although his generic pharmaceutical had made him wealthier than nearly every living person on the planet, Yan's greed left him infatuated with the one man that still outshone him. Living "beneath" Michel Bouchon was unbearable for Yan, and this injustice had torn at his conscience in ways that even his pill's well documented side-effects hadn't.

Frustrated again with the brilliance shown by his adversary, Yan was suddenly struck with an epiphany. *"The masses"*…that was Michel Bouchon's fatal mistake with his cure. There was no money to be made saving the lives of just ten people, but if he could somehow figure out a way to increase production and bring this cure to the entire world, he would crush his foe and make a fortune in the process.

Finally, *he* would be able to supplant Michel Bouchon as the world's richest man!

Lost in thought as he contemplated his next move, one of the dozens of young bikini-clad women roaming the boat approached Yan on the couch and began to seductively rub his leg, breaking his trance.

She demurely purred into his ear, and he forcibly swatted at her hand, yelling, "Not now! I'm thinking!"

Flashing an exaggerated pout, the woman withdrew her hand and slunk away.

With a guttural grunt, Yan rocked his body back and forth, gaining the momentum he needed to get up from the couch.

Strolling the upper deck of his ship shirtless past one of his several pools, Yan's pale and substantial skin reflected the sun like a solar array. His stomach swallowed the top of his bathing suit, while his sandals dragged along the boat's deck as he shuffled across it.

White gloved servants bowed and mumbled as he passed, "Good afternoon Mr. Huen." Yan barely acknowledged their greetings.

He waddled past one of his helipads, pulled out his cellphone from his pocket, and dialed Devlin Archer's number, one he'd sworn never to call again.

"Did you see that?" Yan asked.

On the other end of the line, Devlin Archer answered, "Everyone did."

"My God," Yan continued, "If he's really done it, it'll be worth a fortune."

Skeptically, Devlin asked, "Do *you* believe he's done it?"

Yan snickered, "It's Michel Bouchon. Of course I believe he's done it."

There was an exaggerated pause as Yan carefully weighed his next words - and the potential consequences they might ignite.

Steadfast in his resolve, Yan continued, "I need to know what "it" is, Mr. Archer. Meet me in Buenos Aires. Tomorrow."

"I'll be there," Devlin confirmed.

Yan hung up the phone and stared off the bow of the boat at the clear blue ocean, plotting the next steps he would take on his course to becoming the World's richest man. Was there any limit to what he'd do? Rules he'd break? Opponent he'd decimate?

No, not now that he was so close to finally having the only thing that mattered to him: Michel Bouchon's title.

After a moment Yan's ruminating ended, and he snapped his fingers to summon the nearest servant.

Reverently, a man came sprinting to his side and asked, "Yes, Mr. Huen?"

"Get the jet refueled," Yan demanded.

Timidly, the servant asked, "Which one?"

"The fastest one."

CHAPTER 7

In his early thirties, Gatlin had the physique of a world class swimmer. Tall and sinewy, with the gait of a thoroughbred, the dark-skinned Islander from Tuvalu exuded confidence when he entered a room and commanded respect when he rarely spoke. His neatly cropped hair and clean-shaven face belied a man who kept his appearance, as with everything else in his life, in perfect order. He had often been compared with a Marine or an MMA fighter, but mostly he had been recognized as a man not to be crossed. His eyes had a singular focus, and a rugged determination emanated from his steely gaze.

Gatlin had pledged his life to serve Michel Bouchon when he was still a teenager, and he took his solemn oath seriously - as did thousands of other Tuvaluans who owed their lives and their civilization to the world's most famous man.

With the planet's oceans rising due to unimpeded climate change, their tiny island of Tuvalu, in the middle of the Central Pacific Ocean, had only been a few years away from being submerged and erased from history forever. Lost to a billowing sea, Gatlin and his people owed everything they had and would ever be to Michel Bouchon. Without the man who had, at great sacrifice to his own health, created the Orbital Solar Shade, future Tuvaluans never would have known the beauty of their ancestral homeland or the accomplishments of their proud culture.

Gliding into Layah Golden's office, Gatlin could see that she was transfixed by the images on her computer screen. By her side, as always, Hadron and Cern lay on the floor with their heads resting on their paws.

Deferentially, Gatlin approached Layah and said, "Everything is ready to go."

Still staring at the screen, Layah replied off-handedly, "Good."

After a moment, Gatlin continued cautiously, "Dr. Golden, the spectacle this will create will –"

"Go exactly as Michel planned," Layah finished.

"Yes, Dr. Golden," Gatlin said as he nodded.

Loud percussions and bright flashes jumped from her computer screen and Gatlin couldn't help but glance over Layah's shoulder at the video she was intently watching. He could see the Bouchon Industries' security footage repeated on a loop as militarized drones crashed into the company's roof and simultaneously detonated. Over and over, she replayed their explosions, the screen lighting up from their blasts and then fading to snowy static.

With a sigh, Layah clicked a button on her mouse and the video then switched to a man in a firefighter's suit approaching a bank of computers inside the building's most secure room. Layah and Gatlin watched as he entered in commands, inserted a USB drive, downloaded a file, and then calmly walked out of the room.

"We're still trying to get a positive I.D on who he is, Dr. Golden. With the helmet and face shield on, we haven't been able to attain a clear shot for facial recognition. Plus, those gloves covered his fingers, so we haven't found any prints. In my opinion he is a highly trained professional…and I'll give you two guesses who probably hired him."

Layah clicked another button, and a picture of Yan Huen filled her screen, "I only need one."

Gatlin cautiously continued, "Dr. Golden, with those files now in Yan's hands, is there anything to stop him from copying the Photosynthesuit like he did with the Everwake pill?"

Forlornly, Layah whispered, "Only one. Mr. Bouchon."

With a resigned exhale, Gatlin nodded and headed toward the office door. At the office's threshold, he paused for a moment, turned around towards Layah and said, "I'm sorry you'll be seeing him again so soon."

"Me too."

As he left the office, Layah stared numbly at Yan's image on the computer, at the rotund face of the man whose all-encompassing greed had ensured her life would never be the same. Fury raged inside of her, knowing that his actions, and need to best Michel, meant that soon she would never see her husband again. It was a contingency they had planned for, but one they had hoped would never be needed.

Now, what little time she had left with him, was being stolen by this monster. The man who had already taken so much, was unwittingly about to rob her of the only thing for which her life still held any meaning.

With tears streaming down her face, Layah shut off her computer and let out a deep sigh. She slowly rotated in her swivel chair and found her gaze returning to the large painting that hung on the center of her office wall. It was a simple design but signified a lifetime of work. Black and white with a rainbow-colored eye, it was a depiction of a snake in a circle, eating its own tail.

An ouroboros.

With Hadron and Cern still moping at her feet, Layah bent over and comfortingly pet the dogs.

"It won't be much longer now," she reassured them.

CHAPTER 8

Manhandled by a cadre of security men in dark suits and even darker sunglasses, Devlin Archer took a moment to survey his surroundings as he was patted down in the foyer of the massive mansion. Although he had been a guest in the palaces of kings, emperors, and dictators, even he had to concede that this estate was exceptionally opulent. Flying buttresses arched throughout the voluminous interior of the expansive villa, and Devlin couldn't help but notice several masterpieces by Da Vinci and Picasso adorning the walls.

The gates to enter the compound were manned by a dozen men with machine guns and the sprawling driveway had snaked for nearly a mile through countless vineyards. The black-suited chauffeur sent to retrieve him had remained stoic throughout the drive, giving Devlin time to fully absorb the estate's magnificence.

Once every nook of his body had been searched, Devlin was escorted by six men down a series of lengthy hallways, all lined with Italian marble and baroque statues. Led outside to a lavish pool the size of a professional basketball court, he averted his gaze from the dozens of topless, dark-skinned women frolicking and giggling in the water. Security guards lining the perimeter of the palatial estate were fitted with earpieces, and Devlin assumed, pieces of the 9mm caliber variety.

Escorted to Yan Huen as he waited at a table underneath an umbrella, China's wealthiest man did not rise to greet Devlin as he approached. Instead, he sumptuously took a bite from a mother of pearl spoon that dripped with caviar.

Lowering the gauche utensil, Yan smiled and said, "It truly is fascinating when you think about it, Mr. Archer. I paid more for that one bite than my father paid for my childhood home."

There was an awkward pause as Devlin took a seat and silently waited for Yan to get to the point as to why he had been summoned. Yan raised his eyes and met those of his guest, pulling out the USB drive from his pocket that Devlin had used while conducting his espionage at Bouchon Industries.

With reverence, Yan held the data storage unit in his hand and said, "As always, Mr. Archer, it has been a pleasure doing business with you. I take it you received your payment in full?"

Devlin nodded but remained silent.

The magnate held the drive in front of him and twisted it in his fingers. Sensing Devlin's disinterest, Yan paused for a moment and said, "You have no idea what you downloaded to this drive, do you, Mr. Archer?"

Devlin replied, "I'm paid not to care, Mr. Huen."

Yan smiled, "Of course."

Yan then plugged the drive into the laptop sitting next to him on the table, and on the screen a bulky but futuristic suit popped up in 3D. The outfit looked like something from a sci-fi novel or the video game *Halo*. The animated spec version rotated 360 degrees on screen so the entirety of the ensemble could be seen.

"It is the future, Mr. Archer," Yan began, "The Photosynthesuit. With this technology, mankind will no longer need to eat. We'll be able to convert sunlight directly into energy for the body. Farms, and the immense resources required to run them, will become obsolete. Raising livestock, now the cornerstone of our way of life, will be seen as a barbaric custom from the ancient past, to be derided as much as bloodletting or geocentrism is today. Breakfast, lunch, and dinner – all of those hours wasted to soon become a thing of a bygone era! The entire world will change Mr. Archer…again. Can you imagine how much something like this will be worth?"

"I'm not a businessman, Mr. Huen" Devlin stated flatly.

Devlin's indifference broke Yan's exuberant contemplations, and he quickly returned to the moment.

He closed the laptop and then stared directly at Devlin, "Yes, of course not. My plans for something like this are undoubtedly of no interest to you. But what may be of interest to you, as arguably the world's most sought-after spy, is that I require a man with your particular talents. Again."

"Bouchon." Devlin led.

"Exactly. I need to know what he is working on. And more specifically, what the Ouroboros is."

"Mr. Huen, unless you plan on rigging the lottery, I won't be able to get close enough to find out what he's up to. I'd need to be inside his operation to get the information you're looking for, and no one knows where he is."

"Don't worry about that, Mr. Archer, I will take care of it," Yan said with a roguish smile.

Devlin let the silence hold for a moment as the importance of what Yan had just implied hung in the air. Getting him in, when the entire world was trying to do the same, would be a monumental undertaking, requiring immense financial resources. If Yan were willing to go that far, there was no telling how much he'd be willing to spend.

Devlin cleared his throat, "I see…of course, for a job like this, with this much worldwide exposure, it won't be cheap."

Catching the inference, Yan smiled and said, "Frankly, Mr. Archer, I'm surprised it took you this long to get to that."

With a snap of his fingers, Yan summoned over one of his servants stationed behind him. Without hesitation, the man sprinted over to the table, laid a briefcase delicately in front of Devlin, and slowly opened it. He turned it towards Yan's guest so that he could clearly see the stacks of thousand-dollar bills lining its insides.

Off-handedly, Yan said, "A million dollars. It's yours."

Devlin smirked at Yan, closed the briefcase, and then pushed it back towards the servant.

As he rose from his seat and straightened his suit, Devlin chided "I didn't come here to be insulted, Mr. Huen. Now if you'll excuse me."

Devlin turned to show himself out, and as he began to walk away Yan continued indifferently, "And ninety-nine more like them when you return with what you've found."

Devlin froze, then returned to his without a word.

"I'm listening."

"Mr. Archer, I need to know what Michel Bouchon has discovered, how it works, and where it comes from. Is it another medication like the Everwake pill? Is it shot, like a vaccine? An ouroboros is a snake, so is it some sort of venom? Whatever it is, I need to know. Once you bring back that information to me, my offer stands: I will have ninety-nine more of these waiting for you upon your return."

Devlin smiled, and as he slowly picked up the briefcase, he extended his hand towards Yan, shook it, and said, "Done."

CHAPTER 9

The enormity of Michel Bouchon's announcement captivated the entire world, and wild speculation ran rampant through every walk of life. Families spoke of nothing else at their dinner tables and classrooms dedicated hours on end to calculating the odds of winning. Watercooler gossip in white-collar offices was monopolized by lottery mania, while lunch breaks at construction sites became increasingly passionate forums for debate. Regardless of age, background, or health, only one topic dominated the conversation - and everyone had an opinion: Michel Bouchon.

On television, the lead news story - and every subsequent one - revolved around Michel's cure and the upcoming lottery. Commentators like Art Decker were quick to weigh in, with some believing the impossible was now possible, while others speculated it was all just a scam. "The greatest hoax in human history" was a popular refrain, while others claimed he had indeed found a miracle.

Still, nearly everyone registered - just in case.

With the prospect of a cure found for all diseases, religious leaders around the globe decried Michel's claim as an afront to the Creator, with some asking, "Who does Michel Bouchon think he is, God?"

And while tens of thousands camped out and protested in front of the Bouchon Industries' headquarters, demanding that the cure be available for more than just 10 people, financial channels across the globe became obsessed with the transferable spots and the amount of money they would sell for. Three million? Four million? As with any commodity, their values were speculated on each second, with some outlandishly projecting that they could go for as much as $10 million. By the time the weekend had come for the first drawing, more than

41.2 billion entries had been submitted, with more flooding in by the minute.

With registration fervor gripping every living man, woman and child on the planet, lines stretched for blocks at internet cafes, while those with a Smart phone spent their free time entering submissions.

Truly, the cure behind Michel Bouchon's lottery had gripped the world.

CHAPTER 10

In a cavernous warehouse deep inside Guangdong Province, a thousand exhausted Chinese workers typed furiously at their computers. The terrified laborers did their best to focus on their screens, but they couldn't ignore the black-clad guards who roamed the floor, twirling their batons.

The ceiling of the structure was several stories high, so the tapping sound of their keystrokes echoed deafeningly throughout the enormous building. Only the occasional screamed command by a sectional supervisor punctured the monotony.

Scrutinizing the workers and their supervisors, a thin accountant with horn-rimmed glasses and thinning hair purposefully marched down the long aisles of workers, checking their progress and taking notes on his tablet. Row after row, he roamed, keeping track of registrations on Michel Bouchon's website and the pace with which the workers executed each one.

After completing the last aisle, the accountant wiped his brow with a handkerchief and made his way up a flight of stairs towards a second-story office with large doors labeled *OWNER*. Timidly, the accountant knocked, and from inside a wheezing voice called out "Enter."

As the accountant cautiously walked in, he was confronted by Chi Kwong, an elderly looking Chinese man in his late sixties who dragged an oxygen tank behind him as he slowly ambled. Having started his factory more than forty years ago, Chi Kwong had built one of China's most productive denim manufacturers - an enterprise that rivaled some of West's biggest operations. However, years of treating fabric rolls with indigo dye and other hazardous chemicals had left the tycoon's lungs hobbled from the toxic fumes. Today, he found himself battling Chemical Pneumonia, a diagnosis his doctors had informed him was terminal.

Having exhausted all traditional and holistic medical options, Chi Kwong was now forced to convert his once-thriving vertical manufacturing facility into a hub of computer banks manned by a revolving shift of workers.

Although rich by most Chinese metrics, his four ex-wives had ensured his wealth hadn't reached the upper echelon of his country's elite, and with his funds and health both in decline, he knew it was only a matter of time before both were fully spent.

Chi Kwong was blunt and informal as he addressed the accountant before him, "And?"

The accountant nervously cleared his throat and adjusted his tie, "Each worker is submitting almost 100 entries per hour, Mr. Kwong. That means we're averaging nearly 100,000 registrations per hour. More than two million a day."

"Triple it," Chi Kwong snapped.

The accountant shifted uneasily, "But sir, the workers are typing as fast they can. I don't think they'll be able to make up that sort of –."

Frustrated, Chi Kwong interrupted, "Then hire three times as many workers! I said triple the number, so get it done, now!"

Chi Kwong began to cough heavily as he finished his demand and lifted a plastic mask up to his mouth that was connected to his oxygen tank. He took a few deep breaths and slowly regained his composure.

The accountant empathetically noted his boss' condition, nodded, and turned to walk out of the room before he hesitated.

Terrified, he mumbled, "Mr. Kwong, at this pace, I would be remiss if I did not mention that your funds will soon be completely exhausted. And, even with this many entries, they will represent just a fraction amongst the billions of others. The odds of winning this way will be nearly impossible."

Chi Kwong slowly dragged his rolling oxygen tank behind him to his massive window and stared out at the hundreds of workers who typed furiously below.

Deflated, he asked with a wheeze, "Have you got a better idea?"

CHAPTER 11

With lumbering strides, Darryl chased the young man with the stolen handbag down the crowded Oakland city street. The overweight police officer pursued the thief with as much effort as his nearly 300 pounds could manage, but now in his late forties and only a few months removed from his latest knee replacement, the gap between them widened with every step.

Out of breath, Darryl was forced to stop, slumping over with his hands resting on his knees as he tried to refill his lungs. The perpetrator continued running at full speed, gaining separation, and Darryl cursed the kid's youth as he struggled to contain his panting.

"Come back here you little son of a b –."

From behind Darryl, Charlie came sprinting past at full speed with a broad smile on his face.

Overtaking his partner, Charlie yelled, "How's that diet coming, buddy?!"

Still struggling for air, eyes watering, Darryl croaked, "Screw you!"

Charlie couldn't help but laugh as he turned his attention back towards the criminal in front of him.

Approaching a group of rubberneckers that had gathered on the sidewalk to watch the action, Charlie yelled, "Police! Move!" and the crowd dispersed as he raced past.

The suspect rounded a corner just over a block ahead and vanished from sight for a moment. Charlie reached the corner just in time to catch a glimpse of the thief entering a crowd of several hundred people that had gathered around an outside patio bar.

Charlie sprinted across the empty street and pushed his way into the massive crowd, trying to locate his prey in the herd of bystanders. However, as he entered the dense gathering, none of the patrons gave way, oblivious to his presence or intentions. The people that stood there refused to move, even as he struggled to push past, and in exasperation Charlie yelled, "Police! Out of the way!"

To his surprise, no one in the crowd obeyed his command this time, as they all grumbled and continued to stare at the TV attached to the outside patio bar. Frustrated, Charlie turned to see what everyone was looking at.

"What the hell's happening here?" Charlie asked himself and those around him who could hear.

One of the onlookers gave him an annoyed "Shhhhhh" and then said, "It's Michel Bouchon's lottery. They're picking the first winner's name."

Another onlooker chimed in and whispered excitedly, "The winner's gonna be an instant millionaire!"

In shock and still out of breath, Charlie asked, "I thought those spots were for sick people?"

"They are. But you can sell them. To anybody. For any price! Can you imagine how much some rich jerk would pay for one of those spots?"

Another onlooker vehemently added her own "Shhhh", and the crowd quickly quieted down.

The image mirrored the day the lottery was first announced, with the same singular microphone sitting alone in a secure studio. Inside a small Picture-in-picture, Art Decker hosted a New Year's Eve style countdown, breathlessly announcing "9…8…7…"

A deafening hush fell over the entire crowd who had gathered around the outdoor television. Transfixed, not a word was uttered. As the counter on the screen reached "0", the random number generator at the bottom of the screen suddenly began to spin furiously, until all of the numbers became a blur.

One by one the numerical sequence slowly stopped, until the final number was revealed: "989268010241975."

Total silence gripped the crowd as everyone waited for what would come next. After a few agonizing moments, Layah

Golden appeared on the screen and sat in front of the microphone.

Slowly and deliberately, she tapped a few commands on her tablet and then announced to a world that anxiously waited, "Our first winner is Gilbert Lebedev, of Lausanne Switzerland. Congratulations Mr. Lebedev. Godspeed, and until next week."

As Layah rose and left the microphone, there was a collective groan from the onlookers as they began to disperse from the front of the bar.

"Crap," one of the men groaned, "I must've registered for that drawing like thirty times."

"Me too" another man commiserated. "I could really use the money."

The grumbling crowd slowly headed in their own directions, and Charlie was left standing in his same spot, staring at the TV in contemplative silence. Art Decker and his co-host speculated about the winner's identity, how his life was going to change, and what he would do with his newfound fame and potential fortune.

As Charlie listened, he couldn't help but wonder why money and fame were all these talking heads cared about, and not the fact that this person might actually be ecstatic to be cured of an illness.

With the last few people from the crowd gone, Charlie turned to leave as well when he suddenly found himself standing just a few feet from the thief holding the purse. As cop and robber locked eyes, both waited a split second to see what the other would do first. Charlie quickly feigned reaching for his gun, causing the young thief to turn around and take off, dropping the handbag behind.

Charlie smiled and watched the teenager course down an alleyway out of sight. Now alone, he leaned over and picked up the abandoned clutch. To his dismay, the purse began to shake uncontrollably in his hand, and try as he might, he could not get the quivering to stop.

Reminded once again of his own affliction, Charlie looked from his hand back to the TV as the talking heads continued to babble. Although his entire arm trembled with increased ferocity, Charlie could not help but drift into his own fantasies…and the possibility of winning Michel Bouchon's lottery.

CHAPTER 12

On the gleaming white marble steps in front of Lausanne's Federal Supreme courthouse, a beautiful young woman in her early thirties named Milly Lebedev led her frail and aging father, Gilbert, down to a podium that faced hundreds of screaming reporters. Careful to steady the man who had raised her, the cacophony of camera flashes and hostile shouts from the media was disorienting for the senior citizen, bordering on overwhelming. With the wails of the interrogating journalists growing louder, she gripped her father's arm tight for support and soon found herself questioning if this was the right decision.

Gilbert was in his late sixties, with wisps of gray hair, bushy eyebrows, and thick framed glasses. He hobbled while hunched over, shuffling his feet as he strained to maintain his balance, uncertain where he was or what was happening around him. Although his face belied that of a kind man with a storied past, all that registered in his eyes at this particular moment was confusion and fear.

With heightening apprehension, Gilbert leaned closely to his daughter and whimpered, "What are we doing back here?"

She squeezed her father's hand tightly with a forlorn smile and stepped up to the massive bank of microphones atop the podium. Deliberately she cleared her throat, and the throngs of reporters suddenly fell quiet, enthralled to hear what Milly had to say.

"Thank you all for coming here today. My name is Milly, and this is my father, Gilbert. No words can accurately describe how grateful we are to be here, or how lucky we feel that my father has been chosen in Mr. Bouchon's lottery."

Milly paused for a moment as she wiped away a tear and regained her composure, "Our family is praying that Mr.

Bouchon's cure will help bring my father back - back from the debilitating dementia that has ravaged his mind and body. We do not know what the Ouroboros is, or how it will help, but if there is anyone that can cure my father, it is Mr. Bouchon."

Unmoved by her display of emotion, the hundreds of reporters in the crowd began to scream at the duo again, looking for any additional piece of information to generate a story.

"What type of dementia does he have?!"

"How many times did you register?!"

"Is he the luckiest person on the planet?!"

In the center of the imposing crowd, Art Decker stood with the other reporters, frustrated that he had been relegated to such a menial task by his producers. Surrounded by what he felt were inexperienced journalists struggling to get their feet wet, Art rolled his eyes at the questions they hurled at the dais. He'd cut his teeth doing this sort of grunt work for decades right out of college, and now with the cache he'd built, he should've been back home, spending his well-earned time in front of the camera where he belonged.

For a moment, Art reveled in how this entire spectacle had turned him in to a bit of a media darling. For nearly 10 hours a day, he'd had prime face time on the television, becoming one of the most recognized men in the world. Each day, as his reputation and stature had grown, he'd assured himself that during his next contract extension, his newfound celebrity would provide just the sort of leverage he would need for a hefty bump in pay.

Now, being stuck here with these other no-name reporters, Art considered his time wasted, and frankly a bit of an insult to someone of his caliber. Every minute here was a minute not on the air, and beneath someone with the clout that he, Art Decker, had earned.

Lost in his own grandiose thoughts while being jostled by screaming reporters, Art was unaware as Gatlin brushed past, slipping a cell phone into his suit breast pocket.

At the podium, Gilbert became increasingly disoriented as Milly struggled to answer the barrage of questions slung at her.

Holding his daughter's arm close for support, Gilbert pleaded with her, "I want to go home, Milly."

"We will, Dad, we will."

The mob of reporters, undeterred by Gilbert's obvious discomfort, continued to fire off questions in rapid succession at the pair as Milly labored to respond to as many as she could.

"How long has he been sick?"

"How far has his dementia progressed?"

"What medications has he tried?"

Art began to glance around, searching for how he'd make the quickest exit from this raucous circus. Suddenly, a vibration began to emanate from inside his jacket pocket.

Stunned, he thought, *What the hell?*

To his utter shock, as he reached into his pocket, he found an unknown cell phone and pulled it out to take a closer look. On the screen was a simple text that read "$50 million."

Incredulously, Art looked around at the horde surrounding him, sure that the person who dropped the device into his pocket would be long gone by now. To his surprise, with the entire crowd of reporters shouting questions at Milly in quick succession, one man faced directly towards him nearly twenty yards away. Stoic, the man was tall, dark-skinned, and had a gaze that belied an intensity so powerful that it radiated through the frenzied crowd.

The two men locked eyes for several moments until, without breaking his fixed stare with Art, the man shouted over the others around him, "Was he offered any money for his spot?"

This question, more than any of the others, seemed to rile Milly, and with deep frustration that was visibly apparent, she replied, "We did not register for Mr. Bouchon's lottery to sell our spot. My father is VERY sick, and no amount of money would entice us to sell his chance at a recovery."

Still staring at the man, Art's concentration was broken by the tone of Milly's voice. The question had unnerved her, and instinctually, his need for attention consumed him as he looked at the cell phone in his hand.

With a mischievous smile, he turned towards Milly and shouted over the crowd, "Were you offered 50 million dollars?"

This question physically stunned Milly as she shot a glare into the throng of people, "Who asked that? Who told you that? That is extremely private information that was not to be disseminated."

Art pushed, "So is it true?"

Bewildered, Milly's face reddened as she became flummoxed. She did not answer for a moment, and sensing her unease, the reporters started to frantically press.

"Were you really offered $50 million, Mr. Lebedev?"

"Why didn't you take the money?"

The barrage of attention renewed Gilbert's anxiety, forcing him to grip Milly's hand tightly and stammer, "I… I don't… Milly?"

Milly grimaced and her heart broke at the trauma these questions were causing her father.

Staring angrily at Art Decker, she declared, "That is all of the questions for today. Thank you."

Milly took her father's arm and turned to walk back up the marble staircase of the courthouse, leaving the thunderstruck mob behind.

Still in shock, reporters excitedly surrounded Art, clapping him on the back with shouts of "Way to go", "Attaboy", "Who's your source?" No longer able to see the mystery man through the crowd that engulfed him, Art beamed from ear to ear, and for a moment, forgot how unhappy he was to be there.

Lost in the crowd, Gatlin watched Art become besieged by his colleagues. As he turned to leave the fray behind him, he also smiled. His mission had been accomplished.

CHAPTER 13

By the second week of the lottery, nearly every living person on Earth had heard of and registered for the upcoming drawing. Lottery mania had grown to a fever pitch. No matter the language, culture, or religion, nothing else was discussed on any media platform. With twelve more drawings to go and the lives of twelve more people potentially changed forever, conjecture on just how much more frenzied the worldwide attention would become could not be hyperbolic enough.

Like everyone else, Devlin Archer's television was tuned in as the next drawing was about to begin. Newscaster Art Decker and his guest, renowned hedge fund manager Ian Haynes, passionately speculated about how much the upcoming spot could potentially sell for. Minimizing its financial worth, the New York moneyman focused on its obvious danger and exceptional uncertainty, repeatedly downplaying its value.

"Paying for something like this, with no proof that it works, or even what "it" is, is the very definition of rampant speculation. Despite Michel Bouchon's track record, spending millions of dollars on a promise is hardly a sound investment and not something I'd ever recommend to my clients. Frankly, you'd be throwing your money away."

Art Decker countered, "Are you suggesting, then, that what Mr. Bouchon has claimed is a sham? That there really is no cure and that these spots are actually worthless?"

Exasperated, Ian continued, "What I'm suggesting is that *seeing is believing*. And without any *actual evidence* that his cure works, spending that sort of money could be catastrophic."

Art probed, "Really, Ian? Come now. How much is *your* health worth?"

Self-righteously, Ian responded, "Let me put it this way. The Ouroboros represents a snake eating its own tail, correct?"

"Yes," Art Decker replied, clearly annoyed at this now well-documented detail.

"Well, Art," Ian continued, "The only people that have ever asked 'What is your health worth?'…have been snake-oil salesmen."

Devlin couldn't help but give a snort of acknowledgment for the hedge fund manager's use of imagery. Although clever and undoubtedly successful, he still found the man's irreverence off-putting and smug.

Pulling on his rubber gloves, Devlin crossed the empty warehouse floor he'd covered that morning with commercial-grade plastic. Hired by one of his former clients to interrogate a competitor, Devlin found himself irritated by the bloodied captive's muffled screams as he approached the bound man. Even with a rag shoved firmly into his mouth, the man's wails were distracting, forcing Devlin to pick up the remote and raise the TV's volume.

For a moment, Devlin was transported to a bygone era when he, too, used to scream, all those many years ago. These days, however, he made sure he never screamed, no matter how much pain or agony he had to endure.

Not since prison.

Not since Jorge.

Art Decker and Ian Haynes continued to argue ardently about the value of the upcoming spot, who would win it, and whether that person would end up selling it. As Devlin listened to the two men bicker in the background, he sifted through his trusty bag of "tools", removing a hacksaw and a dull butter knife. Seeing the menacing implements in his captor's hands, the screaming man's eyes widened as Devlin took his time to weigh his options.

Lost in thought as he turned his attention back toward the television, Devlin casually wondered how Yan would pull off the seemingly impossible and secure him a spot as one of The Chosen. With a smile, Devlin had to admit to himself that the tycoon deserved some credit: it wasn't going to be easy.

Refocusing on the task before him, Devlin reached further into the bag and pulled out a hefty blowtorch. Settling on what had recently become one of his favorite instruments in his arsenal, he casually lit it with his lighter and leered at the horrified man who quivered uncontrollably. Purposively, Devlin approached the terrified prisoner, ready to fillet.

With stifled screams echoing through the warehouse, Devlin paused as Layah Golden appear on the screen. Turning his attention towards the television, he and billions of others watched as she started and patiently waited for the random numbers to all click into place. As the last digit "CLICKED" and the final number was revealed, audiences around the world trembled in anticipation of the name Layah would announce.

Tapping methodically on her tablet, viewers in their homes, offices, and stadiums, where games had been paused mid-match, all held their collective breath.

After a few more swipes of her finger, Layah slowly looked up from her computer and monotonously said to the camera, "Congratulations to Zikri Tran of Singapore. You are our second recipient. Godspeed, and until next week."

With a deflated sigh, Devlin – like nearly every person on the planet - felt his fleeting fantasy fade.

As reality set in, Devlin once again began to concentrate on the business before him, and as he turned the knob on the blowtorch to increase its flame, he, like almost everyone else around the world, begrudgingly went back to "work."

CHAPTER 14

In front of his small electronics store on the outskirts of Singapore, shop owner Zikri Tran beamed as he was about to address the throngs of reporters who jostled to get their scoop. With frenetic shouts and relentless camera flashes bombarding him, Zikri basked in the attention of his newfound fame. Smiling to himself, he found it ironic that this kind of publicity was just the sort of boost his boutique would have needed to finally become profitable - had he still needed the money.

After this morning's transaction, he was quite sure that would never be a problem again.

A man of relatively modest means but extravagant tastes, Zikri had always found it difficult to get ahead financially. Lavish trips with his third wife and expensive jewelry for his fifth mistress had ensured that Zikri was always one payment behind on his outstanding debts. Of course, excursions to casinos and brothels hadn't helped either, but deep down, he'd always known that one day his luck would change.

And today had been that day.

As Zikri raised his hands to quiet down the crowd, standing beside him was a tall, indifferent man in a navy-blue suit and dark glasses. Unlike Zikri, the man did not smile. He just stared past the mob of reporters stone-faced, his lips pursed, with his hands folded at his waist. Like a Secret Service agent on duty, the man was uninterested in the chaos directly in front of him and appeared to be more annoyed than elated by the public scrutiny.

As Zikri stepped forward, the balding fifty-year-old addressed the frenzied masses, "Please, please my friends. One at a time."

One of the reporters yelled, "Are you sick?!"

Feigning concern, Zikri said, "No, thankfully not. I've been blessed with perfectly good health."

There was a grumble amongst the crowd until another reported blurted, "Then why did you register?"

"Isn't that obvious? For the money of course."

Immediately, Zikri could tell that his answer hadn't elicited the sort of response he had anticipated. Instead of being congratulated for winning and the astonishing windfall that presumably came with it, his answer had unexpectedly prompted outrage and accusatory questions from the reporters.

"How could you do such a thing!?"

"Don't you have a conscience?!"

Shocked by the judgmental questions, Zikri became defensive, "Pleeease! Everyone registered for the lottery to sell their spot! Don't act like I'm the only one. I'm sure all of you did it too!"

However, the reporters wouldn't relent, and one asked, "But what about the millions of people who are actually sick?"

Deflecting, Zikri replied, "That is for this gentleman here to determine now that his firm is officially the owner of the prize."

Detached, the man in the dark suit remained quiet, motionless.

Pressing, one of the journalists asked, "So you sold your spot?"

Zikri replied, "I did. And I'd do it again. Don't pretend you wouldn't!"

"How much did they pay you?" a voice shouted from the crowd.

Fully basking in this question, Zikri paused to let the drama build and his answer be heard, unencumbered. This was his moment, when all of those people who had said he would never amount to anything, especially his first wife, would hang on every syllable he was about to say next.

Smiling smugly, he said, "That is not something that I wish to reveal, but let's just say that the firm was very…generous."

The reporters then turned towards the man in sunglasses and began peppering him with questions, "What are you going to do with the prize?"

"Are you sick?"

Slowly, the man stepped forward and, for the first time, addressed the crowd, "The prize has already been spoken for and transferred to another recipient."

In shock, Zikri spun around, wide-eyed, "What?"

The man continued, "For the sum of 300 million U.S dollars."

"What?!" Zikri screamed. "That's three times what I sold it to you for!"

Stone-faced, his eyes hidden, the man replied, "Indeed. And the private equity firm of Zatkin, Jacoby and Elliot thanks you. It's been nice doing business with you, Mr. Tran."

The man then turned and strolled away from the crowd of reporters as they screamed after him in a frenzied hysteria. Still in shock, Zikri stared in disbelief as the firm's representative entered a stretch limo, and the chauffeur closed the door behind him. With cameras flashing and shouts ringing out, the press continued to hound the vehicle even as it began to pull away.

As he watched the sedan pick up speed and leave the badgering reporters behind, Zikri felt queasy and cursed the deal he'd made only a few hours earlier, "You…idiot!"

CHAPTER 15

As she rested and watched the TV from her reclining chair in the oncology ward, Kerry Wilson listened as the pundits on the financial news network argued among themselves over the theoretical selling prices of the upcoming lottery spots. Like the commodities market they typically covered, the "experts" debated the value of the ever-dwindling supply of the spots against the ever-increasing demand. One's health could be considered priceless, they argued, and Kerry silently agreed as she adjusted the tape securing the I.V drip into her arm.

In her late thirties with light blue eyes and a smile that lit up a room, Kerry's breast cancer diagnosis had come as an utter shock to the woman who had spent so much of her life monitoring exactly what she put into her body. Prioritizing her vegetarian lifestyle for most of her adulthood had been foundational for Kerry and discovering she had been betrayed by the body she had invested so much time caring for had been devastating.

Now, with her cancer rapidly progressing to stage 4, Kerry had had few options but to participate in experimental trials and allow the administration of powerful chemotherapy treatments. As she continued to watch, surrounded by other patients also attached to IVs, Kerry wasn't sure if it was the chemicals coursing through her veins or the callousness of the television hosts that made her feel more nauseous.

"How much do *you* think the next one will go for, then?" one of the men asked.

"I have no idea," the woman replied, "But I do know that there are more than 3,000 billionaires in the world, so it's anyone's guess what a spot's worth to one of them."

"Agreed" another man conceded, "And after the $300 million the last spot just went for, each subsequent spot is sure to sell for larger and larger amounts."

With her laptop between her legs and a scarf wrapped around her head, Kerry pulled her blanket up over her shoulders. She struggled to adjust in her seat and, as she had for weeks, tried to make herself as comfortable as possible.

Unconsciously, her eyes returned to the table next to her, no longer able to avoid the inevitable. Reaching over, she picked up the letter that had lain there, tormenting her since it had arrived.

Struggling to find the strength to read it once again, she lifted the letter up, scanning the heading, "Petition for Divorce", at the top, just below the legal letterhead. Devastated, she let the letter fall to the floor next to her, unable to read any further.

Overwhelmed by the prospect of countless more chemo treatments, a pending divorce, and a bleak prognosis, Kerry's unflappable strength had reached its limit.

Logging in to Michel Bouchon's website with her laptop, she entered her information, and for the first time since her diagnosis, Kerry began to cry.

CHAPTER 16

Two dozen nuns from the Peterson Orphanage in Perth, Australia, surrounded 11-year-old August "Auggie" Martin as he faced the massive press corps. Sister Carlson consolingly rested her hands on the orphan's shoulders as he fought to prop himself up on the crutches tucked under his arms, all while being bombarded with questions.

Standing before the throngs of journalists in front of their esteemed institution, Sister Carlson leaned close to Auggie's ear and whispered, "Don't worry, my child, this will all be over soon."

Auggie nodded as he steadied himself and bravely met the onslaught of inquiries from the crowd.

Stricken with Flaccid Myelitis as an infant, Auggie's affliction had coursed through his body unabated, sapping the strength from his legs and ultimately forcing him to walk with the aid of crutches. Each subsequent year had seen a further deterioration of his health and prognosis. With the disease projected to take his life long before he ever became a man, there were no delusions throughout the orphanage about Auggie's future.

As the birthdays passed and other non-disabled children were adopted before him, the empathetic Sisters grew more and more fond of Auggie, doting on him with a level of attention that bordered on reverence. Although they never would have admitted it, he had become their favorite, and every evening, they prayed together for God to help Auggie find peace.

Inexplicably, for the women of faith, their prayers had never been answered.

Until today.

Perhaps it was his beaming smile, curly blonde locks, and gifted level of intelligence that had galvanized a nation around him. Or perhaps it was due to the unwavering efforts of the nuns to draw attention to his plight. Whatever the reason, Auggie's story had gone viral, with donations around the country flooding the sisters' charity drive. Nicknamed "The Pride of Australia," he had become an online sensation, and within a week of launching Auggie's endowment, it had miraculously raised nearly 750 million dollars. The contributions collected had been record-breaking, and news outlets around the country had excitedly reported that the money had been enough to purchase the spot from the initial winner in Russia.

Now, through the barrage of questions and camera flashes, Sister Carlson grew weary of the incessant inquiries, raising her hands to quiet down the noise. A hush fell over the crowd as she addressed them with the grace and dignity that had defined her more than sixty years at the orphanage.

"Thank you all for coming today and for the support so many of you have shown. We are forever grateful to all of those across our great country who gave, large and small, to help our young Auggie find hope… in a world that has given him so little. The concerted efforts of our fellow countrymen and women, along with God's good grace, have seen to it that he can now finally be cured. We are truly blessed."

Sister Carlson paused to take a breath, and reporters jumped in with follow-up questions, unconcerned with how crass or cruel their questions were to the young disabled orphan before them.

"Couldn't that money have been used to help more than one kid?"

"What happened to Auggie's parents?"

"Does he have some sort of Polio?"

"Do you believe in God or Michel Bouchon?"

This final question stung Sister Carlson, and her face contorted as it displayed her extreme displeasure at the train of thought.

She replied, "I believe God has bestowed Mr. Bouchon with a gift, and he has bestowed that gift to us. Together, they have created a miracle, and have helped save Auggie's life."

With finality, Sister Carlson assisted Auggie and turned him around, walking up the steps of the orphanage and away from the crowd. As the nuns surrounded and supported the young man in unison, he hobbled up the stairs as reporters shouted follow-up questions behind them.

Standing silently in the crush of reporters, Gatlin was dismayed by the line of questioning from the media and the madness around him. He watched, eyes ablaze, as Auggie left the circus behind him and shuffled back inside the building.

As the mob slowly began to disperse, Gatlin's cell phone rang, and he answered it.

Listening to the voice on the other end, he said with quiet resolve, "I'll be there."

CHAPTER 17

Lying flat on the roof of the *casita*, Gatlin unfolded the duffel bag next to him and methodically pulled out his sniper rifle. Attaching the scope and bipod were easy in the daytime, and Gatlin was thankful this mission wasn't taking place in the dead of night like some of the others he'd been tasked with orchestrating over the years. As far as assignments went, this commission was relatively routine, and Gatlin was cautiously optimistic that everything would go according to plan.

Of course, working in broad daylight had its disadvantages as well. Without the cover of darkness, Gatlin's position was easily exposed, and as the heat of the sun in Jalisco, Mexico began to beat down on the terracotta tiles around him, he found himself beginning to perspire uncontrollably. With each passing minute, the temperature rose, the dizzying heat radiating from the clay shingles beneath him.

Gatlin wiped his brow with his sleeve and positioned himself on his stomach, resting the rifle's mounting on the roof's ledge. From this angle, nearly four blocks away from the town square, Gatlin had a direct line of sight for the shot at the podium. Adjusting the scope of his rifle, Gatlin focused on the stage, slowly swiveling the gun from side to side as he searched for his target.

After a moment, with continuous sweat cascading down his brow and into his eyes, Gatlin once again wiped away the droplets and was able to identify the most recent recipient of the lottery's drawing. Gatlin tightened his jaw as he adjusted the focus on his scope and lined up his crosshairs with Mexico's wealthiest citizen, Umberto Fuentes.

Umberto stood at the podium in front of hundreds of reporters, taking a moment to absorb the enormity of the event and the good fortune that had befallen him. Before addressing the crowd, the jovial billionaire - with a Santa-like laugh and a matching belly - couldn't help but wonder how he had gotten here. Did he deserve to be? And most importantly, what would Maria have said if she had been alive to see it?

Surrounded on the stage by members of his immediate family and heavily armed security guards with bulletproof vests, Umberto reminisced on the path he'd taken to put himself in this position.

A position that promised a future without cancer.

Umberto was the founder of Mexico's largest telecom company and had created his empire through decades of hard work with the unwavering help of his devoted wife. Maria had been his rock, his muse, and his most trusted advisor. And although his fortune was the envy of millions, he would have given it all up, for just one more day with her.

Maria had passed nearly ten years ago due to complications from acute Leukemia, and watching her fade away as she lay in her hospital bed had been gut-wrenching for Umberto. Even with the best medical treatments money could buy and the nation's most esteemed doctors, the love of his life had eventually succumbed to her illness.

Until this week, Umberto's destiny had seemed inexorably tied with his wife's as he, too, found himself fighting for his life. This time, the interloper was colon cancer, spreading ruthlessly throughout his body. With the knowledge that he had only a few months left to live, only the love and strength of his numerous children and countless grandchildren kept Umberto fighting. They were his connection to the past and the last remnants of her.

Over the last year, Umberto had resigned himself to his circumstances and accepted what had evidently been God's will – until he learned of Michel Bouchon's lottery.

Approaching the latest winner was a no-brainer for Umberto. His failing health meant he had nothing left to lose, and the magnate was happy to offer the man just over a billion dollars. With money now meaningless, he would have paid anything if it meant he could spend more time with what remained of his family.

Umberto regained his focus and gazed over the vast crowd, speaking into the microphone and addressing the throngs of people before him, "This is a momentous occasion for me, my family, and all of Mexico. I am proud to represent my country on this historic day."

Reporters immediately bombarded Umberto with questions, each trying to outdo the other, "How much did you pay for your spot?"

"Are you sick?"

"Will you be stepping down as CEO of Mexico Telecom?"

Taking control of the pandemonium, Umberto waved his hands to quiet the crowd, "The amount I paid - and my personal afflictions - are just that: personal. As for my role at the company I founded… I have been given a new lease on life, and I intend to spend as much of it as I can with my family."

The reporters continued to shout a volley of follow-up questions towards Umberto when suddenly, a loud BANG rattled the courtyard.

Instantaneously, one of Umberto's guards who stood beside him crumpled to the ground as screams pierced the crowd and chaos engulfed the onlookers. In total bedlam, the throng of reporters and spectators scattered, leaving only those on stage as targets.

Without hesitation, Umberto flung his large body on top of one of his grandchildren, shielding her from any potential danger.

Covering her head with his meaty arms, he shouted, "My angel! Are you okay?!"

Barely able to speak underneath his weight, the young girl nodded her head, and wheezed, "*Abuelo*, I can't breathe."

Relieved that she was unharmed and now surrounded by dozens of additional guards, Umberto smiled and quickly rolled off the young girl.

Peering across the stage, Umberto saw the wounded guard examine his chest in bewilderment. He pulled out and held up a smoldering bullet mangled by his bullet proof vest, wincing as it burnt his fingers. The guard quickly dropped the crushed slug, and Umberto let out a sigh of relief, knowing the man and his family had survived the assassination attempt.

With the rifle still smoking in his hands, Gatlin anxiously peered through its scope at the guard that had been hit, comforted to see that the man was still moving and okay.

Smiling, Gatlin quietly pulled the weapon back from the roofline - his mission complete.

CHAPTER 18

The news of the day had Art Decker in a euphoria he was sure shone through to the hundreds of millions he knew were watching. The failed slaying of Mexico's wealthiest billionaire, Umberto Fuentes, was just the sort of salacious story the public craved, and he was positive they would tune in *en masse* to learn more. Holding the entire world's attention as they hung onto his every word, Art almost felt like he was floating - and, for a moment, wondered if this was what heaven was like.

With each subsequent lottery pick chosen, the drama had ratcheted up tenfold. Until this afternoon's events, Art hadn't thought the interest in his news coverage could get any more parabolic.

He had been wrong.

A mysterious shooter still at large and a beloved titan of industry's near-fatal demise had intensified the public's insatiable need to know more. Specifically, their need to know more about all things related to Michel Bouchon.

Addressing the camera with his face caked in layers of foundation, Art continued from behind his desk, "Yes, the perpetrator of today's assassination attempt IS still at large and considered extremely dangerous. The Jalisco police have admitted they have little to go on so far, but they assure us that they are examining every piece of evidence and are tracking down all possible leads. This actually reminds me of the time I was embedded in the fifth infantry's forward unit during the battle of Fallujah. You see, as we were taking heavy fire I –."

Art was about to continue but was unceremoniously interrupted by a breaking news announcement, leaving him mid-bloviation and visibly bewildered.

TVs around the world cut to Layah Golden as she approached a microphone. Adjusting a piece of paper, Layah avoided eye contact with the camera as she read from her notes and addressed the billions watching.

"Ladies and gentlemen, as many of you know, today Michel Bouchon's lottery was the cause of a horrific attack on an innocent man. The scene was one of chaos, and a life was almost lost. This is not something Mr. Bouchon ever wanted, as his lottery was created to save lives, not to take them."

Layah paused for effect.

She continued, "It is apparent now that publicly announcing the winners' names each week has put their lives, and those that have purchased their spots, in grave danger. This is simply not a risk we can further accept. It is for this reason that, going forward, all winners and their benefactors will be kept anonymous. We will continue to publicly choose the winning numbers, but those whose numbers are drawn will be contacted directly by intermediaries from Bouchon Industries. They will be presented with the highest bid that has been submitted, and in private they can decide within 24 hours whether to accept or reject the amount offered. Anonymity will protect the lottery winners, as well as the highest bidders, and ensure that the safety of everyone is maintained."

Layah put down the paper she was reading and looked directly into the camera, "We truly wish things didn't have to be this way, but in light of recent events, it is the only way we can protect all of those involved. We hope everyone understands."

As Layah left the microphone, the camera returned to Art, his face brightened in anger as he lashed out, enraged that his golden goose would no longer be laying golden eggs.

"This is an outrage! Anonymity?! This is obviously some sort of ploy to keep these billionaires' illnesses secret! Or at the very least, a way for them to avoid public ridicule over how much money they've spent for a spot."

With his fury on full display, Art hoped his tirade would go viral, and at least for a little while, maintain the ratings he so desperately craved. Of course, deep down, he didn't really care how much was offered for the spots or who won. What he did care about, though, was that everyone *else* did.

With continuous worldwide attention on the drawings, he had, only moments earlier, envisioned reaping the windfall of endless news coverage for the upcoming events. Now, without details like the winners' names or the amounts paid, he would be reduced to speculating alongside everyone else.

Art became apoplectic, the reality dawning on him he would no longer be the center of attention. His face now crimson, he shouted in utter exasperation, "Besides, with complete anonymity and Bouchon Industries wielding full autonomy, how do we even know the bidding process will be fair?!"

As she watched Art's outburst on a TV monitor off-camera, Layah smiled.

They didn't.

CHAPTER 19

The rolling hills of his estate in Tuscany were picturesque - awash in the beauty of vineyards stretching across hundreds of acres, their leaves turning varying shades of burnt amber. As the grapes reached their full maturity, he guessed it would only be a few weeks now before the harvesting commenced and his private label reserves began fermentation.

Smiling, he noted that the size and texture of the fruit were flawless, and he assured himself that this year's vintage would be one of his finest. The serenity and splendor that surrounded him were mesmerizing, and for a brief moment, he forgot.

Until the engine of his wheelchair roared to life and jolted him back to reality.

Mustafa al Farouq grimaced as the exhaust from the gasoline fumes wafted behind him, stifling the pristine air. Although the smell of burning fuel had once been intoxicating for Mustafa, now it only reminded him of a past that no longer existed - and a future that had been stolen from him.

The horsepower of the gasoline engine was necessary when traversing the dirt rows of his vineyard, but he resented its utility nonetheless. More than the combustion engine though, he despised the wheelchair itself for what it represented.

At thirty-five, with a thick dark beard, deep brown eyes, and bushy black hair, Mustafa saw his wheelchair as an albatross - a glaring memorial of what used to be. Once a playboy who had spent his nights at disco-techs and his days racing supercars, he was now just a shell of his former self. The disease ravaging his body had shackled him to the piece of machinery he was now inexorably tied to, with no prospect of ever being able to walk again.

His undoing had begun simply enough some six years earlier, with routine blood work administered by his family's trusted doctor. Although the test took just a moment, the results had been life-altering. *Amyotrophic Lateral Sclerosis*, or, ALS.

Branded as "damaged" by his family, Mustafa had been ostracized overnight, forced to relinquish the aristocracy he had been groomed to inherit. As the eldest son, he had been prepared from birth to run the family's multi-billion-dollar oil empire and maintain the stranglehold it had on power within the Saudi kingdom. But his diagnosis had derailed that path, which had led to his younger brother being touted as the future head of the clan. With no heirs of his own and now no prospect of any, Mustafa had been shunned by the family, left to live his remaining days alone in abject obscurity.

As he turned his wheelchair and headed toward the winery, Mustafa understood what had to be done. Michel Bouchon's lottery was the only way he would be able to regain his health and reclaim his lost legacy. Once cured, he would be welcomed back into the oil empire he had been born to lead and reclaim his lost birthright.

As Mustafa passed by row after row of grapes, he couldn't help but feel a twinge of melancholy. Leveraging his entire fortune to be cured would mean having to sell this place. But once back on his feet, literally, he would have access to his family's financial resources and the means to buy it back a hundred times over.

Revving his wheelchair's engine to top speed, Mustafa sped towards his opulent chateau, resolved to place a winning bid with Bouchon Industries and reclaim his rightful inheritance.

CHAPTER 20

Over the next six weeks, regularly scheduled lottery drawings were televised, and although the randomly generated numbers were chosen for all to see, the winners' identities remained completely anonymous. Regardless of position, status, or clout, no one knew the names of the winners or whether they had decided to sell their spots to those with the means to buy them. When the last official lottery number was announced, a collective groan of defeat could be felt around the world.

The tenth and final winner was chosen, and only the three alternate spots remained to be filled, with many in the media deriding them as "worthless" symbols of false hope. The original winners had presumably been offered immense fortunes, so the press universally agreed they would never give up their spots if they hadn't already. As for the billionaires with the funds to purchase their spots, they too were unlikely to relinquish their stations, as there was undoubtedly nothing that could be offered to them that they didn't already have.

With nothing of substance to report and airtime to fill, increasingly bombastic rumors began to swirl amongst the media outlets. Some alleged that several of the winners had sold their spots for billions of dollars, while others countered that although billions had been offered, they had ultimately been rejected. By the time claims of fraud and lottery manipulation began to permeate, it became harder and harder to distinguish fact from fiction.

As wild speculation and competing conspiracy theories ran rampant, there was one thing everyone could agree on: the only man who truly knew what was happening behind Bouchon Industries' closed doors had yet to utter a single word.

CHAPTER 21

Yan Huen and his accountant sat anxiously in a luxurious office overlooking the ocean. Both had their eyes trained on his lawyer as he lowered his cell phone, smiling.

Unable to wait, Yan blurted out, "Well?"

"It's done, Mr. Huen," the lawyer announced with an exaggerated sigh of relief, "Your blind trust's bid has been accepted. You got the last spot."

Swinging his rotund arm in victory, Yan let out a jubilant yelp as his enormous body thundered across the opulent room.

"Finally!" he bellowed as he picked up a priceless vase and smashed it against the wall in triumph. "I thought we'd never get one. How many weeks in a row have we placed a bid? How many times were they rejected? This endeavor has cost me a fortune!"

Chewing on the end of his glasses, Yan's accountant meekly set them on the desk in front of him and whimpered, "Mr. Huen, along those lines, I would be remiss if I didn't bring to your attention that –"

"What?!" Yan yelled, uninterested in the bean counter's details.

"Well, it's just that the sort of liquidity we'll need to fund your bid will require quite a bit of maneuvering among your holdings. I don't believe we have nearly the level of cash on hand to adequately –"

Yan interrupted the accountant with a flick of his wrist, "Imbecile! That's what a margin account is for."

The accountant looked over at the lawyer, who nodded as if to say, "Continue."

"Yes sir. But…"

Frustrated, Yan screamed, "What the hell is it? Spit it out!"

The accountant continued, "Well sir, it's just that with that much money tied up, you will be highly…leveraged."

Yan's exuberance and overconfidence quickly pivoted to nominal concern, "Leveraged? How leveraged?"

The accountant cleared his throat and tentatively continued, "For the next month? Fully."

Yan sank into a leather couch, his triumph cooling into unease as the scale of what he'd just done began to register. With his company's stock accounts fully margined and his personal reserves nearly depleted, following through would mean putting his entire fortune at risk. Even in this infinitesimally small window, the tiniest of errors now would be disastrous for his legacy and upend the vast empire he had spent a lifetime creating.

Dating back to those early days of counterfeiting with a bottle of bleach and color copier, Yan had trusted his gut, never allowing himself to get over-extended or too big too fast. Maintaining a measured sense of discipline hadn't failed him yet, and for a moment, Yan's better judgment began to emerge.

But then he remembered.

He remembered how much he detested Michel Bouchon and everything the man stood for. His self-righteousness and benevolence sickened Yan, as Michel was revered by the people while he, a titan in his own right, was considered merely an interloper.

Living in Bouchon's shadow had become an unbearable torture for Yan, and if he had a chance to finally overtake his nemesis, he would do whatever it took to do so.

The only thing that mattered to Yan now was Michel's title.

Hoping a semblance of prudence might prevail, the lawyer interjected, breaking Yan's train of thought, "Legally speaking, we can still back out Mr. Huen if you want. We've only *verbally* committed to –"

"Screw it," Yan muttered to himself.

"Sir?" the lawyer stammered.

Lost in his own grandiose thoughts, Yan declared with maniac conviction, "The money doesn't matter anyway, because soon it will all have been worth it. I'll find out what he's invented, how it's made, and I'll mass produce it just like I did before with his Everwake pill. And just like before, he won't be able to stop me! Ten people cured? That's absurd! *I'LL* be the one who brings his cure to the masses, and I'll make a fortune doing it cheaply. Finally…*I'll* be the richest man in the world!"

As his breathing became labored from the exertion of yelling, the enormity of what he was about to do and the amount of money he'd actually pledged finally began to sink in. For the first time in decades, he felt a twinge of uncertainty, and as Yan picked up a glass of whiskey, he sipped it, hoping to calm his nerves.

After a moment, he lowered the glass and took a deep breath.

Staring out of the floor to ceiling windows at the expansive ocean before him, he quietly muttered to himself, "This better work."

CHAPTER 22

Charlie slumped on the couch, his chin resting against his chest, an empty bottle of Jack Daniels in one hand and his service revolver in the other. He stared in silence at the TV in front of him, his eyes glazed from the alcohol, his thoughts swirling, his resolve strengthening.

On his screen, Charlie watched Art Decker and the other media pundits prattle back and forth about the final alternate spot in Michel Bouchon's lottery.

Art declared, "This is it folks! The last spot in Michel Bouchon's lottery will be chosen tonight. With only five minutes left to register, I have to say though, I'm almost happy this spectacle is finally coming to an end. Especially when you consider how much of a letdown these last few weeks have been. Wouldn't the rest of you agree?"

The rest of the panel all nodded in unison, each attempting to inject their opinions over the others.

"Absolutely," one of the women said. "Compared to the almost feverish hype that had surrounded the initial winners, these drawings for the alternate spots have just been sort of…sad."

"I agree" another man said. "Especially for a spot like this one. The third alternate? Who would even want something like that? It's not like any of the other winners would ever give up their spot after how much money they presumably paid. Frankly, I feel sorry for the person that wins. Talk about false hope!"

"Perhaps," Art retorted, "but you can't just dismiss the third alternate spot. Who knows, maybe three of the initial winners will have a change of heart and surrender their spots for a nobler cause and –."

Suddenly, Art Decker burst into laughter, unable to contain himself any longer. "I'm sorry, I'm sorry everyone. I just couldn't keep going with a straight face."

The panel all joined Art in laughter, each joking about how ridiculous it had been to have alternates in the first place. Anyone who had passed up on the millions, or even billions presumably offered for their spot, wouldn't change their mind *now* about being cured. And neither would the billionaires who had spent so much money to purchase their spots. It was folly to keep this charade going any longer.

With nothing of substance left to discuss, they each light-heartedly reminisced about the first month when the identifiable winners had been chosen.

Tears streamed down Charlie's face as he picked up the framed newspaper article about his lost wife and son, stared at the picture, and marveled at how their faces had always beamed with joy. They had been the meaning behind everything he had ever done, or ever would do. They were his motivation to get up in the morning, and to come home safely in the evening.

However, after their passing, Charlie had lived his life with reckless abandon, often volunteering for assignments that others on the force had avoided. Time after time, he had rushed ahead into dangerous situations with little concern for his safety, undeterred by the potentially lethal hazards. Many in his unit had whispered that he had suddenly developed a death wish, and in this moment, he couldn't help but think that maybe they had been right.

Charlie looked around at his dilapidated apartment filled with strewn trash and mildew stains on the wall. The contrast between the picture in front of him and the circumstances he now found himself in became even more pronounced.

With his hand shaking, he gingerly rubbed his finger over their bright faces, and outlined the bow tie his son was wearing. As his hand continued to tremble more and more violently, Charlie's frustration grew, becoming more determined.

With a deep sigh, Charlie looked up to the ceiling and said, "I just can't anymore, you guys. I'm sorry. I'm so, sorry."

Charlie raised the gun to his tilted head, put it in his mouth, and closed his eyes – ready to join his lost family.

With his eyes squeezed together tightly and thoroughly concentrating on what he was about to do, Charlie's senses heightened, and he could taste the metal in his mouth and almost hear the beating of his heart. He noticed the metal had a sulfuric taste, but he was more distracted by the beats pounding in his ears. They were deafening, and slower than he would have thought. Almost as if…

Charlie opened his water-filled eyes and stared above him. He quickly realized the beating sound hadn't come from his chest, but from the ceiling's water leak dripping into the pot right behind him. Charlie sighed in utter exasperation, frustrated by the disruption.

He hadn't discovered inner peace; he'd discovered shoddy plumbing.

Resolved to pick up where he had left off, Charlie tilted his head back and once again put the gun in his mouth. As he was about to close his eyes for the last time, he suddenly noticed something about the leak. Was it possible? The water spot that had been created on the ceiling had formed a shape that looked exactly like the polka dot bow tie his son was wearing in the picture.

Utterly stunned, Charlie slowly pulled the gun out of his mouth and looked back at the picture lying next to him on the couch. The spot above and the bow tie in the picture were IDENTICAL. Shocked, Charlie couldn't believe what he was seeing. In disbelief, he lowered his gun onto the couch cushion next to him. Was this some sort of sign?

Flashes from the TV and animated gesticulations by Art Decker snapped Charlie out of his trance.

"This is it folks! The final minute! Only sixty seconds left to register before the final spot is chosen!"

On the screen, a timer began to count down from sixty, and suddenly Charlie no longer heard the chattering of the broadcasters in front of him or the dripping of water behind him. Though still fully inebriated, he purposefully picked up his

laptop and logged onto the Bouchon Industries
website. He tried to enter the required registration information
like his name, date of birth, and illness, but his hand once again
shook uncontrollably. With all of his effort, and perhaps, he
thought, divine intervention, he clenched his fist and steadied
his hand for just a moment.

As he typed furiously, entering his information into the web
site, Charlie didn't care that it was his first, and only, entry into
the lottery. The odds didn't matter and neither did the fact that
he was hoping to win the third alternate spot. All he thought
about was his wife and son, and how maybe, just maybe, they
were watching over him.

Finishing the last few details of his entry, he hardly noticed
as the final few seconds of the countdown reached zero on the
TV in front of him. Instead, he shut his laptop, wrapped his
arms around his wooden picture frame, and passed out on the
couch.

On the TV in front of him, the numbers of the final drawing
began to spin. Oblivious, Charlie slept, and as he involuntarily
hugged his framed newspaper clipping even tighter, his
handgun slowly slid down his couch and fell to the floor.

CHAPTER 23

Gatlin got behind the wheel of his four-ton SUV and could feel the exhaustion creeping into his body. Having just landed after a fourteen-hour flight, he fought through his crippling jetlag, much like he had done for the last two months. Each country visited had come with its own unique set of challenges, from unfamiliar customs to inedible food.

Still, none of those obstacles had been nearly as onerous as the people he had met.

Regardless of their age, gender, or background, most of the winners he met with had been absolutely vile. Always seeking more money, their greed and selfishness had been the one constant he could rely on no matter the language spoken or the God worshiped. Though Michel had predicted these interactions, Gatlin had still struggled to comprehend that nearly all of the winners he'd visited had entered the drawing solely to sell their spot for a massive payday.

A few, of course, had truly been ill - but once presented with the enormity of the final offer, they couldn't resist the temptation to sell. He found it difficult to denigrate those who had knowingly sacrificed their own health to ensure financial security for their children and their children's children, but he'd still wished it hadn't come to that.

Every "offer run" made his bile simmer and his blood pressure rise, but Gatlin reminded himself that Michel knew what he was doing - and why.

Not only had Michel anticipated transactions like these, but his entire plan hinged on them.

Even with that sort of divine insight, it didn't ease the nausea he felt every time he met with one of the winners. If it hadn't been for the grade schoolteacher, the one person who hadn't allowed money to influence her, Gatlin wondered if he might have found himself giving up on humanity.

But sadly, in the end, she had been the anomaly, the outlier from all of the rest. She was the first and, unfortunately, Gatlin feared, would be the last.

Gatlin let out an involuntary sigh of relief at this thought. Thankfully, whether they decided to take the money or not, this was the final person he would have to present an offer to. He was hopeful it would go as anticipated, but as he fastened his seat belt and lined up his massive vehicle, deep down inside Gatlin feared that, like most of the others, this interaction would not go as planned.

As he approached the car ahead, Gatlin steadied his nerves and braced himself to meet the final winner.

CHAPTER 24

At a stoplight in their patrol car, Darryl again noticed Charlie's hand shaking. For the past several months, the trembling had become more and more apparent, but Darryl had bitten his tongue out of courtesy for the tragedy his partner had been through.

The shaking wasn't the only change Darryl had observed with Charlie. There was a shift in his overall demeanor as well. Once an exemplary member of the force, with sound judgment and measured restraint, since the funerals, he'd become a shadow of his former self. Now, Charlie often acted imprudently when faced with danger and indifference with respect to protocols.

Perhaps worse, though, than the changes in his physical and mental health had been his alcohol consumption. Darryl had never known Charlie to overdrink during the nine years they had worked together prior to the accident, but since that day, he had reeked of a distillery each morning. Darryl didn't know how Charlie spent his nights, but he suspected it was at the end of a bottle.

Trying to cut through the awkward silence and day-after bourbon smell that hung in the air of their squad car, Darryl began with small talk and asked, "Man, they've got me putting in some overtime these days, you know? The station got you working weekends too?"

Staring out the passenger side window, his eyes glazed from his massive hangover, Charlie answered curtly, "Not yet."

Darryl waited a moment, not sure how to broach the subject he'd been wanting to talk about for months.

With a deep breath, he asked, "So when are you going to tell them?"

Still detached, fighting the pounding headache that had consumed him all morning, Charlie responded nonchalantly, "Tell them what?"

"That you're sick."

With a start, Charlie turned quickly towards Darryl, unwittingly clenching his fist to quell his trembling hand.

"How do you know about that?"

"Come on, Charlie, I've been your partner for almost a decade. You didn't think I'd notice your hand?"

Charlie looked down at his fist and whispered, "Jesus, is it that obvious?"

Darryl smiled, trying to break the tension, "Let's just say I wouldn't want you to be my dentist."

Both men chuckled, Darryl's large belly quivering underneath his uniform. They felt some of the anxiety wedged between them melt away, and, for a moment, they forgot about the tragedy Charlie had endured, the illness he was battling, and the demons he was attempting to quell.

For a moment, they felt like things were back to how they had once been, normal.

Suddenly, Charlie and Darryl lurched forward as their car was bumped abruptly from behind. "What the f–?" Darryl asked.

Both men turned around and saw an enormous black SUV nearly on top of them. Now stopped, it rested against their rear bumper, so close that neither man could see into the front windshield.

Exasperated, Charlie turned to Darryl and asked, "Shall we?"

"After you, Dr. Weaver," Darryl deadpanned.

Charlie smiled at the playful inference as they both exited their patrol car.

Closing their doors behind them, both officers approached the vehicle with an air of cynicism.

Darryl asked, "Little early for the bottle, isn't it, pal?"

The man stepped out of the car, ignored Darryl, and immediately locked eyes with Charlie. The smile on Charlie's face waned as an uneasy feeling began to wash over him. The man's gaze held an unnerving intensity, like a cheetah stalking its prey, or a predator ready to pounce.

The man was lean, tall, and in peak physical shape. Perhaps an athlete. Charlie's pulse started to quicken, and he could feel the moisture gathering in his palms. This man was definitely not normal, or Charlie could tell, someone to be trifled with.

Charlie froze. "Easy..." he muttered – more to himself than the stranger.

The two provocateurs maintained eye contact, unmoving as if mimicking a standoff in a Western. Darryl shot a glance back and forth at the two men, sensing a tension that had arisen from thin air.

"What the hell's going on here, Charlie?"

In an instant, the man turned and began sprinting away from the officers down the street at such speed that his body became a blur.

"Shit!" Darryl exclaimed, amazed at the man's quickness, "The guy's a gazelle!"

Just as quickly, Charlie hurdled himself over the trunk of the squad car, sliding across it as his gun-belt rattled against the metal.

Giving chase, Charlie shouted back towards Darryl, "I've got him! Meet me on the other side!"

Having seen this sort of cavalier attitude time and time again over the past several months, Darryl wasn't surprised as Charlie chased the man with reckless abandon down a darkened alley.

Shaking his head, Darryl muttered to himself, "God damn it. Not again."

Regaining his wits, Darryl turned back towards his car, swung open the door, and wriggled himself back behind the steering wheel. He slammed the car into drive and peeled out, tires squealing.

As Charlie entered the alleyway in a huff, he could see the man sprinting towards the far end, nearly fifty yards away.

Like Darryl, Charlie was startled by the man's speed and yelled down the alleyway in a last-ditch effort to slow him, "Stop!"

For a moment, the man at the far end paused his retreat and looked back over his shoulder in a way that, if he hadn't known better, would have felt like an invitation to Charlie. As the two men once again locked eyes, agonizing seconds ticked by before the man turned to resume his getaway. Nimbly jumping on the side of the alley's brick wall, he quickly propelled himself over a wood slat fence that blocked the end of the alleyway. Climbing the walls like a stuntman in a martial arts film, a split second later, the man was out of sight and running away on the far side of the fence.

Undeterred, Charlie refused to relent, and he, too, sprinted down the alleyway and approached the wood slat fence. Surveying his surroundings, he quickly realized that he wouldn't be able to duplicate the feat of acrobatics he had just witnessed in front of him. Propelling himself over the 8-foot enclosure like a spider-monkey wasn't a maneuver his body was built for, so he did the only thing he could think of in the moment and lowered his shoulder to barrel through it.

With an enormous "BANG", Charlie smashed through the fence and fell, rolling on the ground with shattered wood splinters cascading all around him. After a moment of bewilderment, Charlie regained his bearings. While his head slowly cleared, and his eyes attempted to refocus, he saw his quarry standing half a block down the street staring at him as if he were waiting.

Unfazed, the man turned and strolled into an auto repair shop.

Charlie watched as the man leisurely entered the building, muttering to himself, "The balls on this guy…"

Mindful that he was alone on a deserted street without any back-up, Charlie quickly reached for his shoulder walkie talkie to radio Darryl for support.

"Darryl! Do you copy? Come in! I'm on…Webster and 19th Street, do you copy?!"

Listening intently, the only reply he received was a sharp crackling static sound. As he grabbed his two-way radio and examined it more closely, Charlie realized that the fence had obliterated the device. Now inoperable, Charlie ripped it off of his shoulder in frustration and slammed it to the ground.

"Damn it!"

For a moment, Charlie considered following standard protocol and waiting for back-up to arrive. Or, at the very least, to get word to his partner and let him know his exact location. Those were the practical options, to be sure, but as he contemplated the benefits of waiting, like "safety" and" prudence", he suddenly remembered he that he just didn't give a crap anymore. He'd be dead within months regardless, and he decided then and there that he'd rather go down fighting than wasting away in a hospital bed somewhere.

Resolved, Charlie unholstered his sidearm and quickly approached the auto body shop that had a sold sign hanging in its window. Once again, the gun shook in his hand as he walked through the open garage, but this time, he was unsure if it was the disease or his adrenaline that caused the gun to tremble.

Inside the garage, scurrying rodents and reflected sunlight startled Charlie, causing him to swing his gun from one side of the bay to the other. With each step he took, he felt as though invisible attackers were jumping at him from every corner of the repair shop. Although the scares proved to be false alarms, Charlie's heightened anxiety and frayed nerves kept his trembling trigger finger on a razor's edge.

As he finished scouring the inside of the hangar, Charlie noticed a lone door at the back of the garage. The only exit available, Charlie approached it with extreme caution, careful not to make a sound as he gathered that this must have been where his adversary had gone.

Slowly pushing open the door, Charlie saw that it led to a dingy hallway and a series of outdated offices. The décor had a mid-seventies motif, while the carpeting had a smell from decades earlier. A single light bulb dangled from the hallway's ceiling, and Charlie's eyes struggled to adjust as it flickered and buzzed.

The interior's appearance gave the impression of a family-run business that had operated for several generations without the desire or impetus for improvements. Recalling the 'Sold' sign out front, Charlie offhandedly wondered to himself who in their right mind would have bought a dump like this, especially in its current condition.

Charlie quickly snapped back to the moment, slowly creeping down the hallway, his senses operating on high alert. Cautiously poking his head into each room he approached, Charlie scanned their interiors for movement or evidence that his quarry had been there. Every office he searched was empty, and Charlie soon noticed that the door to one suite at the end of the hallway was unlike any of the others.

It was closed.

Charlie cautiously advanced on the door, his gun raised, paused, and then shouted at its threshold, "Police! Come out!"

There was a deafening silence from the other side of the entryway, and Charlie could feel the suboccipital lymph nodes at the base of his skull begin to swell.

"I said NOW God damn it!" Charlie screamed.

Without receiving a response, Charlie took a moment to steady his nerves and then resigned himself to what he had to do.

"Let's do this" he said to himself as he squared his shoulders in preparation to barrel through.

As he took one last deep breath and shifted his weight in order to lunge at the door, a voice suddenly called out from the other side in response, a moment before he propelled himself forward, "We are unarmed."

Charlie stopped his momentum with an exhale and was about to shout another command when a startling thought suddenly occurred to him, "'We'?"

The response confused Charlie, and his mind quickly filled with questions. How many people were on the other side?

Could the man's assurance be trusted? What would he encounter if he did decide to go through?

It didn't take Charlie long to answer his own questions: who cared? With his health failing and his future without hope, in the end, it really didn't matter what happened once he opened that door.

Now unencumbered by concern for his own safety, Charlie slowly pushed open the ingress and declared to all that were listening, "I'm coming in!"

Upon entering the room, Charlie saw the man sitting behind a dilapidated desk covered in disheveled papers and accented by a rotary phone blanketed in dust. On the wood-paneled walls hung low-quality paintings and certifications likely expired by decades. The ceiling boasted light fixtures from the 70s and asbestos protruded from cracks.

Charlie quickly turned his attention back towards the man. His hands were calmly raised, and behind him stood two similar looking dark-skinned men, both loosely clasping their hands in front of them.

Charlie's adrenaline spiked as he shouted commands with his gun still trained on the two potential threats, "Show me your hands, now!"

Both men hesitated, and Charlie could feel his nerves reach their limit as he screamed, "Now!"

The man at the desk kept his eyes on Charlie's and nodded slightly, giving the two men permission to follow the policeman's instructions. Slowly, both men raised their hands in compliance.

For a moment, Charlie finally felt a semblance of calm until the man he had chased said, "I assure you, we pose no threat, Officer Weaver."

With the gun still pointed at the three men, Charlie's legs wobbled slightly in shock, unsure of what he'd just heard.

"What?"

"I apologize for the theatrics, Mr. Weaver, but it was the only way we could meet with you on such short notice, and, more importantly, in seclusion."

Confused, Charlie demanded, "Who are you, and how the hell do you know my name?"

The man continued, staring at Charlie's shaking gun, "We know a great deal about you Officer Weaver. Where you were born, what high school you attended, and even your scores on your Officer's exam. In truth, we know everything about you…including your Parkinson's diagnosis."

"What?" Charlie stammered.

"A terribly debilitating affliction, Mr. Weaver. Our deepest sympathies. A disease that can cause uncontrolled tremors, am I right?"

"Well, yes, but –."

"Then, if you could be so kind…" the man nodded towards Charlie's shaking gun, "Would you mind doing all of us a favor and lowering your firearm? For everyone's safety."

Charlie's eyes left the man for a moment and focused on the extreme shaking of his hand holding the gun, something he hadn't noticed until just that moment.

He lowered it slowly and asked, "How do you know about my Parkinson's? I haven't told anyone about that. Did you speak with Dr. Cohen?"

"Dr. Cohen? I'm afraid not."

"Then how!?"

The man remained silent, giving Charlie a few moments to think through every possible scenario.

Charlie continued out loud, more to himself than the man, "The only other time I've even mentioned the word Parkinson's was…"

"Was…", the man led.

"Was on a registration form I filled out online, but that was for…"

Charlie's eyes widened in shock, and his brain began to swirl.

"Mr. Weaver, it was your registration last night in Mr. Bouchon's lottery which has led to our meeting today. My name is Gatlin, and I am here as a Representative of Bouchon

Industries to inform you that you have won, Mr. Weaver. You are the final winner in Mr. Bouchon's lottery. Congratulations."

Still in a trance, Charlie was unable to comprehend what he had just heard and muttered, "I…won?"

"Your number was chosen during last night's drawing, Mr. Weaver, and therefore, you have been selected as the third alternate in Mr. Bouchon's lottery. Do you know what that means?"

Charlie stammered "I don't know what any of this means."

"It means, Mr. Weaver, that of the billions upon billions of names that were entered into the lottery, yours was chosen. You have been given a chance to be cured of the disease that is now ravaging your body."

Charlie whispered to himself, "I…I don't believe it."

"Believe it, Mr. Weaver. It's true."

Charlie stood in silence for a moment, looking around the room, unsure if he or it was spinning. Was it possible? Could he really have won? Would this nightmare really be just a distant memory soon?

Charlie's mind raced, and his body became numb as he mumbled to himself, "Cured…"

Gatlin cleared his throat, breaking Charlie's reverie, "However, also believe this Mr. Weaver. You are the third alternate, meaning you will only be cured if several of the other initial winners decide to forfeit *their* spots. Remember, many of them have paid handsomely for this opportunity or have already passed on equally life-changing offers. Do I make myself clear?"

Charlie fell silent for a moment as what he'd just heard slowly sunk in. "You mean –."

"I mean, that as the third alternate, *three of the previous winners would have to decline being cured for YOU to be cured.*"

The reality of this statement quickly took the air out of room for Charlie.

"Oh, I see…"

Sensing his moment, Gatlin continued, "Which is why I think you will be pleased with the generous offer I have been tasked with presenting to you today. It seems there is a billionaire out there who is willing to bet that, although unlikely, there is the slightest chance that the last official spot might become available to the third alternate. As such, I am here to make you the following offer. May I?"

Gatlin lowered his right hand and intimated he would reach into his coat pocket. Charlie kept a close eye on him and nodded, his gun still ready to raise at a moment's notice.

Gatlin slowly reached into his pocket and pulled out an envelope. The other men simultaneously lowered their hands as Gatlin pushed the envelope across the table towards Charlie.

"For you Mr. Weaver. All you have to do is surrender your third alternate spot."

Charlie stared at the envelope without moving, but after a beat, he holstered his gun and finally reached down to pick it up.

He slowly and deliberately opened the envelope, unsure what he would find within. Inside, he pulled out a check, and his eyes bulged as he read "One…billion Dollars?"

"Yes Mr. Weaver. A billion dollars. With that much money at stake, you can see why it was imperative to meet with you as quickly as possible. You have a day to decide whether you will accept the payment, but it can be yours now, if you like, with just the stroke of a pen."

One of the men behind Gatlin pulled out a contract from his coat pocket while the other pulled out a pen. They handed both to Gatlin, who slid them towards Charlie.

"All you have to do is sign."

Looking at the check and the contract in front of him, Charlie's mind raced as he began to think of what that amount of money meant. That kind of money - and the freedom it offered – were incomprehensible. He would be able to do what he wanted, go where he wanted, and buy what he wanted. It meant absolute freedom.

Excitedly, Charlie picked up the pen and bent over to sign the contract.

As he did, his hand shook uncontrollably, and Charlie found himself having to steady his right hand with his left. Frustrated,

Charlie closed his eyes, took a deep breath, and focused on stilling his hand so that he could sign his name.

"Come on…" Charlie whispered to himself.

With his eyes closed and fully concentrating, Charlie attempted to calm himself by fantasizing about what he would do with his newfound fortune. As he did, he pictured taking amazing life-changing adventures, visiting wondrous sights in exotic lands, and participating in the exploits that only the world's wealthiest would ever experience.

But as he did, a realization suddenly washed over Charlie.

All those distractions and material objects would be meaningless, if he had no one to share them with.

Slowly, Charlie lowered the pen onto the desk and opened his eyes.

Staring directly at Gatlin, Charlie said, "I'm sorry, but I'll have to pass."

In stunned disbelief, Gatlin probed, "Excuse me?"

Pushing the check back towards Gatlin, Charlie said, "Tell whoever made the offer that they can keep their money."

Still in shock, Gatlin explained, "You understand, Mr. Weaver, that as the third alternate, you most likely won't be chosen. Then you won't be cured of your Parkinson's *or* have the money."

"I understand."

"Then why the hell –."

Charlie interrupted, "What good is any amount of money, if I don't have the time to spend it or a family to share it with?"

Charlie paused, strengthening his resolve. "Thank you for the offer, Gatlin, but I'll take my chances with the third alternate spot."

For several moments, Gatlin sat stone-faced, letting Charlie's decision hang in the air.

Then, a subtle smile spread over the Tuvaluan's face as he replied, "Very well said, Mr. Weaver. I respect your decision."

Gatlin picked up the check and slowly tore it to pieces, "Besides, now I get the satisfaction of telling the entitled billionaire who submitted this offer that, for once, he won't be getting what he wants."

Both men nodded as Gatlin rose from the desk.

The two bodyguards followed him as he approached the back door, where he stopped, and turned towards Charlie, "After all the winners I've met with, it was actually a pleasure to meet you, Mr. Weaver. You're one of the good ones."

Quizzically Charlie asked, "*One* of the good ones?"

With a wry smile, Gatlin said, "Of two."

Charlie followed the three men outside. They opened the doors to the awaiting limousine that was idling and got in.

Closing the door, Gatlin lowered his window and said to Charlie, "Be ready, Mr. Weaver. We will be sending a car for you in 48 hours."

"A car? Where will I be going?"

"To meet Mr. Bouchon, of course."

Charlie's body inadvertently tensed, shocked at what he'd just heard.

Gatlin continued, "Until then, please remain inside of your apartment, and do not tell anyone of what has transpired here."

"Really? Why?"

"For the same reason we met with you in private today, Mr. Weaver, your own protection."

As the car began to pull away, Charlie appealed, "Protection? From who?"

Gatlin met his eyes, "Everyone."

CHAPTER 25

Art Decker sat at the desk in his corner office, romanticizing the last several months, knowing they had likely been the best of his life. The worldwide attention, unparalleled celebrity, and critical acclaim had led to the fulfillment of every ambition he had ever dreamt of. The envy of all in his profession, his career had even soared past those of former media icons like Cronkite or Murrow. Although it was true that in his storied vocation he had interviewed multinational CEOs, superstar celebrities, and infamous dictators, those moments had all paled in comparison to the spectacle of Michel Bouchon's lottery.

Reflecting on the moment the enigmatic cell phone vibrated in his jacket pocket, and the mysterious man who had presumably put it there, brought a smile to Art's face.

For reasons he still did not understand, that man and his small device had unmistakably altered the course of his life. He had become the center of the media world and had reached the pinnacle of his profession. He had been the "insider" that everyone had looked to, and even more prestigious, the journalist with the most sought-after "source." Of course, the identity of the source was just as much a mystery to Art as it was to everyone else, but the rest of the world didn't need to know that.

Now, however, it was all over. There were no more cryptic texts to read, clandestine handoffs in broad daylight, or primetime panels of experts to host. With the lottery now completed and interest already beginning to fade, his days of speculating over salacious tidbits and promoting unconfirmed conspiracy theories had come to an end.

As the cold reality of his waning fame began to set in, Art had to accept the fact that he had peaked. Never again would he come close to the heights he had just achieved over the last several months or the acclaim he had garnered. Even worse was the very real prospect that he might slowly slide back into relative obscurity.

Like a newly minted bride the morning after her wedding, Art could feel himself descending into depression, no longer the center of everyone else's attention.

A blanket of self-pity began to fully engulf the news anchor, until his melancholy was suddenly broken by a vibration that came from inside one of his desk's drawers.

Was it possible?

He sat perfectly still in absolute silence, not allowing himself to feel what would undoubtedly be false hope and yet, listening intently just to make sure.

A second buzz confirmed his most fervent desire. Frantic, Art dove into his pants pocket and scrambled to find his keys. Fumbling with them for a few agonizing seconds, he unconsciously let out a sigh of relief as he found and inserted the elusive key into his desk drawer's lock. Wrenching it open quickly, his eyes lit up as he beheld what had become his most prized possession: "The" cell phone.

Grabbing the phone without hesitation, Art was unable to breathe as he gaped at its screen. Feverishly examining the text message that was displayed, the enormity of what he was reading began to take shape.

Reflexively, Art mumbled to himself, "Oh, my, God."

Slowly lowering the cell phone his mind raced as he tried to process what he had just read. Instinctively, he quickly snapped back to the present as he spotted his producer, Jerry, walking past his office door.

Jumping to his feet Art shouted, "Jerry! Get me on camera, now!"

Startled, Jerry asked, brow furrowed, "Now? For Christ's sake, Art, it's Primetime and –."

Incensed, Art interrupted with a scream, "God damn it, I said NOW!"

Rattled by Art's conviction, the Producer quickly acquiesced and said, "Ok, ok, fine. Jeez. Which program should we break into?"

With a maniacal glare in his eyes and a burning heat under his skin, Art seethed, "All of them."

CHAPTER 26

Sitting alone in her opulent estate in Woodside, California, Shira Eisenberg watched the news unfold on her television, struggling to suppress her horror and outrage.

In her late forties, with curly dark hair, pale white skin and waif-like build, the social media pioneer was stunned as she listened to Art Decker expound on her life's most intimate details. Shockingly however, not only were the finer points of her personal history being exposed, so too were the bios of the other winners in Michel Bouchon's lottery.

How had he known?

Having taken every conceivable precaution to maintain her anonymity, she had intended for her private life to remain just that, private. But now, her identity, and the amount she had spent on her spot had somehow been leaked to the media. Dripping with faux concern, the press had been quick to point out the irony of one of social media's most iconic figures having her personal data publicly exposed.

Labeled "The Dirty Baker's Dozen", Shira and the other twelve recipients were castigated by the media for their perceived narcissism, with many in the press arguing that they had "squandered" obscene amounts of money in the pursuit of their own self-interest. At the forefront of this ridicule, was of course the man who had broken the news, Art Decker.

"It's simply disgusting if you ask me," Art Decker admonished his panel of guests planting his flag atop the moral high ground. "Just think of how many mouths that could have been fed with that kind of money. How much good could have been done in the world?"

"Hear, hear," one of the panelists concurred.

"And yet," Art continued, "these oligarchs had the audacity to spend billions of dollars for a single person's health. It truly is sickening."

Shira rose and paced nervously in her living room, glancing out of a skylight at one of the helicopters that circled overhead. They had been noisily hovering above ever since the news had first broken, joining the hordes of protestors camped at the front gate of her compound.

"Vultures," Shira raged to the empty room.

Having dropped out of college early, Shira had interned at a tiny start-up pioneering a radical new idea: social media. Biding her time until she could find a "real job", Shira had admittedly thought the idea was absurd, and only something that kids of her generation would play with while wasting time. In many ways, she'd been right.

Over the years, however, as the company grew from a handful of employees to more than 50,000, she had seen her career and personal fortune balloon.

It had been argued in the media that her dedication and hard work had cost her her marriage, but she constantly reassured herself that that trade-off had been worth it. Today, those same skeptics had crowned her one of the wealthiest women in the world, with presumably everything she could have ever wanted.

They had been mostly right. She did have just about everything - except a healthy pancreas.

When she had first heard about Michel Bouchon's lottery, she'd known from the very outset what she would do. With the cancer eating her away from the inside, Shira had had precious little time to debate the morality of whether her health was worth the fortune she'd spend. Her doctors had given her the grim prognosis, warning her that her days were numbered. And yet, even with such a bleak diagnosis, the indelible drive that had fueled her meteoric rise had also compelled her to do whatever it took to save her life.

Let them judge, Shira mused as she glanced back at the television - she *would* live.

As she anxiously waited for her ride to meet Mr. Bouchon, Shira couldn't help herself as she intently watched the biographies of the other winners. Like everyone else on the planet, she found herself fascinated by their stories.

"Art, just to be clear, you can confirm that Oman Disden, the notorious Sudanese Warlord, spent in excess of $6.5 billion for his spot?"

"Through my exclusive sources, yes."

One of the other panelists asked, "Where did he even get that kind of money, Art?"

Art smiled to himself, having waited for this planted question. His staff had dug up some statistics that morning, and he was looking forward to passing them off as his own. "Great question. You see, in that part of the continent, bloody conflicts between warring factions have resulted in a massive proliferation of weapons sales. Why, in the last eighteen months alone, it is estimated that more than two million guns have been funneled into the region, generating by some accounts more than $3 billion in trade. Wars are expensive, and Mr. Disden has apparently been the primary benefactor, acting as the principal arms dealer for that corner of the globe. In a way, it reminds me of the time I interviewed some of the armed revolutionaries in Columbia known as FARC. You see, there I was, in the jungle surrounded by a rag-tag ensemble of freedom fighters who only wanted to –."

Shira tuned him out, pacing the room, uninterested in his personal anecdotes and blatant self-aggrandizement. He was clearly an egotistical moron who was only concerned with hearing his own voice. However, as much as she despised him at the moment, Shira had to admit the man did deserve a fair amount of credit. After all, he had been right. She *had* spent $4 billion for her spot.

After several minutes of grandstanding, Art Decker finished his display of pomposity and returned to covering the intimate details of the winners' profiles. Resist as she might, Shira found herself completely engrossed by the back stories he revealed and the minutia of these now infamous figures' lives.

Clinging to every word, she couldn't help but wonder if the New York hedge fund manager was possibly as arrogant as was being portrayed, or if the business practices of the Indian telemarketing founder had really been as questionable as had been inferred.

Of course, Shira watched with a fair amount of skepticism. She had, after all, been labelled by these same talking heads as emotionless and robotic. Nothing could be further from the truth she had assured herself, perhaps unconvincingly. After all, her twenty million followers meant otherwise, didn't they?

As the panelists fought to talk over one another, Art Decker interjected, "Of course, predictably, the three alternate spots sold for much less than the ten original spots. Was anyone surprised by that?"

"I wasn't," one of the panelists offered. "I mean, think about it. Why would any of the original winners EVER give up their spots? Especially now, after your bombshell report and the worldwide exposure that's come with it. Frankly, those alternate spots should be worthless."

"Worthless?" One of the other panelists chirped in, "Hardly. Just ask legendary movie star Cynthia Swift. She must have thought they were pretty valuable since, according to Art's source, she reportedly paid nearly $2 billion for one."

"Don't you mean her husband paid?" another panelist pettily added.

"Regardless of whose pocket it came from, that amount of money was still spent."

Another panelist offered, "I guess. I just wonder what would have caused someone with such a seemingly perfect life to spend such an obscene amount of money."

"Perhaps things aren't always as glamorous behind the curtain as they are made out to be."

"Speaking of the inexplicable," Art interjected, "I think we all can agree though that the biggest mystery surrounding Michel Bouchon's lottery has to stem from the final spot, wouldn't you concur?"

The entire panel nodded, before one member sarcastically quipped, "You mean the mystery of why that cop turned down a billion dollars?"

The coterie of panelists all laughed, with one proclaiming over the ruckus, "What an idiot!"

"I know, can you imagine passing up that much money for the THIRD alternate spot?" another added.

A third jumped in, "Exactly! As if three of other winners would give up their spots!"

As the laughter continued to rage, Art whispered in a serious tone.

"No, I meant the last of the *original* winners."

Suddenly, the nastiness around the table became unnervingly quiet as all breathlessly anticipated how Art would proceed. The panel, and the viewers at large, hoped that his "source" had disclosed new, previously unheard-of information that would shed at least *some* light on who the unknown winner was and how much they had paid.

"As we all know by now, that spot was purchased by a blind trust, and as such, is the only one I was unable to gather any information about. Who the recipient is or how much they paid wasn't something my exclusive source could reveal…and I'm sad to report, that initial shroud of secrecy remains in effect."

There was an audible groan from the men and women who sat around the table, which likely mimicked the reaction of the viewing audience around the world.

Art continued, "But, if you consider that each subsequent spot sold for larger and larger dollar amounts, with the first known spot selling for $100 million and the ninth selling for more than $11 billion, it's anyone's guess how much the *tenth* spot went for. Truly, that final piece to Michel Bouchon's lottery is a gripping mystery that remains to be solved. And when it is, mark my words, *that* will be the biggest news story to come out of this entire spectacle."

As curious as Shira was about all of the winners, again, she had to admit that Art Decker was right. Like everyone else, all she could think about was who was behind the final spot and how much they had paid. Wild speculation had run rampant all day and night on every news channel as potential names and possible afflictions had ceaselessly been bandied about. Like a shout in an echo chamber, each subsequent rumor had reverberated with increasing ferocity until nothing else was discussed on television but the secrecy surrounding the identity of the person behind the blind trust.

Shira zipped up her travel bag and prepared to meet Mr. Bouchon. She smiled, knowing that unlike everyone else on the planet, she was about to find out.

CHAPTER 27

Charlie sat on his couch watching the madness unfold on TV, wondering if he had made a mistake. Over the last 24 hours, prognosticators on every channel had moralized their disdain for the billionaire winners they claimed were simply buying their way out of misfortune, but to his surprise, they had expressed abject contempt for him as well.

Labeled a 'moron' and a 'fool', speculation mounted as to why he had passed on the billion-dollar offer. Some had said it was because he'd been greedy and wanted more money, while others had argued that he might have indeed been ill. All agreed, though, that he'd squandered his chance. As the third alternate with little hope of being cured and now with no money to show for it, Charlie got the feeling that the consensus regarding his decision was universal: he'd chosen poorly.

He rose from his seat and peaked out of his curtains at the dozens of news vans that lit up the darkened streets outside of his apartment. Simultaneously, he heard a live play-by-play of his action from the TV behind him. Scores of cameras were trained on his building, and he had been trapped inside ever since word of his win was leaked. Like a zoo animal, Charlie had become nothing more than an oddity to be gawked at and photographed by the media.

He quickly drew the curtains closed as reporters on the television commented on his appearance and speculated on what they believed was going through his head. They, of course, had no idea what he was thinking or how he desperately wished his wife and son were with him now. The armchair psychiatrists on the screen frustrated Charlie, and soon, he found himself ruing the decision to have registered in the first place. The lottery had turned his life into a horrifying spectacle, and once again, he glanced at his handgun, wondering if that wasn't the easiest way out of this circus.

Just as his mind drifted towards the darkness, there was a knock at his front door.

Over the screams of reporters, held back by Tuvaluan guards stationed at his entrance, a familiar voice called out, "It's me, Charlie. Can we come in?"

Charlie peeked through the peephole and quickly opened his door for Gatlin as a barrage of camera flashes turned his front door into a makeshift discotheque.

Blinded by the lights, Charlie covered his eyes as scores of reporters screamed, "Charlie! Charlie! Charlie!"

Stunned and unable to see clearly, Charlie quickly closed the door behind Gatlin as he and two of his men brushed past him into the apartment, leaving the mob of reporters outside.

Instinctively, Gatlin took stock of the run-down apartment while his compatriots quickly spread out, securing the remaining rooms.

Rubbing his eyes to help them readjust, Charlie offered, "It's just me. There's no one else here."

Gatlin remained stone-faced as he slowly paced around Charlie's living room, stepping over empty whiskey bottles and past overflowing trash cans.

"Standard protocol, Mr. Weaver."

After a few moments, the first man returned and reported, "Clear." Gatlin huffed an acknowledgement as he looked over some of the pictures hanging from Charlie's wall.

Seconds later, the second man returned from Charlie's bedroom and hesitated.

"Well?" Gatlin asked, his gaze remaining fixed on the pictures that adorned Charlie's mantel.

"Clear sir, but you're not going to believe this…"

After a momentary pause, Gatlin urged, "Spit it out, son."

Glancing at Charlie, the second man continued incredulously, "This guy still sleeps."

Holding the framed newspaper article in his hands that detailed the loss of Charlie's wife and son, Gatlin reverently lowered it back onto its shelf. He slowly turned to look directly at Charlie, and for the first time, Charlie could sense a glimmer of empathy emanate from the man who had, to this point, shown none.

With his eyes still locked on Charlie, he addressed his younger compatriot and solemnly replied, "Not everyone wants to stay awake."

A silent reverie hung in the room between the men, the emptiness filled by the blaring TV and the news reporters continuing to babble incoherently. Gatlin looked towards the TV and, as they had for hours, listened to the pundits who once again chastised Charlie for his inexplicably "poor decision."

Unruffled by the never-ending avalanche of slights, Charlie picked up the remote from his couch and turned it off.

Unsure how his host was holding up, Gatlin consoled, "I'm afraid the media hasn't exactly been kind to you these last few days, have they, Mr. Weaver?"

Dropping the remote back onto his couch, Charlie sighed and said, "I'm used to it…I'm a cop."

Gatlin smiled, appreciating the man's perspective and courage under such extraordinary circumstances.

"Good to hear. You ready to get out of here then?"

Charlie took a deep breath, "Just give the word."

"We've got a plane ready to go now, so pack your things. Toiletries, medicines, and bring enough clothes for three days. You've got 15 minutes."

Charlie nodded and began to head towards his room when he suddenly remembered a question that had been running through his head non-stop over the last 48 hours.

Turning back towards Gatlin, he asked, "Care to tell me where we're going?"

Gatlin maintained eye contact, the seriousness of his response radiating from his face, "I can't, Charlie, for your own protection."

"Protection." There was that word again. Gatlin hadn't exaggerated the first time he'd warned him, so Charlie decided not to push. In that moment, only two days ago, Charlie had

had little to no inkling of how his life was about to change or how prophetic that advice would end up being. Now, with things outside descending into chaos, he was grateful for the men Gatlin had stationed around his building and for the *protection* they had provided.

Charlie threw his personal items like clothes, shoes, and Dopp Kit into a rucksack. He glanced around his apartment, wondering what his life would be like when he saw it again. Would his hand still shake? Would he be taking a different medication or some kind of shot? And perhaps the most random question of them all: would the guys at the station ever stop busting his balls for passing up on so much money?

With that last thought beginning to recede, the smile it produced also quickly began to fade, as Charlie snapped back to reality and the more likely scenario that awaited him. One where he, as the third alternate, would just end up back where he was at this very moment – still sick, stuck in this dingy hovel, with only his handgun to look forward to.

Shaking his head to clear it, Charlie squared his jaw and forced himself to resist the negativity he'd so easily given in to these last several months. With great effort, he reminded himself just how lucky he was because, unlike the hundreds of millions around the globe who were battling their own diseases, at least he had a *chance* at curing his.

Charlie steadied himself and walked out of his room with his bag in his hand. In his living room, Gatlin and his men waited for him before leading him to the front door.

Gathering themselves for the onslaught of reporters on the other side, Gatlin paused and said to Charlie, "One last thing. Your cell phone."

Confused, Charlie asked, "What about it?"

"You're going to have to leave it here, Charlie."

Reluctantly, Charlie asked, "Really?"

Gatlin nodded and said, "No electronic devices at all, Charlie. It's the same for all of the winners. They simply aren't permitted where we're going. As a matter of fact, do you have anything else that's electrical? Radio? Camera? Key fob?"

Slightly rattled by the request, Charlie thought for a moment and then shook his head, "Not that I can think of…"

"Then, if you wouldn't mind…" Gatlin said, extending his hand.

Charlie reached into his pocket and pulled out his cell phone, handing it over to Gatlin, who then placed it on Charlie's couch.

"It'll be right here when you get back."

Once again, Charlie wondered off-handedly how different his life might be when that occurred.

Gatlin reached for the doorknob and continued, "Alright then. Are you ready?"

As Charlie was about to nod, a thought struck him and he said, "I think so, I've got everything I need to – wait!"

Charlie quickly spun around and approached his cabinet full of liquor. As he walked towards the alcohol, he resolutely passed the half-emptied bottles on their shelves and made his way to the homemade shrine of his family that rested above his mantel.

Gently picking up the newspaper clipping of his family in its wooden frame, Charlie delicately placed the framed article into his bag and said, "Now I'm ready."

Gatlin smiled and then immediately refocused. Taking a deep breath, he said, "Then stay close to me, Charlie, and follow us to the limo. It's going to be a gauntlet out there."

The moment Gatlin opened the apartment's front door, the cascade of flashes popped in such quick succession that, to Charlie, the brightness felt as though it were emanating from the beam of a powerful spotlight. Like they had when he had first been diagnosed in the doctor's office all of those months ago, Charlie's ears began to ring so loudly that he felt the sound reverberate through his skull.

The cacophony of questions shouted at him by reporters were imperceptible over the deafening ring inside of his head. Hands grabbed at him from every direction, and all Charlie could see were the dark suit backs of the security men as he was whisked through the hordes of screaming people.

Charlie kept his head down and moved in unison with the group as they reached the awaiting limousine. With the rear door open, Charlie was forcibly pushed inside like a head of state escaping a would-be assassination attempt. Gatlin quickly followed him inside and slammed the door behind him once they were both safely in and secure.

From the interior windows of the car, the two men could see the hundreds of shrieking journalists as they all pressed against the glass, each one trying to capture that elusive font-page picture. With dozens of hands pounding menacingly on the car windows and their vehicle beginning to shake violently from side to side, for a moment, Charlie couldn't help but wonder if Gatlin carried a sidearm.

The limousine honked loudly and began to move forward. Gatlin straightened his suit lapel and kept watch through the window at the remaining guards who maintained their positions behind, facilitating an escape route for their car.

"We made it," Charlie sighed, thankful to be on the move.

"Hardly," Gatlin grimaced.

Pulling out a microphone connected to a walkie-talkie inside of his suit, Gatlin announced, "We're on the move."

"Copy," came the response.

Charlie looked around bewildered as the vehicle gained speed, "'Hardly'? What do you mean?"

"Look," Gatlin replied, pointing out the window.

Next to the limo, five or six cars chased and paralleled theirs, frantically snapping pictures and streaming live video. Charlie watched as they brazenly wove through traffic, with little regard for other motorists or the safety of pedestrians.

Looking up through the tinted sunroof, he noticed that even at night, he still had to shield his eyes. Hundreds of feet above their vehicle, swarms of helicopters simultaneously shone their spotlights, illuminating his car like a beacon in a tumultuous sea.

As the limousine led a trail of paparazzi through the streets of Oakland, residents, who had been watching the spectacle live on their televisions, came pouring out of their houses to shout encouragements to Charlie. Some held signs while others jumped and waved. Charlie couldn't help but smile. He had patrolled these streets countless times in the past, but he had never seen them quite like this before. Unabashed support gushed from the public he'd spent years serving and protecting, and, as he had that first day he'd donned his badge, Charlie couldn't help but feel an immense sense of hometown pride too.

The limo entered a private entrance to the Oakland airport, and the line of cars that had chased them were stopped by airport security, unable to pursue any further. Surprisingly, though, Charlie could still see the helicopters as they continued to follow, hovering in synchrony above the airfield.

"So much for restricted airspace," Charlie muttered to himself.

The limo sped along the airport's tarmac, approaching a massive hangar, and quickly entered through two towering doors that automatically closed behind them. Once inside, the car screeched to a halt in the center of the well-lit hangar, directly in front of five private jets.

Charlie got out of the car with Gatlin and instantly a security team of Tuvaluans hurriedly greeted them, with one politely but firmly asking, "If you wouldn't mind, please raise your hands in the air, gentlemen. We need to check you for any devices that might be transmitting data."

Exasperated, Charlie asked, "Again? You can't be serious. Fellas, we've been together practically every second."

As a member of the security detail ran a wand over his clothing and bag, a loud screeching sound emitted, and everyone froze in their tracks. The hangar was filled with a palpable silence as the security guard gingerly reached into Charlie's coat pocket and pulled out a tiny electronic tracking device.

"Practically," he said with disdain.

"Unbelievable," Charlie gasped. "Someone outside of my apartment, on the way to the car, must have reached through the crowd and —."

Uninterested in "The how", the man dropped the device on the ground and stomped it with his foot.

The security guard then looked at Charlie and said, "As you can see, Mr. Weaver, every attempt will be made to breach our security, which means we haven't much time. So please, if you would, pick a number between one and five."

Stunned by the request, Charlie stammered, "What do you mean?"

"Please, time is of the essence, Mr. Weaver. Pick a number."

Charlie hesitated for a moment and then said, "Three?"

"'Three' it is. This way, Mr. Weaver, if you will follow me."

The security detail quickly shuffled Charlie to the middle airplane of the five. As he walked up the steps, the team of guards stood watch at the base of the staircase, with only Gatlin following him aboard.

Inside the sumptuous fifteen-passenger airplane, Charlie took his seat in a plush dark leather chair that swiveled and reclined. He couldn't help but be impressed by the polished armrests of mahogany and brass window plating.

"So, this is how the other half lives," Charlie deadpanned as he took in his surroundings.

"It's how Mr. Bouchon lives," Gatlin replied while taking his seat.

Charlie's brow furrowed as he continued to examine the plane's interior and noted that all of the windows had been blacked out.

Seeing Charlie's concern, Gatlin offered, "It's just a precaution, Charlie, so the press doesn't know which plane you are in."

Charlie replied passive-aggressively, "And so I don't know where I'm going."

Charlie's aircraft rolled out of the hangar with the others in a single file line. The five planes taxied across the tarmac, revving their engines simultaneously in preparation for takeoff.

With his private jet in to position behind the others, a Tuvaluan stewardess approached Charlie deferentially and asked, "Would you like something to drink, Mr. Weaver, before we get going?"

Out of habit, Charlie was about to ask for his "go-to", a whiskey on the rocks, when he paused for a moment and turned his head.

Looking at the picture frame poking out of his opened bag on the seat beside him, he said, "No, thank you. I'll pass."

The flight attendant nodded her understanding and continued past, but Gatlin took note. He remembered the countless liquor bottles he'd seen strewn throughout Charlie's apartment and wondered if it was possible that, having been given the opportunity of a lifetime, their guest was turning over a new leaf.

Had a change of heart been triggered in Charlie?

Exhausted and unaware of Gatlin's observation, Charlie kicked off his shoes, closed his eyes, and reclined his chair back to settle in. Before the plane had even reached the runway, the man, whose body had spent the past 48 hours in a constant state of alertness, quickly succumbed to fatigue as he drifted off to a much-needed sleep.

The flight attendant took her seat and buckled in for takeoff. She looked over at Charlie as he slept and sighed, whispering to Gatlin, "So peaceful, watching him sleep. I'd almost forgotten what that looked like."

With intrusive helicopters still hovering nearby, the first plane bounded down the runway and took off into the darkness of the night sky. As each took flight and banked in their own direction, the tens of millions around the world who watched had no idea which plane carried Charlie.

Or, like the man himself, where he was headed.

CHAPTER 28

Something wasn't right.

As Yan Huen anxiously paced the balcony of his sumptuous Hong Kong Penthouse with a glass of Dom Perignon in his hand, he couldn't shake the feeling that he was missing something. Unable to pinpoint where his anxiety stemmed from, he knew there was a piece to the puzzle that eluded him, or perhaps more accurately, that just didn't fit.

Had he taken everything into account? Was there an angle he had miscalculated?

Having spent his life scratching and clawing to advance his position, Yan's insatiable competitive drive had fueled his never-ending quest to win at any cost. In order to dominate, he had devoted decades to sharpening his unique gift: the ability to see the entire field long before others had even stepped onto it. This uncommon ability had been the foundation of his success and the primary reason why he'd always had an advantage over his competition.

Now, however, for some unknown reason, he felt a twinge deep inside that he hadn't felt since his initial foray into counterfeiting as a youth.

Things inexplicably didn't make sense.

If the newscasters were to be believed, the African arms dealer had paid a little more than $6 billion for his spot. Although certainly a sizeable amount, it was nowhere near the $11 billion that Yan's blind trust had offered for the same spot. Even more confounding was the report that the Oil heir from Saudi Arabia had spent $12 billion for the next spot, while he had offered more than $25.

Weren't these spots supposed to go to the highest bidder?

For a moment, Yan cast aside his unease as he congratulated himself on the one thing that had gone as planned: his foresight.

Setting up the blind trust in the first place had shown prudence and had allowed him to protect the fundamental cornerstone to his plan: his identity. While those other fools had allowed their information to be exposed, compromising themselves and their bids in the process, he had taken great care to ensure he remained anonymous.

Of course, that sort of legal insulation had come at a great cost, but the rewards for uncovering the mystery behind Michel Bouchon's cure would be well worth the money he had spent.

As he stood on his balcony's ledge lamenting his attorney's fees, the topic of expenses forced him once again to acknowledge the reality of the money he'd spent on the spot itself. His accountant had been right. Pulling together that much money at one time had completely leveraged his holdings, and at that exact moment, he was uncomfortably exposed.

With each successive spot becoming more and more valuable, the prices skyrocketed from one week to the next. Unable to place a winning bid again and again, Yan had ultimately been forced to shell out more than $72 billion for the final spot - a fortune that hadn't been easy to obtain.

Borrowing against his assets and emergency credit line approvals with his banks had, thankfully, given him the funds he'd needed. And, although his outstanding loans were massive, Yan took solace in the fact that in less than a week, his banks would once again allow him access to the liquidity needed to keep his operations afloat.

All he had to do was make it one more week.

His die cast, Yan took a deep breath and relaxed, satisfied that after all of his legal and financial maneuvering, he had done it. He had secured a spot, and as he had with the Photosynthesuit, he would soon possess the secret of the Ouroboros.

And yet, Yan still couldn't shake the fact that things just didn't make sense. If those spots were supposed to go to the highest bidder, why *hadn't* his blind trust's bids been accepted? Time after time, *he* had placed the highest bids but still hadn't won. With his identity and nefarious intentions hidden behind the veil of the trust, what possible reason could Michel's team have had for not accepting his larger and larger bids each week, *unless…*

Suddenly, Yan's eyes widened as a nightmarish scenario quickly swept over him. Paralyzed, he involuntarily dropped his drink over the ledge, the crystal champagne glass and its contents tumbling eighty stories to the sidewalk below.

With his mouth agape and his vision blurring, Yan's legs began to weaken as he quietly whimpered to himself, *"Oh my God…"*

CHAPTER 29

Over the next thirty-six hours, their planes took off and landed four more times, with each successive pitstop culminating in an aircraft exchange inside a massive, windowless hangar. Switching planes was designed to throw off would-be followers, and by the time they landed at the final airport, Gatlin was confident they'd been successful in shaking any potential tails.

Asking the winners to choose random numbers at each location had been Layah's idea, and Gatlin could see the logic behind implementing such a strategy. That kind of arbitrariness meant no definitive flight plan and had almost certainly secured the privacy she envisioned.

As their plane finally rolled to a stop, Gatlin couldn't help but give an involuntary sigh of relief. The effort required to ensure their "disappearance" had been enormous. Scores of airplanes, drivers, pilots, security personnel, hangars, and flight attendants in a multitude of countries had to be arranged to ensure the lottery winners' furtive transportation.

The logistics had indeed been massive, but worth it if it meant the concealment of their final destination.

Establishing absolute stealth had been paramount to the undertaking's success. Gatlin knew that the small percentage of Tuvulans who had volunteered and pledged their lives to Mr. Bouchon's project were the only ones he could fully trust to safeguard history's biggest secret.

As Charlie disembarked, he noticed the protocol differed slightly from the routine they had established at the other airports. Gatlin led Charlie out of the hangar and hustled him towards a state-of-the-art helicopter that awaited them on a desolate tarmac.

With his bag in his hand, Charlie asked sarcastically, "Are we there yet?"

"Almost," Gatlin replied, "Last one."

Approaching the twelve-passenger helicopter, Gatlin glanced around in the darkness and was reminded just how barren this place really was. Without any buildings or lights for reference, they could have been literally anywhere on Earth, which not coincidently, was just how Mr. Bouchon had planned it. The winners weren't supposed to know where they were or even which country they were in.

At least not yet.

After getting a glimpse at the confusion on Charlie's face, Gatlin could see that part of the mission had so far been accomplished.

As Charlie and Gatlin grabbed the handles of the Airbus H175, its massive rotors spun in a deafening whir just above their heads. Instinctively, both men ducked as they stooped to get on board.

The chopper lifted off from the helipad into the pitch-black night sky, but unlike the interiors of the airplanes, the windows of the helicopter were uncovered. Concealing the apertures was apparently unnecessary, as the cabin's inner lights and the signal lights outside were the only things visible for hundreds of miles in every direction.

Gaining speed as it took off into the darkness, Charlie strained to see any discernable landmark out of the helicopter's window. After a few moments of futility, he eventually acquiesced, leaning back in his seat and crossing his arms in obvious frustration.

"I can't see a God damn thing."

"That's the idea," Gatlin replied impassively.

Gatlin could see the annoyance on Charlie's face and smiled, knowing it wouldn't be much longer now until at least a few of his questions were answered.

Settling into his own seat, Gatlin glanced out of his window just in time to see a partially illuminated fence below that bore a warning sign he'd become all too familiar with.

It read:

"Bouchon Nuclear Power Complex
Radio-Active Contamination Area

KEEP OUT!"

Even at its top speed, the flight lasted nearly an hour in the expansive pitch-darkness until, with little warning, the pilots began to descend, expertly landing on a large painted "H" below. Isolated in the emptiness of the night, only the dim light from the helipad shone, illuminating a path to a small electric car and driver that awaited them.

The two men carefully exited the helicopter, unable to hear each other over the roar of its rotors. Gatlin pointed towards the car, and both men headed in that direction, fighting the wind and sand churned up by the aircraft's blades.

Spitting the silica particles out of his mouth while holding his rucksack, Charlie paused as they approached the car, curiously bending down to pick up a handful of sand.

As he let the grains fall through his trembling fingers, he shouted to Gatlin over the noise, "Sand? Where the hell are we?!"

"Come on, get in the car, Charlie!" Gatlin shouted in reply, fighting the sandstorm and howl of the helicopter behind them.

Once they reached the car, both men quickly jumped in and shut the doors behind them. Charlie secured his bag on his lap, and Gatlin tapped the driver on the shoulder to let them know they were ready. As they drove away from the helipad, Charlie watched the helicopter take flight and vanish into the night sky behind them. It vanished into the vast darkness as the landing pad's light dimmed to black.

For less than ten seconds, the car traveled along a bumpy path until it came to a slanted embankment that descended toward large steel doors that led to an underground bunker.

With a push of a button on the car's visor, the driver signaled the twenty-foot-tall doors to engage, and slowly, the mammoth entrance opened before them. As they entered the windowless subterranean garage, nearly a football field in size, the car was driven to the side and parked at a charging station.

The garage was completely empty but for a man and a woman awaiting their arrival. They approached the car as Charlie, Gatlin, and the driver got out. While Gatlin walked around the vehicle and approached Charlie, the driver made sure to insert a charging cable into the side of the car.

"You ready?" Gatlin asked.

Obviously flustered, Charlie replied, "For what?"

"To meet the other winners, of course!" the woman interjected as she and her companion converged on the car.

Extending her hand, she continued, "My name is Debra, Mr. Weaver, and let me be the first to welcome you to Mr. Bouchon's research facility."

Wearing a white lab coat and glasses, Debra was dark-skinned and dark haired, just as most Tuvaluans were in Gatlin's family. His first cousin, she was diminutive in size but had a glowing smile and a pleasantness to her face that radiated energy. Like a lighthouse that illuminated the unknown, a genuine friendliness emanated from Debra that had always allowed others to feel at ease.

Gatlin noticed Charlie give him the side-eye as he deadpanned, "Nice to meet you, Debra. Maybe YOU can tell me where the hell we are."

Exchanging looks with Gatlin, Debra replied, "That is something Dr. Golden will be sharing with you at dinner, Mr. Weaver, along with a great deal more, I imagine. I take it you must be hungry after such a lengthy journey?"

"Starved."

"Well, it's perfect timing then. Dinner is about to be served, and there, you'll have a chance to meet all of your fellow winners. My understanding is they are eager to meet you as well."

As Charlie replied with a sarcastic "Great,", Gatlin got the distinct impression that the man wasn't one to be awestruck by some of the world's wealthiest people. In fact, it was almost as if he felt disdain emanating from the cop. Was it possible that, unlike many of the others here, Charlie wasn't a sycophant when it came to the bank balances of others?

Whatever the reason for his apparent aversion towards the .0001%, Gatlin didn't care, it just made him like the man even more.

Noting that the driver had begun to rummage through his luggage, Charlie warily asked, "Looking for something specific, buddy? I left anything of value back at home."

Sensing his uneasiness, Debra interceded, "Sorry about that Mr. Weaver. We just have to check to make sure you don't have any contraband. I hope you understand."

"Contraband?"

"Yes. Electronics. Metal. Or anything that produces fumes. You'd be surprised by some of the things a few of the other winners thought were appropriate to bring into our facility. One gentleman even brought a baggie of medicinal –."

"Got something," the driver called out from behind them.

Stunned, the group turned towards the man as he dramatically lifted Charlie's electric toothbrush out of his Dopp Kit and showed it to the group.

"My toothbrush?"

Debra sighed. "Yes, Mr. Weaver. Again, I'm sorry. Anything electronic must be confiscated. Where we're going, we absolutely cannot have any outside electronic devices, even something as innocuous as your toothbrush."

Noticing he was still staring at it, Debra continued, "But don't worry, Mr. Weaver. We'll be returning it to you when you leave. Now, let's go meet the others."

Debra took Charlie's arm and began to lead him away from Gatlin, who remained with the car.

Noticing his absence, Charlie stopped in his tracks and turned back towards his traveling companion, "Wait, aren't you coming, Gatlin?"

Gatlin smiled and shook his head, "I'm afraid this is goodbye, Charlie. For now."

"For now? Does that mean I'll be seeing you again?"

Gatlin sighed deeply and said sheepishly, "You're the third alternate, Charlie, and my job is to ensure the safety of our winners to and *from* the facility. So…"

Getting the inference, Charlie finished, "So, in all likelihood, you'll be seeing me sooner rather than later."

"Sooner than I'm sure we both would like it to be. Good luck Charlie. I really *am* rooting for you."

Debra once again took Charlie by the arm, and along with the two other Tuvaluans, led the police officer to a lone elevator at the far end of the hangar.

Traveling with Charlie had been a pleasure, and Gatlin had grown fond of him over the past two days. But knowing what lay ahead of him made Gatlin suddenly feel a slight pang of melancholy. He hoped everything fell into place for Charlie and that he wound up actually being cured. But after meeting most of the other winners, Gatlin conceded that his chances were exceptionally slim.

As the finality of that certainty struck, Gatlin quickly snapped out of his thoughts and reminded himself of what he was there to do.

Turning his attention back to the electric car, he stuck with the plan and unplugged its power cord.

CHAPTER 30

As Charlie, Debra, and the two other Tuvaluans got on the elevator, the first thing he noticed was that its control panel had only two buttons, labeled "Hangar" and "Facility." Debra leaned past Charlie to push "Facility", and instantaneously the elevator began to move.

Charlie watched the digital numbers above the elevator doors begin to count. They moved so quickly that, at first, he was unable to tell if they were going up or down. Soon, however, their direction became apparent as his inner ear told him they were descending.

The digits climbed rapidly (45, 62, 77), and Charlie grew uneasy. "How far down are we going?"

Debra smiled and replied, "Mr. Bouchon's facility is more than a thousand feet below the surface. We've only got a little further to go, Mr. Weaver."

The elevator continued to plummet for nearly another minute, causing Charlie's ears to depressurize and eventually pop. With the number totals above the door continuing to increase, he suddenly felt a wave of claustrophobia sweep over him. Taking a deep breath to steady his nerves, Charlie forced himself to remain calm and allow the feeling to pass.

The elevator finally came to a stop, and as the doors slowly opened, Charlie was immediately blinded by a pure white glare. Blazing incandescent lights from the ceiling reflected off a glossy white tiled floor, creating a radiance he imagined might be comparable to the one found at the Pearly Gates. Covering his face, it took a moment for Charlie's eyes to adjust after they had become accustomed to the darkness above.

Once his eyes adjusted, Charlie stood transfixed by the sight before him. Although smaller, he stood in yet another hangar, whose walls were lined with dozens of small tuk-tuks.

Apparently made of translucent Lucite, their wheels were rubber, while their seat cushions were clear, inflated plastic. Not a single piece of metal could be seen on the vehicles, and even the wheels' spokes were see-through. Plastic pedals attached to thick rubber bands appeared to be the method of propulsion, and Charlie could see that the facility indeed took enforcement of their "no electronics or metals" code seriously.

Standing beside one of the tuk-tuks was a Tuvaluan, who, like Debra, wore all white. He waved to the group as they exited the elevator, and the four occupants headed his way.

As they crossed the hangar, Charlie took stock of the room and couldn't help but notice a loud humming sound that emanated from the ceiling. Locating the source of the sound, Charlie spotted a four-foot-wide cylindrical tube that vibrated slightly.

For a moment, Charlie wondered what it could be until Debra broke his musings and motioned towards their awaiting carriage, "After you, Mr. Weaver, and watch your step getting into the Invisi."

"Invisi?" Charlie asked, stumped by the name.

Debra giggled, excited to explain, "Yes, named after Wonder Woman's invisible jet. Cute, don't you think? It's a convenient way to get around here, especially when you consider how expansive the facility is."

"How big *is* this place?"

Debra paused for a moment, considering how to answer, "Massive."

The four of them hopped aboard their Invisi, as Charlie placed his bag on his lap to settle in for the ride. Once in their seats, Debra nodded to their driver, and the man began to pedal the vehicle out of the hangar.

The fivesome journeyed down a long, well-lit tiled hallway and Charlie soon got the impression that they were traversing through miles and miles of underground catacombs. Each hallway was teeming with smiling Tuvaluans in white lab coats who walked along the side of the walls and waved as they passed. Noting the pleasant demeanor of everyone they encountered, Charlie got the feeling that this was a community that had spent years underground together.

"Everyone seems quite happy here," Charlie noted.

"We are," Debra replied.

As they rounded a corner, Debra continued, "This is the staff's wing, where our living quarters, recreation rooms, and eating facilities are located. We have more than two thousand members of our staff here, all of whom have volunteered to dedicate their lives to Mr. Bouchon."

Continuing for several more minutes, their hallway eventually opened to an enormous cavern of luscious green vegetation the size of several square miles and tended to by scores of Tuvaluans. There were countless rows of plants watered from plastic sprinklers that hung four or five stories above, as well as acres of trees laden with fruits and nuts. Water cascaded onto the flora below as artificial light poured in from every direction, illuminating the colossal greenhouse and ensuring that the plants were well-fed.

"This is our farm, where all of our food is grown" Debra explained. "With our aquifer, we have enough water to grow and sustain ourselves for centuries, if need be."

"With that much water…it must be huge."

"It is."

Charlie looked around in awe as they drove through the middle of a field, asking, "This is incredible. But you said it was your 'farm', where are the animals?"

Debra smiled, "We live a vegetarian lifestyle here, Mr. Weaver. Gases and waste from animal by-products would damage our fragile ecosystem here underground. Everything in the facility must be kept clean and completely sanitary at all times. It's one of the reasons why we don't allow smoking here. Fumes of any kind would contaminate our sterile environment."

As they left the fields behind them and entered another hallway, Charlie couldn't help but notice the cylindrical tube attached to the ceiling above them - identical to the one he had seen getting off the elevator. In fact, the four-foot-wide plastic piping had been attached to the ceiling of every hallway they had traversed so far. Other than the exertive grunts of their driver, its humming was the only constant sound he had heard in the entire facility.

Charlie was about to mention this observation when Debra suddenly signaled to the driver, who immediately stopped the Invisi in front of a door labeled "Storage." One of the Tuvaluans took Charlie's toothbrush and got out of the Invisi, approaching the door with the "contraband" in his hand.

"This is the storage room, Mr. Weaver, where all contraband is held for safekeeping. Again, not to worry, we will be returning it to you shortly."

Leaving the man behind as he entered the room with Charlie's toothbrush, the four of them continued aboard the Invisi until they approached another wing, which Debra explained was designated for the guests.

"Here you'll find your accommodations, Charlie, along with a lounge area, auditorium, and dining facility. Everything you will need during your stay here with us and – ah, here we are! Home sweet home."

The Invisi approached a long corridor of nondescript doors and Charlie could see that they each had a label above them. As the driver rode past several, he suddenly came to a halt as Debra pointed to the word "Weaver" above one of the entryways.

Once stopped, the other Tuvaluan got out and, without warning, relieved Charlie of his bag.

"Hey!"

Debra smiled as the man approached the door with the name "Weaver" above it and walked in with Charlie's bag.

"Not to worry, Mr. Weaver. You will find your things waiting for you in your room after you return from dinner."

The Invisi's driver continued past the other rooms, where Charlie saw the names of some of the winners he had heard so much about over the past several days. "Al Fouroq," "Eisenberg," "Disden." These had been the names on every living person's lips - was he really about to meet them?

For the first time since he'd arrived, Charlie began to feel a real sense of dread. He couldn't help but wonder what the people he was about to meet were like or what quirks their personalities would reveal. Were they nice? Would they accept someone like him? Last week he had eaten at Taco Bell…twice. Would he even be able to relate?

Regardless of his ability to connect, Charlie just hoped that their obscene wealth didn't trigger the trauma he struggled each day to suppress.

Would interacting with them just remind him of losing his wife and son?

The Invisi came to a stop in front of two massive doors that were tended to by a pair of friendly-looking Tuvaluans. Debra got out and said, "This way, Mr. Weaver. Let's meet the other winners."

Leading him to the large double door, Debra hesitated a moment and looked Charlie empathetically in the eyes, "Ready?"

Charlie took a deep breath, looked at the enormous doors, and then back to Debra, exhaling, "Let's do it."

Debra smiled, squeezed Charlie's hand, and then nodded to the Tuvaluan attendants, who slowly pulled open the imposing doors.

They swung outward and revealed an enormous circular room with a massive Lucite chandelier hanging at its center. Below the extravagant light fixture was the largest round table that Charlie had ever seen, translucent, like nearly everything else in the facility.

The faces of the most famous people on Earth were seated around the table, and as they noticed his presence, their conversations suddenly became quiet as all eyes turned towards Charlie.

Awestruck by the sight in front of him, Charlie stood paralyzed for a moment as he took in the room's grandeur. At equidistant intervals, doors lined the walls while travertine tiles covered the expansive floor.

Nearly fifty feet from where he stood, the table's guests remained quiet until Layah Golden broke the silence and called across the voluminous room, "Mr. Weaver, please, come join us. You're just in time. Dinner is about to be served."

Slowly, Charlie began to walk towards the table, the sound of his steps reverberating in the silence. As Debra stood in the doorway watching him approach the others, the two Tuvaluan staff members gently closed the giant double doors soundlessly behind him.

CHAPTER 31

While unpacking, Devlin tried to ignore the persistent hum from the conduit attached to his room's ceiling. He'd heard it from the moment he arrived and, after feeling its vibration, was beginning to wonder, all of these hours later, if it was some sort of cruel torture device. Devlin chuckled mischievously, imagining how such an irritating contraption might become part of *his* repertoire one day.

Refocusing, Devlin began to mentally catalog some of the features he'd seen so far on his tour of the facility, just in case those sorts of specifics were needed when he eventually met back up with Yan for his payday. Over the years he'd learned that even the most minor nuances had often made the biggest impact when finalizing compensation.

Devlin wanted to ensure nothing was left to chance on a job of this magnitude.

That sort of attention to detail and Yan's insistence on anonymity had forced Devlin to pull out all of the stops on this assignment. Creating false IDs, establishing fictious residences, and utilizing his entire network of operatives had safeguarded his identity. The preparation had been painstakingly detailed, but he assured himself all of that effort now meant that he could conduct his mission with impunity.

The tour of the facility had been incredible, and had he not been there to pillage the man's genius, Devlin might have found himself admiring the scope of the operation that Michel Bouchon had created. Fully staffed with devoted personnel, seemingly unlimited food and water, and accommodations for all, the facility was its own self-contained unit – one with no need for interaction with the outside world.

Its sustainability was truly remarkable.

As Devlin reviewed the minutia of the facility over and over in his mind, he found himself unable to move past one section of the complex that he had become obsessed with: the storage room.

Forced to surrender his cigarettes, Devlin's craving for nicotine made it increasingly difficult to focus on anything other than the alcove that held his stimulants captive. As his foot began to shake from withdrawal, Devlin accepted that it would only be a matter of time before he found himself pilfering that room to retrieve the fix his body so desperately craved.

Devlin's rumination was broken by a sudden knock at the door, and as he answered it, an overly pleasant Tuvaluan greeted him from the other side, "Good evening, Mr. Archer. Just a friendly reminder. They're still waiting for you in the dining facility. Dinner is about to be served."

Regaining his composure, Devlin gruffly replied, "Give me a minute."

"Of course Mr. —," the Tuvaluan began, as Devlin callously closed the door in the man's face.

Listening closely as the footsteps of the busybody echoed away, Devlin tried the door handle again and smiled. As it had been on every occasion prior, the door was unlocked, and Devlin let out an involuntary sigh of relief at the naivety of his hosts.

He still couldn't believe that everything here had been kept wide open and, even more shocking, that there were no cameras to record any of their movements. Devlin chuckled to himself, knowing that he could move unbridled throughout this facility. It would only be a matter of time before he would use that laissez-faire attitude towards security as a weapon against Michel Bouchon.

And yet, even with complete autonomy, for some reason Devlin still couldn't shake the suspicion that he was being watched. He wasn't quite sure why that inkling had persisted, but it was a sense that had endured from the moment he'd arrived. Over the years, his skills and experience had taught him to trust his gut, and now something deep inside warned him to watch his back.

Worse than his paranoia of being watched, however, was his crippling sense of déjà vu. As he fought to quell the anxiety that had taken hold in the deepest recesses of his mind, try as he might, those former days of abject terror continued to creep back unabated. So many hundreds of feet underground, Devlin couldn't help but feel trapped, a tension he hadn't felt since his time in prison.

Those two years of incarceration in Panama had felt like decades, with each day's trauma building on the nightmare of the one before. The constant wails of his cellmates had robbed him of sleep, while the mold in his food had emaciated his body. He could still smell the rotting sanitation that lingered throughout the entire complex and feel the bugs that crawled over his body in the darkness of night. Every day, he fought to repress those memories.

Every day, he lost.

Of course, although those horrors had been traumatizing, they had paled compared to the interactions with his cellblock's guard, Jorge.

It wasn't the nightly beatings that Jorge had inflicted that still terrified Devlin because, after the first several months, he had grown numb to the diminutive man's early evening visits. It hadn't even been the incessant psychological warfare that Jorge had inflicted either, giving Devlin false hope over and over again that his government had come to release him. In time, Devlin had simply accepted his fate.

No, it was the billy club that Devlin remembered most. The billy club that Jorge had used day and night, in an attempt to break not only Devlin's bones but his spirit.

Most nights, when he was alone and lost in his own thoughts, Devlin could still hear the "thwap" of that club, and involuntarily, he'd arch his back in anticipation for the inevitable blow that had always come. The bruises on his outside had, over time, obviously healed, but it was the mental damage those pummelings had caused that had stuck with Devlin for the decades since they had first been administered.

However, from the horror of those constant beatings, psychological traumas and physical abuse, Devlin had learned a valuable lesson that he'd employed then and vowed to continue until his very last breath: never to scream again.

Screaming implied weakness, fragility, and defeat. Worst of all, though, Devlin had come to recognize that a victim's screams were often what gave an abuser the most pleasure. Like a drug, Jorge had beaten and tormented his victims not for the sense of power, but for the high he achieved when hearing their wails.

Over time, Devlin had realized it was the screams that Jorge wanted most from his prey, and so, he pledged to deny his browbeater that one satisfaction. As the months dragged on, Devlin accepted his beatings in absolute silence, maintaining his self-control and robbing Jorge of the pleasure of hearing him scream.

As Devlin reflected on the man his prison experience had hardened him into, he reminded himself that he hadn't entered the penitentiary as a typical criminal in 1988, but as a computer programmer working for Naval Intelligence. Sent by his superiors to assist Panamanian dictator Manuel Noriega as he manipulated his country's general election, Devlin's hacking skills had been instrumental in nullifying the final results. Ultimately, Devlin's efforts had thrown into question the validity of the nation's vote, and as planned, Noriega had retained power.

However, when it became apparent that the U.S government had decided to invade Panama the following year to initiate a regime change, the dictator had pre-emptively thrown Devlin into jail, labeling him an enemy of the State and a spy. By the time the U.S had removed Noriega from his position of authority and extradited him abroad, Devlin had spent months in jail, given little assistance from the administration and even less hope.

Fearful of exposure for interfering in a foreign election, the U.S government had left Devlin to rot, essentially branding him a casualty of an operation that had gone awry. Betrayed, Devlin ruminated in his cell day after day, vowing, that if he ever got out, to never re-enter traditional society again.

It was during one of these days, as Devlin fumed in the prison's rec yard, that his opportunity to retake his life had presented itself. As the other prisoners exercised and the guards patrolled the parapets, Devlin sat against a wall, mindlessly observing the city's trash float in the air near the outer barbed-wire fence. It was there that he had first heard, then spotted, what would ultimately turn out to be the key to his freedom.

Devlin noticed an aluminum can as it danced along the ground among the candy wrappers and trash bags that blew in the wind. He watched it closely as a gust caused it to spin and tumble, and inside of his head, Devlin shouted, "This way!"

For a moment, the can had rolled in the opposite direction, and as Devlin's heart sank, he was reminded of the futility of hope. But just then, the breeze had shifted, and, as if by providence, the can had come skipping back toward the fence. With a strong waft behind it, the can was pressed up against the outside of the wire fence, pinned there four feet above the ground, tantalizing Devlin with the word "Fanta" printed across its side.

With little time to waste, Devlin quickly scoured the yard to ensure no guards or other prisoners were looking and stealthily crawled towards the fence. Quickly reaching the chain link on all fours, Devlin's eyes bulged as the wind abated and the can began to slide down the side of the fence, potentially rolling away for good. Instinctively, he shot his forefinger through a gap in the wire, and with his long, crusty fingernail, months in the growing, he was able to barely snag the mouth of the open can. Holding his breath so as not to drop his treasure, Devlin then stuck his other forefinger through a gap, gripped the bottom of the can, and pulled it tightly against the fence.

With great difficulty, Devlin angled several of his fingers through the fence and, with enough force, was able to crush the can small enough to pull it through a space in the chain link. With his heart racing and little hesitation, he quickly slipped the crushed can into his pants as a wave of relief washed over his body.

Undetected by either the guards or his fellow prisoners, Devlin took a deep breath and began to devise his plan to escape.

On cue, Jorge had come to Devlin's cell to torment him that night, just like he did most others. Perhaps it was because of his height or the color of his skin, but regardless of the reason, Devlin had always seemed to draw most of Jorge's attention. The guard had, on occasion, singled out some of the other twenty men in the holding cell, but to their relief, it was usually the American who had taken the brunt of the beatings.

As Jorge approached, he pulled out his billy club and jabbed it into Devlin's ribs to wake him up, "Get up, it's time!"

Devlin groaned but didn't move. Jorge struck Devlin with the billy club again, but this time much harder. As he'd been groomed to do, Devlin slowly stood up and begrudgingly faced the wall.

"That's more like it, Blue Eyes" Jorge said breathlessly.

As Jorge put the baton under his arm to roll up his sleeves, Devlin quickly spun around and raked the torn edge of the aluminum can across the guard's neck. Jorge's eyes widened in terror as he grabbed his throat, choking on the blood gurgling in his mouth.

Gasping uncontrollably for air as he fell to his knees, Jorge's tongue swung wildly in a futile attempt to scream. With his throat filled with fluid, he clutched helplessly at his neck as his life seeped from his severed jugular. Instinctively, but to no avail, he applied pressure to the ruptured artery with his hands, struggling to stop the quarts of blood that gushed through his fingers.

For nearly a minute he fought death, until with one final curdling wheeze, Devlin's tormentor unceremoniously collapsed into a heap on to the prison floor.

Without hesitation or remorse, Devlin quickly bent over and grabbed Jorge's billy club as it lay in an ever-growing pool of blood next to his body. As the other prisoners looked on in shock, they began to shuffle slowly towards the open door of their cell, opportunistically hoping to make an escape.

Noticing their intentions, Devlin hissed, "Wait! Not that way. There are too many guards, and you'll never get out without any weapons."

One of the prisoners asked incredulously, "So? What do we do then?"

Fighting to catch his breath and with a fire in his eyes, Devlin said, "I'll show you."

Jorge's now lifeless body lay at Devlin's feet, and as he raised the billy club above his head, he violently pounded on his former oppressor. The terrifying noise he had grown to fear over the years now sounded like freedom, and each time he brought the billy club down against Jorge's corpse, the "thwap" it made reverberated throughout the cell.

Devlin beat on Jorge's remains like a rabid animal, causing blood to ooze from every wound, and eventually reducing Jorge's body to a bloody pulp.

After several minutes, exhausted and out of breath, Devlin paused, standing above the pile of meat like a Neanderthal having just made his kill. Terrified, the other prisoners gaped at Devlin in horror, petrified of the man who looked as though he were possessed by Satan.

Sensing their shock forced Devlin to quickly regain his wits, and immediately he began to remove Jorge's clothes. Mopping up the blood with the guard's uniform, Devlin then carried the soaked pieces of clothing over to the cell's window, tying a piece of fabric around the metal bars lining the hole.

With the dripping shirt tied in a knot, Devlin then picked up Jorge's billy club, placed it between the blood-soaked garment and, with each hand on opposite ends of the baton, began to twist it with all of his might.

Incredulously, the other cellmates looked on, each becoming more and more skeptical of what Devlin was attempting to do. One by one, they slowly crept towards the cell door, unconvinced there was a method to Devlin's madness.

Straining with every ounce of strength he had remaining to twist the baton, Devlin noticed out of the corner of his eye that the other inmates were about to flee and shouted, "Wait! Look!"

The prisoners hesitated for a moment in their tracks and, to their astonishment, could see what was beginning to happen to the bars that had barricaded their window. Unbelievably, the old, sea-corroded rods began to slowly bend inward toward themselves where the wet clothing was most tightly leveraged, creating an opening. As Devlin continued to turn the billy club, the space between the bars grew larger and larger with every creak.

"Dios Mio!" gasped one of the prisoners.

Devlin kept twisting until he no longer had the strength to continue. He then tied a second piece of Jorge's blood-soaked clothing around another set of bars next to the first ones and repeated his previous steps. These shafts too began to groan and bend, and soon, there was an opening large enough for the emaciated men to crawl through.

Dripping with sweat, Devlin turned back towards the men as several of the convicts uttered prayers and crossed themselves in disbelief, looking at him as though he were Moses having just parted the Red Sea.

Devlin seized the moment to implement the final piece of his escape plan.

"Take off your clothes. All of you. And tie them together. We'll use them as a rope to get out of here," Devlin ordered the men.

Quickly they followed his instructions and hurriedly began to undress. One by one they fastened their pants and shirts together into a lengthy rope, and after tying it to the window's bars, they soon had a homemade cable that stretched from their cell down to the street below.

Devlin kept a look out as the half-naked men filed through the opening and shimmied down the rope to the base of the building. Sprinting in different directions into the night, Devlin watched as the murderers and rapists he had lived with for years disappeared down the dark alleyways and empty city streets.

With the last of his cellmates gone, Devlin slowly lowered himself down the rope with a smile. He assumed it would be the escape of the hardened criminals that the authorities would focus their efforts on recapturing, and he took solace in the belief that someone like himself would hardly garner any notice. With a little luck and a lot of guile, Devlin was confident that he would be home before the end of the week.

He'd been right.

There was another knock at the door, and Devlin's musings were quickly broken.

Opening the door, the same Tuvaluan stood before him and pleaded, "Mr. Archer, I apologize, but we really must –."

Walking out and closing the door behind him, Devlin said, "Yeah, yeah, I get it. Let's go meet some rich assholes."

CHAPTER 32

As Charlie slowly approached the circular table, he noticed three empty seats and hesitated, unsure which one to take. A gaunt but naturally beautiful woman in her early thirties, with long flowing blonde hair and a welcoming smile, patted a chair beside her and motioned for Charlie to join her.

Recognizing her as Kerry Wilson, the first-grade teacher, Charlie headed towards her as she offered, "Here you go, Charlie, you can sit next to me."

Charlie smiled and reached for the seat beside the now emaciated beauty. Although outwardly her sunken eyes belied a fierce battle that her body was waging against a presumably terminal disease, she had an inner glow that radiated a wholesomeness that he hadn't felt since....

Across the table, a thin, bearded man wearing a white turban, whom Charlie recognized as the Indian billionaire Rami Singh, forcibly interjected "Actually, the placard says he's to sit over here with m–."

Speaking in her teacher voice, Kerry cut Rami short and said, "I'm sure he'll be fine here, Mr. Singh. You won't be issuing any seat citations, will you, officer?"

With a bashful smile, Charlie sheepishly shook his head and pulled out the chair next to Kerry, catching the inference. Like everyone else at the table, he understood that the details of his background were well known. Art Decker's exposés had seen to that for all of them. Their biographies had become fodder for the world to mock, with every facet of their lives scrutinized and dissected.

As he sat down at the lavish table, he and Kerry exchanged an extended glance, as she raised her skeletal hand and said, "It's nice to meet you, Charlie Weaver, of Oakland, California."

Taking her ethereal hand and lightly shaking it, Charlie was momentarily speechless, struck by the sparkle in her eye and irreverence exuded from her rambunctious personality. The delicate touch of her clasp stunned Charlie, and for a second, he thought he might have been staring at a ghost, if not for the striking color of her blonde hair.

Composing himself, he said, "You as well, Kerry Wilson of Oshkosh, Wisconsin."

Both locked eyes for a moment, their hands embraced, when an excited voice from the other side of Kerry rang out, "I'm Auggie. Nice to meet you, too."

Auggie stretched out his arm to shake Charlie's hand, his Lucite crutches rattling against his chair.

Breaking his trance with Kerry, Charlie gently released her hand and shook the young boy's. "I recognized you, Auggie. It's nice to meet you, too."

With a courtesy nod to the others at the table, Charlie repressed his revulsion towards their garish wealth and took a moment to acquaint himself with his place setting. The enormous round table was replete with plates, glasses, and chopsticks, all made of Lucite. White cloth napkins sat atop the dinner plates, while a massive bouquet of white lilies was pristinely arranged at the center of the table.

The ambiance, much like the entire facility itself, was sterile, and Charlie began to wonder if this sort of cleanliness was an environment that lent itself to surgeries. Were they being prepared for an operating room? Would this be their last meal?

Charlie's thoughts were cut short as Layah addressed him from across the table, "Welcome, Mr. Weaver. We are so happy to have you here. We're waiting for just one other guest to join us, and then dinner will begin."

Next to Layah sat Hadron and Cern, whose tongues hung from their mouths as they panted in synchronicity. If Charlie hadn't known better, he would have sworn the dogs were smiling.

"Sounds good," Charlie said as he took inventory of the others sitting around the table. He recognized their faces from their bios on TV.

The African arms dealer, Oman Disden, sat a few seats from Charlie, and he was surprised to see that the man's scowling face was exactly as it had appeared on the broadcasts he'd watched over the past several days.

Next to him sat Chi Kwong, the Industrialist from mainland China. As he inhaled deeply from a carbon composite tank that rested next to his seat, Charlie couldn't help but feel for the man whose every breath appeared to be labored.

Mustafa al Fouruq sat directly across from Charlie, and he gathered that the oil magnate heir was seated in a wheelchair as he settled in lower than everyone else at the table.

The only person Charlie didn't see was the mystery winner that all of the news stations had been obsessed with since the moment the names of the Chosen had been released. Not knowing who the final person was had drawn even more attention to the unexplained enigma, as, day and night, reporters had debated ad nauseum over who that winner might turn out to be. Speculating on the identity of the person behind the blind trust had become a worldwide preoccupation, as everyone wondered who he was or if it was even a "he" at all.

Charlie continued to examine those around the table, like Umberto Fuentes, Shira Eisenberg, and Gilbert Lebedev. His reverie was broken when hedge fund manager Ian Haynes nodded towards one of the two empty seats at the circular table and asked Layah, "And where is our host, Mr. Bouchon? Will King Arthur be joining us this evening?"

Slightly off-put by his inference to the circular table, Layah replied, "Mr. Bouchon is indisposed at the moment, I'm afraid. But he will be joining us later."

"How convenient," Ian replied, suspiciously.

In her late forties, with impeccably groomed auburn red hair and manicured nails painted to match, the world-renowned actress Cynthia Swift said breathlessly, "This is all so mysterious. This whole complex, our rooms, this meal…it reminds me of that spy film I did, *The Trinity Adventure.*"

From his seat, Rami squealed, "I loved that film!"

Accustomed to a never-ending stream of flattery and adulation, Cynthia replied automatically, "Yes, well thank you. It's always nice to meet a fan."

Rami continued, gushing, "I might be your biggest fan! You were so beautiful back then!"

Cynthia, humbled by what she perceived as a slight about her age, felt her bravado deflate as she slowly sank into her chair. Pulling out a pocket mirror, she brushed her hair with trembling fingers as her cheeks flushed red.

Confused by what was happening around him, Gilbert turned towards Layah and asked, "Will we be eating here tonight?"

Layah looked at the other guests, then back at Gilbert, and said compassionately, "Yes, my dear. Dinner will be served shortly."

"I don't like cooked peas, you remember, don't you?"

Layah smiled and glanced at the others, "Yes, Mr. Lebedev, we have your preference sheet. No cooked peas for you."

With a devilish smile, Gilbert said, "Mr. Lebedev? Call me Gilbert, Layah."

"Of course, Gilbert," she said as Hadron rested his snout on Gilbert's arm.

Several seats to his right, Charlie couldn't help but notice Ian staring at him, as if boring a hole. After several moments, Charlie became uneasy and turned towards the banker, his patience having grown thin.

"Yes?"

Looking around mischievously as if he were about to divulge a monumental secret, Ian said, "I'm sorry, but I've been dying to ask you, as I'm sure every news station on the planet has: what on Earth possessed you to turn down so much money for your spot?"

"Excuse me?"

"I mean, a billion dollars…for the *third* alternate spot? And you said, 'No'? That just blows my mind. It doesn't make any sense!"

"That amount of money isn't that absurd," Cynthia blurted. "I have the second alternate spot and paid more for mine than that."

With an amused smile, Ian chastised, "No, I don't imagine you, or perhaps more accurately, your husband would think that amount of money is obscene. But for most regular…pardon me, I mean, working-class people, that is an astonishing amount of wealth. And since I, for one, am sure as hell not going to give up my spot after everything I've been through and the money I'VE paid, what makes you think any of us here would, Mr. Weaver? I mean *third* alternate, Jesus…How on Earth could you have possibly turned down all of that money?"

Charlie could sense that all of the eyes around the table were on him, and he began to feel a little defensive as his chest tightened.

The absolute arrogance of this man as he flaunted his wealth reminded Charlie of the trial.

As he was about to unleash on Ian and the rest of the monied elite at the table, Kerry jumped in and said, "Probably for the same reason I did, Mr. Haynes. What's the point of all of that money if you don't have the time or family to spend it on? Does that sound about right, Mr. Weaver?"

Shocked at how accurately she had described his own thoughts, Charlie's blood pressure began to normalize. He looked at Kerry with gratitude for having defused the moment, nodding, "Yeah, something like that."

As Ian gave a "humpf" and resumed finishing his champagne, Umberto couldn't help but stare at Charlie, overwhelmed with pity for the man who didn't have a family to go back to.

From across the table, Rami Singh chided, "What do you know of the value of money anyway, Mr. Haynes? Some hedge fund manager YOU must be. I watched you countless times on the Financial News Network downplaying the market price of these spots. You said they were 'overvalued' and not worth the billions that were being paid."

"Indeed, I did. Your point?"

Rami chuckled to himself and continued his rebuke, "Shows what you know. Apparently, you had no idea what you were talking about!"

Ian lowered his glass and looked directly at Rami, "Is that so?"

With a confrontational gleam in his eye, Rami replied, "Yes, it is. I'm the first alternate and paid more than three billion dollars for my spot. There are others here who spent much, much more than that."

"I'm sorry to hear that," Ian smirked.

Frustrated by Ian's cavalier attitude, Rami asked, "What is that supposed to mean?"

"It means I made those VERY public comments on TV to keep their values suppressed. It's how I paid a tenth of what you did…for an *actual* spot."

Rami spit the tea he was consuming out of his mouth at this statement and glared at Ian from across the table.

"Son of a bitch."

Surprised by the curse word and the flow of the conversations occurring between people with such diverse backgrounds, Auggie asked, "Do all of you speak English?"

Oman involuntarily burst into laughter, and after catching his breath, the African warlord teased, "Of course, Auggie! All billionaires do!"

This comment broke the tension from Ian's confession, and all the magnates around the table chuckled, sharing in the levity of Auggie's naivete. Embarrassed, the young boy melted into his chair.

Charlie leaned across Kerry and consoled Auggie, "Don't worry, bud, I was wondering the same thing."

At that moment, Rami Singh turned ghastly white as he stared across the room at the man standing in the doorway whose silhouette was outlined by the light behind him. Could it be? Was it even possible?

As the large double doors closed behind him, Rami felt his stomach turn and his throat tighten as he whispered to himself, "Oh dear God."

In the doorway stood Devlin Archer, the man whose identity everyone on Earth had spent the prior week speculating about. One by one, the guests at the table became quiet as they all turned to look at who Rami had become transfixed by.

Lifting their heads up, Hadron and Cern began to growl in unison.

Devlin remained motionless, unconcerned with anyone else in the room except Rami. Locking his blue eyes with the Indian billionaire's brown ones, Devlin's mouth didn't move, but his facial expression screamed, "Keep. Your. Mouth. Shut."

"Come, Mr. Archer, join us, please," Layah offered amiably across the room, piercing the resounding silence.

His trance broken by Layah's offer, Devlin began to saunter across the room towards the table. The contingent of guests remained silent as his shoes clicked on the tiled floor, the sound of his steps reverberating off the walls of the circular room. Charlie couldn't help but notice that the man had a gait that exuded supreme confidence.

Although he hadn't with Charlie, Ian quickly rose from the table and glided towards Devlin with his weaselly hand outstretched.

"Good evening…Mr. Archer, is it? I'm Ian Haynes."

Devlin slowly raised his hand and shook Ian's, surveying the room, but paying particular attention to Rami.

"Hi."

Ian continued, "And here I thought I knew everyone with deep pockets. I don't believe we've met before."

Rami gulped and thought to himself from his seat, "*We* have."

Devlin and Rami continued to lock eyes, and then Devlin said off-handedly to Ian, "No, we haven't."

Ian recognized the accent and continued to fish, "Ah, a fellow American. Glad to have you. There are several others of us here, as I'm sure you already know. Archer? Is that of the Rhode Island Archers?"

"No", Devlin said curtly as he walked past the sycophant and over to the table.

As he sat down next to Rami, Layah tapped her champagne glass to get everyone's attention, including the scorned hedge fund manager who remained shocked that he had just been so utterly disregarded.

While everyone turned their focus towards Layah, Rami whispered to Devlin out of the side of his mouth, "What the hell are you doing here?"

Devlin's response was equally quiet and blunt, "Working."

Layah continued to tap the glass, and as the murmur descended into silence, she said, "Now that we are all here, let us raise a glass."

At that proclamation, Layah picked up her champagne glass and held it up. The rest of the guests at the table followed suit, holding their glasses in the air and in the direction of their hostess.

Layah continued, "You have all come here from great distances and from diverse backgrounds but with a similar desire. To once again, be healthy. Here is to you, The Chosen, and to Mr. Bouchon's cure, the Ouroboros."

Although frustratingly confused, and still unsure what the Ouroboros actually was, all of the guests clicked glasses with those next to them. Rami lowered his champagne without taking a sip.

Layah set her glass down and quickly clapped her hands to break the awkward silence, proclaiming, "Let's eat!"

At her declaration, a dozen Tuvaluan servers quickly entered from doors along the walls of the circular room, their hands filled with trays. One by one, a steady stream of staff approached the Chosen and gently placed plates on the table. Colorful fruits and sauteed vegetables were arranged before the dinner guests, with heaps of rice and aromatic sauces hissing with steam.

"It smells delicious," Auggie purred as he watched the scores of plates stack up on the table.

"Thank you, Auggie," Layah said. "These are some of the more popular dishes of our facility's personnel, the Tuvaluans. On their island, these are traditional delicacies, and we are fortunate enough to grow all that you see in front of you right here in our facility."

Out of the corner of her eye, Layah kept an eye on Devlin and continued, "Of course, one day, we hope that we won't need to eat any food. That is Michel's vision."

This comment caught Devlin off guard as he served himself, but Chi Kwong was first to respond with a scoff.

"Not eat? Ridiculous."

"Perhaps…" Layah said with a devilish grin.

Oman picked up his chopsticks, and, with great difficulty, attempted to eat the rice set before him. Frustrated, he eventually threw them down in exasperation, opting to pick up the grains with his hands from his plate.

Auggie asked, "Who are the Tuvaluans anyway? And where do they come from?"

"Great question Auggie. I was wondering the same thing," Shira added. "Plus, gauging from the number of unmarked planes we took here, the heavy security, and its remoteness, this facility's existence is obviously being kept secret. The privacy you've managed to create here must have been a monumental undertaking."

"As if you know anything about privacy…" Ian deadpanned under his breath to the social media tycoon.

Giving Ian side eye, Shira continued, "Anyway, yes, who are these Tuvaluans, and how do you keep so many of them from leaking this facility's purpose or location?"

Layah smiled as she said, "The Tuvaluans are from Tuvalu, a tiny island in the South Pacific that would have been wiped off the map forever if it hadn't been for Michel Bouchon's Orbital Solar Shade. Climate change was causing the oceans to rise, which would have engulfed their nation, erasing their entire civilization from history. They revere Mr. Bouchon, and owe everything they have or ever will have, to him. It is a debt they believe can never be fully repaid, and many of them have therefore pledged their devotion to him, vowing to always be at his service. That is who they are, Auggie, and the loyalty of those that have volunteered to be here, Ms. Eisenberg, is unequivocal."

"Is their loyalty why I haven't seen any cameras here in the facility? Why every door is unlocked? You trust the Tuvaluans unconditionally?" Umberto asked.

Layah smiled and replied, "We do."

She continued, "And it is also why we trust all of *you*. You are all here for the same reason: you, too, believe in what Michel has set forth to achieve. It is why some of you have spent fortunes to be here and why others have turned them down. Because regardless of your backgrounds, your nationalities, or your bank accounts, you are all her for the same reason: your health. Your desire to be cured unifies you, and it is why we sit at a round table this evening. Here, you are all the same. Here, you are all equal."

Ian rolled his eyes at Layah's progressive soliloquy.

"But, if I may be so bold, Dr. Golden, gauging from your appearance, I am guessing you yourself aren't Tuvaluan. What has prompted YOUR loyalty?" Mustafa asked.

"Let's just say we all have our reasons for wanting to see Mr. Bouchon's vision become a reality."

Devlin scrutinized Layah's facial features carefully as he listened to her talk. Over the years, he'd learned, like a good poker player, to read the "tells" of his opponent. Had her comment about no longer needing to eat been directed toward him? And if so, did she know who he was and what he was really doing there? He couldn't be sure, but Devlin made a mental note to keep a close eye on her just in case.

He *was* sure, however, that the movie star was not who she appeared to be. She gave the impression of an innocent damsel in distress, but unlike the rest of these rubes, he could tell that she was most dangerous one of them all.

Especially wearing those earrings.

He had noticed their gleam from across the room the moment he entered. The blue stones attached to her ears were meant to complement her outfit's motif, but he'd instantly recognized them as Chalcanthite, or Copper sulfate. Once mixed with liquid, they almost instantaneously created a deadly toxin.

In the past he had had the opportunity to utilize their fatal effects on several occasions, eliminating targets when stealth had been required rather than blunt force. What she'd planned to use them for now, or on whom, was anyone's guess, but Devlin made another mental note to be sure he kept his distance.

Leaning towards Cynthia in an effort to get a read, he whispered, "Beautiful earrings by the way. A radiant shade of blue."

Cynthia's body instinctively tensed, and Devlin knew his hunch was right.

"Oh, these old things. Just something I'd picked up overseas…"

Rami could feel the child staring at him for what felt like an eternity until finally he had enough and turned towards the boy.

Pointing at his turban, he asked, "I see you have an interest in this young man. Is that so?"

Auggie nodded, still transfixed by the wrap.

Annoyed, Rami continued, "I see. Well, it is called a turban. A profoundly important symbol of my Sikh religion. As are many other parts of my ensemble that you see here, including my kacchera, kara, and –."

"I used to wear hats too. Many hats!" Gilbert excitedly interjected loudly over the conversations that had permeated the room.

The table became quiet as the guests turned towards the man who had obviously lost his intellectual faculties some time ago.

Feigning politeness, Rami asked, "Is that so, Mr. Lebedev?"

"Yes, many hats."

A huge smile spread across Gilbert's face as he beamed with pride, but just as suddenly as his enthusiasm had erupted, he quickly became melancholy. He lowered his head in apparent shame, "But, not anymore. Not…anymore."

There was an uncomfortable silence at the table for a moment until Mustafa interceded, "What a coincidence. There's something I don't have any more either…my gas-powered wheelchair."

"Gas-powered?" Shira asked.

"That's right. It's been impounded. And they had the audacity to call my chair "contraband" of some sort. Like it was a drug shipment! Now all I've been left with is this manual one made out of Lucite. It's simply barbaric!"

Excited to empathize, Auggie pointed to his Lucite crutches and exclaimed, "Me too!"

Mustafa waved him off, uninterested in the difficulties of the boy.

Layah interjected, "I'm sorry you feel that way, Mr. al Farouq, but as you were undoubtedly told when you arrived, we cannot have any foreign fumes or metal in the facility. The carbon dioxide your vehicle produced was enough to potentially contaminate the fragile ecosystem we have built here."

Mustafa pointed accusingly across the table at Chi Kwong, "Then why can he have that?!"

Having kept to himself since the moment he arrived, a shocked Chi Kwong lowered his mask and glared at Mustafa, "What?"

"Those tanks! They must be producing some sort of gas!"

Chi Kwong snarled, disgusted that his shame had been broadcast so publicly in front of the others, and by a man with such ignorance.

"They are you idiot. Oxygen. The same stuff you breathe. I just need a more concentrated form."

Mustafa sulked, flailing his hands in exasperation.

"Gentlemen, please," Layah said as she stood, "We have all made sacrifices to be here. And it is these sacrifices that bring me to the point of this dinner, and the reason why you are all here. The Ouroboros."

Silence fell across the table and all eyes turned towards Layah.

Layah held the quiet for an exaggerated period of time, punctuating the importance of what she was about to say.

"You are here to be cured, and for those that want to, you will be. But know this: the cost to be cured by the Ouroboros will be far greater than anything you have paid so far."

As those around the table exchanged worried glances, Ian asked incredulously the question they were all thinking, "What is *that* supposed to mean?"

Layah continued, "It means, if you want, you *will* be cured…but you will never be able to see your family or friends again."

There was a palpable silence as those around the table once again looked inquisitively at each other and digested what Layah had just said. Only the constant background humming remained as they absorbed this new and disturbing information.

Umberto Fuentes was the first to speak, "Excuse me?"

Looking at the faces around the table, Layah said, "I understand your shock, but this is the price that must be paid to be cured. It is also the reason why we have chosen alternates. We know for some of you, this stipulation may be a bridge too far."

Layah backed away from the table and said, "So, please, enjoy some cocktails in the lounge this evening, think about what I've just said, and take until the morning to decide. By tomorrow, let us know if this is indeed what you truly want and if this price is one you will be willing to pay."

With a stunned silence hovering over the table, Ian Haynes blurted out, "What the hell? This doesn't make any sense. How can we be expected to make a momentous decision like this based on nothing but…faith? Can't you at least tell us what in the world the Ouroboros is, considering our fates are so inexorably tied to it?"

"Yeah!" Mustafa chimed in.

Layah's lips pursed, unmoved by the hedge fund manager's concerns, "I am sorry, but I cannot. That is, not until tomorrow."

"Why?" asked Shira.

"Protecting the nature of the Ouroboros is fundamental to its success. It's why you were brought here under such extraordinarily clandestine circumstances. Its secrets can never leave this facility. Only those of you who stay can know what it is."

Nodding towards Rami, Cynthia, and Charlie, she continued, "That means that for the alternates, I'm afraid that if spaces do not become available by tomorrow, this will be 'good-bye'. You will be escorted home in the morning, and I am sorry to say, we will be unable to share with you what the Ouroboros is or allow it to cure you."

A finality hung over the table as the reality of their circumstances settled upon them.

Layah turned to walk away, hesitated, and repeated a version of the phrase that the world had labeled as her catchphrase, "Godspeed, and until…tomorrow."

Layah began to leave with Hadron and Cern when Umberto jumped from his seat and motioned towards Layah, "Dr. Golden…wait. I do not need until tomorrow. I've already made my decision."

"Oh?"

Umberto continued with finality, "You can count me out."

Ian Haynes became apoplectic. "What the hell are you doing, Umberto?! You've spent a fortune for your spot – you're going to just throw that away?"

Umberto turned and looked directly at Charlie.

Maintaining eye contact with the policeman the entire time, he said, "I am truly a blessed man, Mr. Haynes, and am lucky to have a family. They are more important to me than any amount of money. I would rather spend my last remaining months with them than an eternity without them."

Shaking his head in bewilderment, Ian whispered under his breath, "Idiot."

"Very well then. Anyone else?" Layah asked the deafening silence that blanketed the table.

Unable to look into the eyes of their fellow winners, many at the table sat in embarrassed silence, ashamed they, too, were not jumping at the chance to spend more time with their families or friends.

Sensing the awkwardness, Layah continued, "So be it. The rest of you then have until tomorrow to decide. Mr. Fuentes, if you will follow me, please, we will have the helicopter take you back to the airport."

Layah and her four-legged companions led Umberto away from the dining table. The rest of the winners sat quietly in their seats, pondering what they would ultimately do.

Oblivious to the magnitude of the moment, Gilbert asked, "What's happening? Are we going now?"

Charlie nodded towards Umberto and said, "He is."

As the massive doors to the room closed silently behind Umberto, Charlie leaned across the table towards Rami and took the opportunity to congratulate him, "Way to go, bud."

In shock and unsure if what he'd just seen had really happened, Rami mumbled, "Does this mean…?"

Charlie replied, "It means you've gone from first alternate to one of the winners. Congratulations, Rami."

As the realization of his good fortune began to sweep over Rami, he jumped from his seat and shouted in exaltation, "I've won! I can't believe it! I'm going to be cured! ME! I must be the luckiest person on Earth!"

While several of the others took their turns praising his providence, Cynthia gazed blankly ahead, staring at Rami as he jumped around like a demon possessed. She was happy for the man but, at the same time, exceptionally jealous. She understood that with Umberto gone, she was now one step closer as the next alternate in line, but would any of these others follow in the telecom mogul's footsteps?

It was possible that one of these other people would back out like Umberto had, but if they didn't, she'd be forced to implement her backup plan. Otherwise, she would be heading home in the morning, uncured and two billion dollars poorer.

Desperation began to overwhelm Cynthia, causing her to glance at the others around the table, looking for a potential target. Other than the cop who was behind her in order, anyone of these remaining people could be the one. But who?

For a brief moment, Chi Kwong wondered if, by not offering to leave, like Umberto, he was being selfish and only thinking of himself. That thought quickly vanished as he remembered he only had spoiled kids and a greedy wife waiting for him back home. Going back was the last thing Chi wanted, and he began to fantasize about starting his life over again. This time, with a younger wife that appreciated him and perhaps more children, ones that doted over him and actually listened. With his health restored, he would definitely do things differently this time around.

Chi soon began to smile. Never see his family again? He would have paid extra for that.

As Devlin digested the ultimatum he had heard from Layah, he scoffed at her naivete. Did that woman really think that he would never re-engage with society or collect the money that was owed to him by Yan? Her pronouncement had obviously been an exaggeration, and whatever pill, laser, or nano-technology Michel Bouchon had invented, its secrets would be escaping this tomb with him – one way or another.

Nothing would keep him from collecting his payday.

Nothing.

Resolved, Devlin examined the faces of the others around the table, and out of curiosity, wondered what they were thinking. Would any of *them* back out? From what he'd seen so far, he doubted it. These people were too greedy and selfish to give up their spots, even if it did mean never seeing their friends and families again. No, he was quite sure they'd do whatever they could, at any cost, to be cured by the Ouroboros.

Acknowledging the temerity of the other winners quickly drew Devlin back to the moment and forced him to confront the more pressing matter at hand - Cynthia's jewelry. Was *she* willing to do anything to be cured? Desperate times often called for desperate measures, and she had undoubtedly brought those poisonous stones with the intention of using them.

As he stood from the table and shook her hand, she flashed a fake Hollywood smile, leaving Devlin with little doubt of one irrefutable truth: No matter what the Ouroboros turned out to be, in this facility, it wasn't the most dangerous snake.

CHAPTER 33

Entering his room for the first time, Charlie saw it mirrored most areas of the facility. It was sparse and sterile, with a dull humming sound reverberating from a cable attached to his wall. Like the prison cells he had sent countless criminals to over the years, it had little to offer in the way of amenities, having apparently been built for functionality.

Trying the door once again just to be sure he hadn't been locked in, he involuntarily sighed in relief when it opened without resistance. The room may have resembled those that were found in jail, but unlike those, he could come and go as he pleased.

Charlie smiled as he noticed a makeshift bed assembled in a corner of the room on the floor. Although it was simply a pile of blankets with a few stuffed shirts tied together as pillows, Charlie appreciated the effort.

Charlie spotted a note on top of the quilts and picked it up. It read: "We apologize for the crudeness of the bed, Mr. Weaver. It was the best we could do on such short notice."

For a moment, Charlie wondered if any of the other guests had been offered similar sleeping accommodations and then quickly realized that most billionaires probably thought sleeping was a waste of time. They undoubtedly saw those precious hours as a valuable commodity, not to be squandered on something as unproductive as sleep. People with that much wealth had places to be and empires to run.

And sometimes, he thought as he looked at the picture of his wife and son that stuck out of his bag, families to destroy.

With its tiny bathroom, shower, closet, and desk, Charlie could only imagine how the billionaires were adapting to such spartan accommodations. Without the luxurious comforts he was sure that they were accustomed to, Charlie guessed these rooms didn't feel like going from first class to coach for them, but from private plane to cattle car.

As he unpacked his bag, and now-partially-empty Dopp kit, he pulled out the few shirts and pants he had taken with him. Placing the picture frame that held the clipping of his family on the desk, he set it next to a newspaper he had been given on one of yesterday's airplanes.

Charlie smiled as he read the front-page headline that blared, "Who is behind the mysterious blind trust?" He found it amusing that he actually knew.

His brow furrowed, however, as he recalled his initial impression of Mr. Archer, one that hadn't inspired confidence. Having spent the better part of the last decade interacting with criminals, there was something about the man that Charlie just didn't feel comfortable with.

Trusting his gut, something he had relied on repeatedly over his career, it warned: This man isn't who he says he is.

Charlie fought to control the instinctual detective inside of him. He turned over the paper with a concerted effort, accepting the reality that in less than 24 hours, the man's true identity probably wouldn't matter anyway. Uncovering some misperceived ulterior motive or hidden agenda was pointless, especially given that, in all likelihood, he would be sent home, never to see the mystery man, or any of the other winners, again.

The near certainty of seeing these people for the last time struck Charlie suddenly as he fondly reminisced about his interaction with Kerry Wilson at dinner. She wasn't like most of the others here and had a warmth to her that left an indelible impression. There was a kindness to her and a glimmer in her eyes that brought back memories for him of a life, and love, recently lost. With a heat beginning to burn in his chest that he hadn't felt for some time, Charlie turned towards the picture frame sitting on the desk. He felt conflicted, wondering if he could ever love again.

Charlie shook his head, hoping to clear it. He left the desk behind him and approached his closet to put away his clothes. Inside, he was surprised to find a plastic hanger with a futuristic white jumpsuit and "Weaver" stitched into the lapel. As he examined the trappings more closely, Charlie chuckled at how much it resembled something an astronaut would wear, adorned with an American flag patch and heavy plastic zippers.

Charlie couldn't help but wonder what in the world this outfit was for and where he might be asked to wear it. Were the winners being sent into space? Was this whole facility some sort of launching pad?

If so, Charlie hoped these suits were more protective than the one Michel Bouchon had apparently worn while overseeing the construction of the Orbital Solar Shade. It had been widely speculated that after spending so much time on site during its assembly, the toxicity of the metals he had been working with was ultimately responsible for his terminal diagnosis. Without the proper protective gear, Michel Bouchon's attempts to save the planet had, in turn, sealed his own fate.

As he shut the closet door with a trembling hand, Charlie took a deep breath and conceded that, in the end, he didn't care what the suit was for.

He just hoped he'd be around long enough to find out.

CHAPTER 34

While unpacking at her desk, Kerry rummaged through her bag, her frail body - and guilty conscience – still reeling from Layah's ultimatum at dinner. If she stayed, she might be cured – but she'd never see her family or friends again. Was that actually something that she could do? Would she really sacrifice every relationship for the sake of her own health?

Struggling with a choice that had no easy answer, Kerry found herself drifting back to the day when her doctor had first shared the horrific news: she had been diagnosed with breast cancer. Having discovered the disease after it had reached stage IV, her oncologist had warned her that the chance of recovery was nearly impossible. Even with state-of-the-art chemotherapy treatments and radioactive ablations, he had been genuinely apologetic as he let her know that the prospects of her survival were infinitesimal.

Somberly, he suggested that she make preparations to ensure the quality of what little life she had left.

Always a fighter, Kerry had ignored the odds and the dire predictions the experts had leveled at her. Instead, she had opted to start experimental chemotherapy treatments and battle for the life that was on the verge of being stolen from her. Without fear or hesitation, she had defiantly confronted the disease ravaging her body, resolved to leave no stone unturned in the quest to restore her health.

Due to subsequent chemo treatments over the next several months, her lustrous hair, eyebrows, and eyelashes had inevitably fallen out. Numerous surgeries to remove unhealthy tissue had shaken her fragile confidence as her body's exterior was permanently altered. And, with experimental medications administered daily, her skin's elasticity had soon degenerated as it hung from her body and turned nearly translucent. Infirm and skeletal, she had vowed to resist the ever-present temptation to give up and promised herself that she would continue this struggle until her very last breath.

Her husband had not been so strong.

More debilitating than the diagnosis, treatments, or side effects was the separation that had ultimately ensued as her prognosis grew bleaker. The financial burdens resulting from her treatments and the dramatic changes to her proved too much for Kerry's husband to take and had eventually led him to petition for divorce. Unable to cope as his wife had become a shell of her former self, he had forsaken his wedding vows, leaving her at her darkest moment to fight for her life alone.

When she had miraculously won a spot in Michel Bouchon's lottery, as with the other winners, she was offered an obscene amount of money. With her health rapidly in decline, however, and her divorce from the only family she had finalized, Kerry realized that there was nothing any amount of money could buy that was more important to her than her health.

At dinner, she had expressed such sentiments when coming to Charlie's defense by rhetorically asking what good money was if he didn't have the time or family to spend it on. She had offered that response to explain Charlie's decision, but in truth, she had really spoken for herself.

With little time left and no one to go back to, Kerry knew that she would opt to stay.

CHAPTER 35

Rami sat on the floor of his room in the Sukhasana position, his legs tightly crossed, and his palms pressed together. Lost in meditation, he focused on Layah's dinner-time proposal and the ramifications of never seeing his friends or family again. Clearing his mind was essential to Rami's inner peace. As he whispered the Shanti mantra, a calm washed over him – his first in months.

Although forsaking his loved ones would be heartbreaking, Rami reminded himself that just being in a position to accept Layah's proposal had been a blessing, especially given his circumstances only an hour earlier. Before Umberto had backed out, Rami had resigned himself to being unable to spend time with his loved ones ever again anyway, so at least now, he could do so with the knowledge that he would be cured.

Regardless of Layah's "cost," he was in a much better position now than he had been that morning.

Rami felt a familiar warmth on his beard, a sensation he had become all too accustomed to since his initial diagnosis. He instinctively wiped the blood that began to drip from his nose onto his dhoti. Even with the most advanced treatments and best doctors in India, his bloody sleeve reminded him again of the brain tumor that continued to metastasize. Rapidly growing unchecked beside his brain stem, the glioblastoma was beginning to push on the outer walls of his skull, distorting its shape. Although his turban hid the burgeoning deformity from those around him, it could not conceal the physiological effects of the lump on his body. Bloody noses and the inability to control basic bowel functions not only embarrassed Rami but became daily reminders of his impending demise.

Wiping away more blood, Rami couldn't help but smile at his luck. It was indeed a divine miracle, a gift that he did not intend to insult Vishnu by discarding. With God's grace, he had become one of the final ten winners, and with a little more, he would soon be cured.

Basking in his good fortune and bright future, Rami allowed his thoughts to drift. In doing so, he suddenly recalled his encounter with Devlin Archer and relived his paralyzing fear. What on Earth was HE doing here? He certainly didn't have the kind of money necessary to purchase a spot, and especially not the last remaining spot, which had presumably sold for the most money.

Benefactor or not, whatever Devlin's reason for being here, it wasn't a good one.

Sure, Rami thought, he had used some of Devlin's "services" in the past, but that had been a long time ago when he was just getting his business started. And, although it was true that some of Devlin's intelligence gathering had ultimately helped Rami take down his biggest rival, he would have been just as successful without the spy's help. Wouldn't he?

Rami couldn't be too sure, but regardless, he knew that today, his company was India's largest telemarketing firm. Through his hard work, he reaped the enormous financial benefits he deserved. As to whether it would have grown as exponentially without Devlin's help, this was unknowable. Rami saw no reason to ponder outcomes that did not exist.

He preferred to live in the moment, and in this moment, Devlin presented a threat.

Rami changed out of his blood-stained clothes and prepared to leave the room. He took an extra minute to adjust his turban in front of the bathroom's mirror and fine-tuned his ensemble, ensuring he looked presentable.

Securing his ceremonial kirpan, a four-inch blade that he kept hidden inside of his headdress, Rami took a deep breath and focused. Confronting Devlin to find out what he was up to would be risky, especially given the man's history. But even though Rami knew better than most what the spy was capable of, now that he was one of the actual winners, he vowed that nothing would stop him in his quest to be cured.

Even a man as dangerous as Devlin Archer.

CHAPTER 36

Charlie placed a water bowl in front of Hadron and Cern, watching with a smile as the powerful German shepherds enthusiastically lapped the water. The sound of their slurps, along with the background humming from the cylindrical tube above, was the only noise in the dining room, and their reverberations cascaded off the walls of the circular room.

Bending down to gently pet their heads, he noticed as he rubbed them that, for the first time in a long time, his hand no longer shook. Perhaps it was the calming presence of such majestic animals that steadied Charlie's frayed nerves or the fact that he had spent so many years with the same breed when he had worked with the K-9 unit, but either way, his trembling had stopped momentarily, and Charlie was happy for the reprieve.

As he continued to stroke the dogs and scratch behind their collars, his mind drifted to his wife and son and how much he wished they were here so that he could talk to them now. They would know the answers to the questions that had tormented him since Layah's stipulation at dinner. Would they think he should keep on living without seeing anyone else he knew ever again? Or would they have hoped that an actual spot didn't become available, so that *they* would see him again soon?

Lost in his thoughts, Charlie didn't notice as Kerry entered the dining room, watching from behind as he petted his new friends. After a moment, both dogs lifted their heads simultaneously from the bowl and acknowledged Kerry, causing Charlie to turn around and see her for the first time.

Slightly embarrassed that she hadn't announced herself sooner, Kerry said, "Sorry, I didn't want to disturb you."

"It's okay," Charlie replied, "I was just doing some thinking."

"You're not thinking of backing out, are you?"

Charlie couldn't help but smile at the irony of her question. "Well, since there's still an alternate ahead of me, I don't think I'll have much say in the matter, anyway. But, if I did have a choice, I was just thinking about how not having anyone to go back to might have made it easier to decide to stay."

Kerry probed, "No one?"

Charlie took a long look at Kerry and saw the deep-rooted kindness in her eyes that he had first noticed at dinner. She wasn't like the self-absorbed bluebloods he'd met so far, and Charlie got the impression that, unlike the others, she actually seemed to care. As she continued to lock eyes with him, he became more and more confident that her compassion was genuine and her warmth sincere.

Since the accident, he had never spoken at length about that day, not to his partner Darryl, the therapists his precinct had assigned, or even to himself. But there was something about Kerry's warmth that felt real, and for the first time, he found himself letting down his guard and sharing what had transpired.

"It happened a little over a year ago. My wife and 10-year-old son were headed home from one of his classmate's birthday parties when they were killed by a driver who was under the influence. The driver, it turned out, was a billionaire venture capitalist who had just left a party of his own. Apparently high on cocaine, he had hit them head-on with his SUV…killing them instantly."

"I'm so sorry" Kerry offered.

Charlie took a deep breath and continued, "With all of his financial resources, he'd been able to hire the best defense attorneys in the country, and after a trial that had lasted barely a month, he got off scot-free. I'd lost everything I'd ever loved, and he was inconvenienced for less than 30 days."

In an effort to comfort him, Kerry gingerly put an arm around Charlie's slumped shoulders.

"It's just so ironic when I really think about it. I spent my entire career catching criminals and putting them away, always confident that justice would be done. But when I needed justice for me and my family, well…let's just say I lost my loved ones and my faith in the system that day."

Kerry rubbed Charlie's shoulder, hopeful it would bring him a semblance of reassurance.

"I'd always dreamt of raising our son the right way and one day retiring on a tropical island, surrounded by crystal clear blue ocean and sandy white beaches. Watching sunsets from a beachside bungalow was the paradise I'd always dreamed of…even though I knew it was a silly, unrealistic fantasy on a cop's salary."

Staring at the double doors that led to the hallway, Charlie continued, "But after that day, everything I had ever wanted or dreamt of had been stolen from me. All because of some…obscenely rich…scumbag."

Kerry turned to look at what Charlie was staring at and asked, "Is that why you're not hanging out with the billionaires in the cocktail lounge?"

Startled back to the moment, Charlie answered, "What? No. I have a…"

Again, Charlie looked in Kerry's eyes and could see that, unlike his own, there was no judgment in them for his past indiscretions.

He confessed, "You see, the day after I buried them, I began to drink."

"That's understandable," Kerry consoled.

"No, not really. I took it to the extreme. It was so excessive that I got to the point of wanting things…to end."

Kerry solemnly whispered, "Oh, I see."

Charlie paused, regaining his composure after just admitting out loud for the first time something he had not been able to admit even to himself.

"But in the end, it was Michel Bouchon's lottery that saved me. Because whether I end up being chosen or not, it showed me that I actually did want to live. And once I had accepted that, deciding to cut out alcohol was easy. It's why I don't drink anymore."

"Good for you Charlie, that's definitely something to be proud of," Kerry said with a compassionate twinkle in her eye.

Charlie smiled, "Of course, I'm only on day three."

Kerry chuckled and said, "Well, you've gotta start somewhere."

Self-conscious that he had been rambling only about himself, Charlie asked, "What about you? Are you thinking of backing out?"

For a moment, Kerry thought about sharing the details of her terminal illness and the cowardice of her ex-husband, but instead she decided to keep the conversation light and chided, "You'd like that, wouldn't you?"

Both Charlie and Kerry laughed, their eyes lost in each other's. For the first time in longer than either of them could remember, they didn't subconsciously dwell on the diseases coursing through their bodies, the sudden and traumatic disintegration of their families, or the unanswered questions about the enigmatic Ouroboros.

For a moment, nothing else existed but each other.

Their trance was broken, however, when across the room they heard a distinct scraping on the tiled floor. Surprised, they both turned to look and simultaneously saw Auggie hobbling across the expansive dining room on his Lucite crutches.

"Auggie!" Kerry exclaimed, "Come here and join us."

Auggie forced a smile as he made his way to the massive round table and sat down next to Charlie.

Charlie put a reassuring hand on Auggie's shoulder and asked, "How are you holding up, bud? Lots for a young man to think about, wouldn't you say?"

"There sure is," Auggie whispered, his head bowed as if depressed.

Sensing something was off, Kerry probed, "What's the matter, Auggie? Are you worried about the decision Dr. Golden asked us to make?"

Auggie's eyes began to water as he shook his head and said, "I don't have any family to go back to, and all of my friends always leave whenever they get adopted. But…I *would* miss the nuns. They've always taken such good care of me."

Consoling the boy, Kerry offered, "We'll take care of you too, Auggie. We promise."

Auggie wiped his runny nose and then deliberately looked up at Kerry. "Do you mean it? I'm so scared."

Kerry nodded and then paused for a moment without speaking.

After a pause, she met Charlie's gaze and slowly removed her blonde wig, revealing the bare, vulnerable truth beneath.

"It's okay, Auggie. We're scared too."

CHAPTER 37

Rami marched into the cocktail lounge with purpose, eager to confront Devlin and uncover his true intentions. He paused as he entered, wholly unfamiliar with the surroundings. His religion had forbidden him from drinking alcohol, and Rami suddenly realized that this might be the first time he had stood so close to this much liquor before.

White tufted chairs lined the lounge's equally white walls. The center of the room showcased a massive circular wet bar made out of Lucite, its multiple layers stacked with crystal decanters filled to the brim, their facades sparkling from the lights above. Rami had to admit that there was an ethereal beauty to their intricate glasswork. While some were filled with dark liquids, others were clear, and not for the first time, Rami conceded to himself, he had no idea which was which.

Several members of the Tuvaluan staff canvassed the Lounge. One approached Rami and asked, "May I get you something to drink, Mr. Singh."

Preoccupied, Rami dismissed the man curtly and said, "No, none for me."

Scouring the room for his target, Rami noticed that most of the other winners had already arrived, each enjoying a glass of their favorite spirit. Shira and Oman shared a lively conversation in one corner, while Chi Kwong socialized with Mustafa al Farouq in another. As hearty laughs rang out around the room, for a brief instant, Rami wondered if perhaps he had been missing out by abstaining all these years.

This thought quickly faded, however, as he spotted his quarry sipping a cocktail on a couch across the room. Rami steadied his nerves and made a beeline, ready to challenge the man whose reasons for being here were undoubtedly nefarious.

Ian Haynes intercepted him as he crossed the room, extending his hand in best wishes, "Congratulations again, Rami. What an incredible stroke of luck!"

With his eyes locked on Devlin, Rami said meekly, "Thank you."

Ian continued, "I guess that three billion you paid for your spot was money well spent after all! Between you and me, though, I still can't believe Umberto did that, can you? I mean, good for you and everything, Rami, but what an idiot. Am I right?"

Impatient and no longer listening to what the moneyman from Wall Street had to say, Rami brusquely pushed past him and said, "If you'll excuse me."

Although stunned by the man's rudeness, Ian shrugged. Beside him, a Tuvaluan offered a glass of champagne, which he gladly accepted.

Sitting by himself as his foot shook from withdrawals, Devlin noticed Rami the moment he had walked in. Following the man's brisk gait toward his couch with his steel blue eyes, Devlin adjusted himself to make room for his obviously ill-tempered guest. Devlin patted the empty seat next to him, sliding over on the couch.

"Care to join me?" Devlin offered sarcastically.

Rami abruptly sat down, quickly surveying the room to make sure no one was looking or listening, and then turned to Devlin, hissing under his breath, "I don't know what you're up to, Devlin, but I don't want anything to do with it, do you understand? Don't mess this up for me!"

With a fiendish smile, Devlin played with his accuser and replied, "What would possibly make you think I'm up to something?"

"I know you, *Devlin Archer*, or whatever the name you're using this week is. Better than any of these people, I know exactly what a man like you is capable of."

Taking a sip from his drink, Devlin intensely locked eyes with Rami and said, "Yes, you do."

Momentarily intimidated, Rami regained his courage and said, "Mole, spy, or whatever, this is my one chance to live, Devlin, and you are NOT going to rob me of that."

Devlin finished his whiskey and playfully chided, "Come on, a person can change, can't they, Rami? I'm not that guy anymore."

Incensed that the operative wasn't taking him seriously, Rami subtly reached into his turban and quickly pulled out his Kirpan, flashing the sacred knife towards Devlin. "You are *not* ruining this, do you hear me? Not after everything I've been through and the money I've spent!"

Devlin lowered his eyes towards the four-inch blade and then around the room to see if anyone else had noticed their interaction. Having faced deadlier weapons and more dangerous foes, Devlin remained unfazed by the obviously idle threat.

Nonchalantly he asked, "After all of these years, Rami, is that any way to treat an old co-worker?"

Shaking with fury, Rami said, "Co-worker? That was years ago, and all I did was hire you for a job!"

"A job that made you a fortune."

Defensive, Rami seethed, "I was already rich!"

A sly grin crept onto Devlin's face. "Yes, but I made you WEALTHY."

Momentarily stunned and unable to refute Devlin's logic, Rami replied, "Listen, I won't sit here and let you –."

Suddenly, Rami's eyes widened as he stopped mid-sentence and discreetly slid his Kirpan back inside the folds of his turban. Devlin turned to see what the telemarketing tycoon was so enamored with and saw that it was the gorgeous Cynthia Swift entering the lounge.

She was radiant in a tight blue sequin dress. It was clear she had spent a considerable amount of time in front of the mirror, perfecting her make-up and beautifying her hair. Most notable to Devlin, her matching blue earrings glimmered from the incandescent lights, giving him the impression that the actress was truly dressed to kill.

The lounge suddenly became quiet, as all eyes in the room turned towards the movie star, giving her the attention she so desperately craved.

Sensing his opportunity to distance himself from Rami, Devlin swiftly rose from his seat and made his way to greet her. He was well practiced in pouring on the charm, a skill he had perfected over the years when seducing countless women.

"Mrs. Swift, welcome. You look absolutely stunning this evening. Please, come and join us."

Cynthia took Devlin's hand and glided across the room as Rami sat starstruck, gazing in awe.

When she reached Rami, she extended her hand and demurred, "Mr. Singh."

His mouth agape, Rami took her hand and stammered, "Uh…Cynthia, I mean, Mrs. Swift. So nice to see you again."

"Please, call me Cynthia."

Rami blushed, unable to properly speak, "Cynthia. I. Yes…"

Devlin guided her to his seat, and as she sat down next to Rami, he offered, "I was just going to get us some drinks. Can I get you something?"

Cynthia smiled. "Whiskey, neat. Thank you."

Devlin continued, "And you, Rami?"

Still transfixed and apparently no longer encumbered by his religious convictions, he mumbled, "The same."

Devlin turned and left the pair, knowing that Rami was hooked. Like a black widow, she had trapped her prey, and after Rami's veiled threat with his knife, Devlin could see the benefits of helping this spider with her catch. The Sikh billionaire's suspicions towards Devlin's intentions had turned Rami into a potential threat, and the sooner he was out of the way, the better.

Devlin poured the drinks at the wet bar and brought them back over to Rami and Cynthia, catching the tail end of their flirtations.

"So, what brings such a vision as yourself here anyway? I'd always imagined your life to be perfect."

Cynthia, giggling amorously, replied, "Well, things aren't always as they seem."

With slow and provocative gestures, Cynthia raised her dress with perfectly manicured fingers, alluringly showing off her sublimely sculpted legs. Brown blemishes had begun to appear along her calf and thigh, dotting them like spots on a Cheetah.

Guiltily, Cynthia explained, "Too much time by the pool, I'm afraid."

Handing the two paramours their drinks, Cynthia seductively asked Devlin, with her dress still raised, "Mr. Archer, you'll be joining us, won't you? I've always found the more to be… the merrier."

Jealously, Rami hissed, protecting his prize, "I'm sure he has other more pressing matters to attend to, don't you, Mr. Archer?"

Rami thought he was asserting his dominance, but Devlin knew he was sealing his doom.

Nodding, Devlin said, "I'm afraid Mr. Singh is right, Mrs. Swift. I'll be retiring early tonight. I bid you both a pleasant evening."

Devlin could see her disappointment as he turned to leave, but with Rami firmly in her clutches, he was confident that soon she wouldn't care. It was only a matter of time now before she had her victim, and the one man who knew his identity was no longer a threat to expose him.

Crossing the room and heading for the door, Devlin was once again ambushed by a now inebriated Ian Haynes. Eager to brown-nose and learn more about the mystery man behind the blind trust, he blocked the spy's escape path, forcing him to engage.

"So, my friend, I don't think we really ever got a chance to connect at dinner."

Annoyed and eager to leave before the fireworks began, Devlin curtly replied, "No, we didn't."

Oblivious to the disdain in Devlin's response, Ian continued, "It really is quite amazing that we haven't run into each other before. You weren't at Prince Riyad's 40ᵗʰ birthday party in Dubai last spring, were you?"

Devlin glanced over Ian's shoulder at Rami and Cynthia, watching as she giggled flirtatiously. Brushing her hair with her hand, she cleverly removed a blue stone from one of her earrings.

Devlin smiled, "No, I must have missed that one."

"Too bad," Ian continued, "That was one hell of a party. I was a big fan of the giraffe races and trapeze artists, but of course, my date couldn't stop babbling about the celebrities. It actually reminded me of the Oscars last year. You see, I was at this afterparty in Malibu when my good friend Sting said to me —"

Uninterested in anything this windbag had to say, Devlin continued to observe the interactions between Rami and Cynthia, watching as she adroitly dropped the stone into the unsuspecting man's drink.

Lifting her glass with a seductive smile, he could just make out her toast. "Cheers!"

Rami lifted his glass in response and said, "To health!"

"To health," Cynthia ironically responded.

Both touched glasses before taking a sip, Cynthia's eyes never leaving her intended victim as Rami involuntarily winced at his first sip of alcohol.

Ian could tell his small talk with the blind trust winner wasn't going anywhere, so he pivoted and asked, "So, tell me, Mr. Archer, what brings you here? What's your affliction?"

Listening to the hedge fund manager in the periphery, Devlin watched Rami's eyes begin to widen as he grabbed helplessly at his throat. Choking on his tongue, Devlin could see that the poison had already begun to take hold and knew mere seconds remained before he entered his death throes.

Wanting to end the conversation with the braggadocio quickly, Devlin put a hand seductively on the man's shoulder and said, "AIDS."

As his eyes widened and his body tensed, Ian glanced at the hand on his shoulder and said, "Oh, I see. I…"

Devlin quickly brushed past Ian, who now stood petrified, and said, "If you'll excuse me."

Rushing to Rami's "assistance", Devlin dropped to his knees in contrived concern.

"Rami! What's wrong?"

Rami wheezed and gasped for air.

Knowing it was already too late, Devlin shouted to one of the Tuvaluan servers, "Get him some help! He's choking!"

The Tuvaluan sprinted out of the lounge as Cynthia screamed in feigned terror. Turning towards the commotion, everyone in the room watched in horror as Rami's mouth began to foam and his nose gushed blood.

With his eyes bulging and his body convulsing in spasms, Rami pawed at his neck in a vain attempt to regain his breath. Devlin softly lowered him to the floor and on to his back to make him more comfortable. Rami grabbed at the spy's lapel, shaking uncontrollably as he did. His body prone on the floor, Devlin leaned closely over him until the two men locked eyes, and sadistically, Devlin gave him a wink.

Rami's body twitched feverishly at the provocateur's prodding, just as several Tuvaluans in medical gear rushed through the door. Ripping open Rami's tunic, they began compressions on his chest in a desperate attempt to save the tycoon's life.

Struggling to breathe as his body shook, Devlin once again bent over and lowered his face just inches from the billionaire.

Rhetorically, Devlin asked loudly so that everyone else could hear, "What was that Rami? What did you say?!"

Now close enough to the man's mouth to cover his face, Devlin acted as if he were absorbing Rami's final pleas, "Are you sure?!"

After a moment of "listening", Devlin slowly sat back up on his knees and pointed dramatically at Cynthia, "He said it was her!" he shouted in mock disbelief.

There was an audible gasp in the lounge as the entire room turned towards Cynthia.

She stood and backed away, raising her hands defensively while she stammered, "What? Don't be ridiculous. This isn't *my* doing!"

Challenging her response, Devlin continued, "He said it was."

With her cheeks now matching the color of her dress, Cynthia rationalized, "The man is obviously ill. That's why he's here in the first place!"

All eyes turned back towards Devlin as he stared in spurious shock at Rami's drink on the table. With great deliberation, he reached for the glass and dramatically emptied Rami's Whiskey onto the table, knowing the Chalcanthite wouldn't have had a chance to fully dissolve.

In the middle of the puddle sat a single blue stone.

Everyone in the lounge stared at the rock and then back at Cynthia.

Chi Kwong was the first to speak and pointed, "Look! The stone from her earring. It's missing!"

With the blue gem from one of her earring studs clearly removed, Cynthia was caught, her acting skills unable to absolve her of her crime.

She sputtered, "But...but. I would never. It wasn't me!"

Immediately, the Tuvaluans servers grabbed Cynthia by the arms and began to carry her out of the lounge. Hysterical, she screamed and flailed her spotted legs as the men dragged her out of the room like a mental patient bound in a straitjacket.

"No! You can't do this to me! I'm Cynthia Swift! Do you hear me? I'M CYNTHIA SWIFT!" she cried out, her voice cracking with righteous indignation.

As all eyes were focused on Cynthia's histrionics, Devlin utilized the commotion to take advantage of the opportunity. Having cupped his hand behind Rami's head in feigned compassion, Devlin deftly slipped his hand inside of Rami's turban and quickly removed the Kirpan from the headdress atop the man's now lifeless body.

In a matter of seconds, the master pickpocket was able to tuck the weapon inside of his sleeve, without any of the others noticing his deception.

With the Kirpan now secured, Devlin couldn't help but feel a twinge of guilt. He hadn't needed to out Cynthia as the culprit, but her bombastic reaction was exactly the distraction he'd needed to procure Rami's dagger. Was her expulsion and the loss of her husband's nearly two billion dollars really worth him having the only weapon in the facility?

Devlin smiled as he thought to himself, "Yes."

Devlin mimicked the distress of those around him, conveying faux concern as the Tuvaluan medical staff continued to work on reviving Rami. Devlin chuckled internally, knowing it was a pointless endeavor. Trying to resuscitate Rami now was a fool's errand, as Chalcanthite was one of the deadliest substances on Earth. Its effects were almost instantaneous, which unsurprisingly, was why it had always been one of the more popular tools in his arsenal.

No, Rami was gone.

Having obtained a knife and eliminated his only threat in one fell swoop, Devlin took a moment to revel in his own cunning.

He had quite *literally* killed two birds with one stone.

No one could stop him now.

Basking in his own self-satisfaction, Devlin's smugness was short-lived. Without Rami to distract him, his withdrawal symptoms quickly took center stage. As his foot twitched uncontrollably, the inflamed nerves in his body snapped him back to the moment, demanding he get out of there and away from these people.

Devlin slowly exited the lounge, leaving the Tuvaluans to ineffectually resurrect the body of India's wealthiest man.

Knowing the chaos he was escaping from was just the diversion he'd need for his privacy, Devlin headed for the one place where he could find a remedy for his nicotine-induced shakes: the storage room.

CHAPTER 38

Layah couldn't tear her eyes away as Rami's face disappeared beneath a solemnly placed blanket. His lifeless body, now shrouded, was gently rolled on a Lucite gurney towards her, and a wave of grief washed over her. Her vision blurred with tears, but she valiantly fought to hold them back, seeking solace in Hadron, who whined and nudged her hand in a futile attempt to console her.

Overwhelmed with sorrow, Layah couldn't deny that things were not going as planned. Until this evening, every detail had been meticulously devised, but the unscrupulous greed of one of the alternates was something neither she nor Michel had accounted for. Blindsided by Cynthia's actions, Layah's mind swirled with doubt, and for the first time, she began to wonder if Michel was doing the right thing.

Michel's plan was never meant to harm anyone, let alone lead to someone's death. Would Michel want any of this to continue if it meant risking even a single person's life?

Layah wasn't sure, but he would let her know one way or the other tomorrow.

The Tuvaluans wheeled Rami down the hallway, and Layah brushed her fingers along his arm as they passed, whispering, "I'm so sorry."

Leaning against the wall to steady herself, she struggled to maintain her composure. Gatlin approached her with deference and rested a sympathetic hand on her shoulder, breaking her reverie. She straightened, regaining her resolve.

With as much conviction as she could muster, Layah declared, "We stick to the plan."

"Of course, Dr. Golden."

"We've come too far, and we're too close now to…"

Overwhelmed with emotion, Layah's voice quivered as she wrestled with the guilt of what had just transpired, and perhaps more distressingly, what was yet to come.

Reassuringly, Gatlin rubbed her back. "Everything is ready to go, Dr. Golden. After tomorrow, this will all be in the past."

Observing the winners as they gathered to console one another in the lounge, Layah couldn't help but prophesize, "It won't be, for them."

CHAPTER 39

Charlie tossed and turned in his makeshift bed, his mind unable to find solace in sleep. An endless stream of thoughts coursed through his head as he speculated about what the morning would bring. Going home wasn't something he desired, but it had become all but inevitable at this point. None of the other winners seemed willing to relinquish their spots, and frankly, Charlie couldn't blame them. Even if he'd had the option to back out, in his failing condition, he doubted he would have. A life without family or friends was still a life, and besides, he didn't have either.

Leaving this place also undoubtedly meant facing an endless barrage of questions back home from countless news outlets across the globe. He imagined that for the few remaining months of his life, he would be hounded daily by the media's insatiable appetite for each minute detail of his experience.

Regardless of their cravings for salacious gossip, however, Charlie wondered what he would be able to reveal. He still didn't know what the Ouroboros was, where he'd been taken, or if Michel Bouchon was even still alive. He, like everyone else, remained in the dark, and for all he knew this entire experience could have been one highly elaborate farce.

Yet, despite the mysteries and uncertainties, Charlie couldn't help but feel grateful. Whether he was ultimately cured or not, he would still be leaving here with something he hadn't come with: hope. Hope for a life, regardless of how brief, where the thought of a woman and child brought him joy instead of unfettered grief. Kerry and Auggie had revived his soul, which he thought he had forever lost all of those months ago.

Charlie smiled, lost in the pleasure of how comforting his time with them had been. His joy, however, was bittersweet, knowing that in just a few short hours he would likely never see them again.

A knock at the door startled him out of his dream-like trance.

In the darkness, he called out, "Hello?"

From the other side of the door, Debra's familiar voice desperately implored, "Charlie? Are you awake? I need to speak with you right away. It's urgent."

Groggily, Charlie rose from his "bed" and flipped on the lights.

Dragging his feet along the floor, he approached the door and slowly opened it, confused. "Debra? What time is it? Is everything ok?"

Debra's eyes watered as her lower lip quivered, "Charlie, there has been a terrible tragedy. Rami Singh has been murdered."

Shocked by the revelation, Charlie's adrenaline spiked, "Murdered? How? By whom?"

"It was Cynthia Swift, Charlie. We're still trying to figure out exactly how it happened, but it looks like she poisoned him."

Charlie's police training and natural instincts reflexively kicked in, "Poisoned? Okay, then the area is now considered a crime scene, and we'll have to keep it sterile. Let's cordon off a perimeter while a forensics team can be brought in to –."

Debra raised her hand and interrupted him, "Charlie, we're past that. Cynthia has already been removed from the facility along with Rami's body. Both of them are gone now, so…don't you see what this means?"

Still in shock and unable to grasp Debra's inference, Charlie stammered as he began to pace, "Gone? But, she'll have to be questioned, and possibly arrested if –."

"It means you're no longer an alternate. *You're* one of the winners now."

Like a lightning bolt, Debra's words struck Charlie and froze him in his tracks, leaving him speechless.

"Charlie…you're going to be cured."

Unable to fully register what Debra had just told him, Charlie stood paralyzed, incapable of formulating a cogent response, "Cured?"

"I just came to let you know, Charlie. Someone had to. Now, please try and get some sleep so you're ready for the morning. You'll be meeting with the other winners in the auditorium, and there, Michel Bouchon will introduce you to the Ouroboros."

Stunned by everything he had just heard, Charlie stammered, "I…I don't know what to say."

Debra offered a reassuring touch, "I'm happy you've won, Charlie. I'm just sorry it was this way."

As Debra turned to leave, sensation slowly retuned to Charlie's limbs. Watching her walk away down the empty hallway, he quietly mumbled, "Yeah…*me too.*"

CHAPTER 40

Devlin walked down the corridor, reveling in his own genius. He conceded that the only person who might think this day couldn't get any better was that cop from Oakland. With two other winners now eliminated, the man had just been promoted to the final spot in Michel Bouchon's lottery.

Devlin refocused as he reached the storage room. Cautiously glancing around to make sure he was alone, as he had so many times since arriving, Devlin couldn't shake the feeling that he was being watched. Quickly he spun around, trying to catch the boogeyman he was sure was tailing him. As before, he found himself staring only at an empty, sterile hallway. Once again chalking up his paranoia to his days in prison, Devlin turned his attention back towards the storage room door and stealthily slipped inside.

Devlin shut the door and, with practiced care, took inventory of his surroundings. He couldn't help but notice that the room looked like a police evidence locker. The walls were lined with alloy shelving holding items in plastic bags labeled "Contraband", while the entire enclosure was encased in a metal mesh-like structure.

It took Devlin a minute to piece together why the room felt so foreign - until he realized that it was the first place he'd seen in the facility with any metal. Almost everything else here, he had observed, was either made of plastic, glass, carbon fiber or Lucite. Only in this room did he see anything that contained steel.

Was the metal pen that enclosed the room some sort of Faraday Cage?

Examining the shelves more closely in search of his cigarettes, Devlin took stock of some of the "Contraband" confiscated from the other winners. An electric toothbrush was in a cubby marked "Weaver," car keys on a shelf labeled

"Wilson," and lightweight aluminum crutches in another marked "Martin." He picked up a bag, sniffed the inside, and smiled, returning the contents marked "Medicinal" to the receptacle labeled "Haynes."

Continuing to take in his surroundings, he noticed in a corner of the room sat Mustafa's gasoline-powered wheelchair. Devlin remembered he had complained about having it confiscated at dinner, but now he could see why. If the cop couldn't have an electric toothbrush, this piece of equipment, and the fumes it would undoubtedly produce, would certainly not be permitted. The chair was bulky with a powerful engine in the back, and Devlin shook his head at the fact that the oil magnate had gone with a gasoline powered wheelchair instead of an electric one.

At least the man was consistent.

Not for the first time, Devlin wondered why they couldn't have metal or electronics in the facility in the first place. What was so important that these items had to be impounded, and what did they have to do with the Ouroboros?

Devlin's train of thought was cut short when he noticed a shelf with his name on it, which held his box of cigarettes and lighter inside of its own plastic bag. Excitedly, he pulled out the bag and removed a cigarette with a sigh of relief. After popping it in his mouth and lighting it, Devlin sat down to take a drag, lifting his head towards the ceiling in anticipation of the rush from the nicotine stick. He inhaled deeply, letting the smoke exit his mouth slowly. He could instantly feel his body begin to calm, his jitters starting to subside. It was pure bliss - and after the success with Rami, it almost felt like an after-sex smoke.

Devlin let his pale blue eyes wander around the room as the intoxicant coursed through his veins when suddenly his heart skipped a beat. Above him, he noticed a fire sprinkler protruding from the ceiling and instantly froze, terrified that his smoke would cause an alarm to go off.

That shot of adrenaline quickly subsided, however, as he recalled having set off these sorts of fire suppression systems many times in the past. As he'd found out when he lit that warehouse on fire in Pakistan, these sprinklers weren't triggered by smoke but by heat. Smiling, he recalled that blaze fondly and the enjoyment he'd felt watching the munitions depot burn.

Devlin relaxed as he finished his cigarette in the blissful silence and seclusion of the room, lost in his former exploits.

After several minutes and with his nerves steadied, Devlin left the room and walked back towards his own. Now satiated, he strode with a purpose, reinvigorated for tomorrow's big reveal.

From a shadowed doorway down the hall, Gatlin eased his head out, watching the interloper as he made his way down the corridor. With every fiber in his being, Gatlin fought the urge to rush over and confront the man who was obviously up to something.

Doing so, however, would contravene what Layah had asked, so instead, he took a deep breath and did what he was supposed to do: Stick to the plan.

CHAPTER 41

In his room, Ian Haynes paced back and forth, unable to shake the image of Rami convulsing on the floor. The memory rattled him more deeply than he cared to admit. On a number of occasions, Ian had found himself in similar circumstances, albeit due to a myriad of illicit substances he had consumed. He was no stranger to moments of foaming at the mouth, but witnessing Rami's lifeless body being wheeled away brought back memories for the hedge fund manager he'd tried desperately to repress.

In his high-stress role of managing billions of investors' dollars, Ian had, from time to time, relied on the "help" of science to cope. Some ingestants had been used to calm his nerves, while others had given him the energy to continue for several days on end. There was a delicate balance between the two, and occasionally, he had navigated that channel poorly. Like Rami, he too had ended up on a gurney, unresponsive and covered in his own secretions.

Ian's volatile lifestyle had, over time, taken its toll on his health. Years of late-night schmoozing with clients, indulging in a variety of narcotics, and consuming copious amounts of alcohol had slowly poisoned his body. Years of exposure to these toxins had ultimately proven fatal.

Living like a billionaire hedge fund manager had come with a cost, and that price had been his liver.

After months of treatments he'd kept hidden from investors, the cirrhosis had eventually chewed away most of his already damaged liver. He no longer had the luxury of waiting for a donor transplant, which was why he had taken one of his few remaining options and purchased a spot in the lottery.

It had been easy for Ian to tell the world the lottery spots were worthless, especially when his only other alternative had been to hire an organ harvester to remove a healthy liver from an unsuspecting "volunteer." In the end, having someone abducted overseas would've cost far less, but as he did with every significant financial decision he made, he analyzed the pros and cons of each option. The pro of stealing an organ was cost savings, while the con was potential imprisonment.

Ultimately, Ian took the least reprehensible route, not because of some moral conviction but for self-preservation. He wasn't built for prison, and he came to accept that paying for a spot was just the cost of doing business in this business called "Life."

Now that he was here, giving up when he was so close wasn't an option. After all he'd done - from the money he'd spent to the public he'd misled - Layah's ultimatum had barely registered. Limited time left to spend with his family, and the prospect of suffering immense liver pain for the last few months of his life, made his choice to stay an easy one

Content with his rationale to proceed, Ian once again thought about Rami's body as it had twitched on the floor. Although horrifying, this time only one thing ran through his mind: Better him than me.

***

Oman Disden sat lost in thought at the desk in his room. He also recalled Rami's lifeless body as it lay on the lounge floor. Over the decades, Oman had seen countless corpses and, as a consequence, was unmoved by the sight of a man fighting for his last breath. Death was a daily part of his arms business, making Oman indifferent to it - unlike the others.

Except for one man.

Oman had noticed as the chaos erupted, one person in the room who hadn't looked nearly as shaken as the rest: the man behind the blind trust. Oman couldn't be sure, but reading the man's facial features and eyes, he sensed that he had seen the loss of life before. The man wasn't afraid of death or the horrors of inflicting it.

The man had ultimately reminded Oman of himself, which only meant one thing: he was dangerous.

Danger was a way of life for Oman, having sold countless arms to warring tribes throughout his and neighboring countries. Oman's weapons had caused the bodies of perhaps millions to litter the jungles, frequently resulting in the systematic killing of entire villages and small towns. Oman had become numb to those horrific massacres, so Rami's death held little significance.

His mind moved past the evening's hysteria and returned to Layah's warning of never seeing his family or friends again. Could he do such a thing if it meant being cured?

Of course he could.

Oman hadn't taken even a moment to deliberate on Layah's stipulation, as he hadn't had any real friends or family since his youth.

Although he had survived countless firefights in jungles, after being abducted as a child, most of his friends hadn't. They were cut down in wars before they ever reached their teens - casualties of tribal conflicts, their memories and friendships long since gone.

As for family, he had never seen his parents again after the kidnapping, and the progression of his Multiple Sclerosis had left him unable to conceive. No, he had no family to go back to, but even more significant, no chance of starting one as things stood now.

For his life and legacy to continue, Oman resolved that his only chance was here, to be cured by Michel Bouchon's Ouroboros.

CHAPTER 42

The next morning found Charlie exhausted. His survivor's guilt had kept him awake throughout the night, musing in the darkness of his room over what Rami's death had meant for *him*. Alone with just his thoughts and the ever-present humming sound that radiated from the pipe attached to his wall, his conscience had torn at him, screaming that he should never have won this way. Without the tragic murder of an innocent man, the reality was that he wouldn't have found himself in the position he was in now, moments away from being cured.

Was it even right to win this way?

He paused in front of the auditorium doors, watching his Tuvaluan chauffer pedal away in an Invisi. Charlie took a deep breath to steady his nerves, unsure what the others would think when they saw him. He, of course, had nothing to do with the evening's events, but as a former alternate, would they wonder about him in the back of their minds?

Had Cynthia simply beaten him to the punch?

Two Tuvaluan attendants opened the doors to the large theater, and Charlie found himself standing at the back of an auditorium that sat several thousand. It was a massive room with countless rows of Lucite seats and a large plastic dais at the front. On the stage was a single translucent podium with an immense projection screen behind it. The room resembled an amphitheater but without the kitschy warmth or congenial ambiance. Taking in the cavernous space before him, Charlie became acutely aware of just how many Tuvaluans inhabited the facility.

Most of the seats were unoccupied except for the eight that were taken by the remaining winners. Mustafa sat in his wheelchair, prominently positioned in an aisle. The Chosen were spread throughout the auditorium, seated apart from one another, except for Kerry and Auggie who sat together.

As he stepped through the threshold of the doors, all eyes turned toward Charlie. He couldn't be sure, but he saw suspicion in the faces of some and apathy plastered on others. Only Gilbert did not turn to look at him. The man sat still, hands clasped, and facing towards the front.

Charlie and Kerry locked eyes, and she waved to him to come and join her and Auggie.

As he made his way over to both of them, he passed by Ian Haynes, who said sarcastically under his breath, "Congratulations."

Unsure how to respond, Charlie just nodded and continued past, taking a seat next to Auggie.

Kerry reached across Auggie, took Charlie's hand, and whispered, "I'm glad you're here."

Sheepishly Charlie replied, "I just wish it was under different circumstances."

At that moment, Layah walked through a side door along the auditorium wall, and immediately, everyone turned towards their benefactress. She strode towards the stage with conviction, Hadron and Cern close at her heels.

She climbed the pulpit steps in the deafening silence, her footsteps reverberating throughout the auditorium. Like an ASMR video, the sounds of her clicking heels echoed hypnotically through the still auditorium, and Charlie could feel the hairs on his arms begin to stand up.

Layah reached the podium at center stage and stood silently for a moment, peering out over the ten winners to survey those still remaining. Her eyes swept over the room, jaw clenched, every feature taut with purpose. She gripped the lectern and dropped her gaze to the notes before her.

Clearing her throat, she began, "I know last night was traumatic, and a terrible shock for all of us, but what I am about to reveal to you is the greatest invention in the history of mankind. With that comes inherent risks and unforeseeable dangers. EVERYONE on Earth wants to know what I am about to share with you, and some are willing to pay any price to uncover it."

Devlin shifted uneasily in his seat.

"So, before I continue, I must again reiterate, once I reveal the cure of the Ouroboros to you, you will never be able to see your family and friends again. Is that understood? This is your last chance. Anyone who would like to leave, *must do so now.*"

There was a long silence as the winners turned their heads in search of any hesitancies in the others. Chi Kwong noticed that some of the remaining winners looked scared and almost guilty that they'd never see their loved ones again.

"Fools," he thought.

Layah continued, "Very well then, let's begin. *I introduce to you, Mr. Michel Bouchon.*"

Layah pushed a button on a remote that sat atop the podium, and the room slowly darkened. The large screen behind her lit up with the image of the most famous man on the planet. In his early sixties, with greyish blonde hair, kind eyes, and an inviting smile, Michel Bouchon resonated warmth as he addressed the audience.

The Chosen sat in stunned silence on the edge of their seats. Hadron and Cern whimpered excitedly at the screen.

"Hello, friends, and welcome. My name is Michel Bouchon, and I can only imagine what it has taken for you to be here today. You are the final ten winners of my lottery and have undoubtedly come from great distances and diverse backgrounds to be here. Although different in many ways, you have all come for the same reason – to seek a cure for the diseases ravaging your bodies. Rest assured. you've come to the right place."

Charlie and Kerry glanced over at each other, squeezing one another's hand.

Michel continued, "In the past, I have created medications to conquer sleep and satellites to stop global warming, but today, ladies and gentlemen, is about the future. I am excited to present to you my greatest invention yet, the Ouroboros. Mankind's first Time Machine."

With his jaw dropped, Devlin leaned forward in his seat and mumbled to himself, "What. The. Fuck?"

A large painting of a circular image appeared on the screen: a black snake eating its own tail. The snake gradually dissolved into a circle that resembled a hula hoop. Inside the ring, two white dots slowly diverged from each other at the top of the hoop and began moving around the circle in opposite directions.

Michel spoke over the depiction, "The Large Hadron Collider, on the French/Swiss border, is the world's largest particle accelerator, and until recently, was the most complex machine ever invented. With a circumference of *sixteen miles*, it smashes together nanoparticles at nearly the speed of light. Millions of times smaller than a single grain of sand, these particles collide with so much energy that they create matter, the building blocks of the entire universe. This is how modern science believes the Big Bang was achieved."

The two white dots converged at the bottom of the circle, coinciding with a large flash that lit up the room.

"The Ouroboros works in much the same way."

The screen now had a much larger circle with just one white dot. It began to spin around the circle, gaining speed with each revolution.

"Except, instead of a circumference of sixteen miles, the Ouroboros has a circumference of *a thousand miles*. And instead of spinning microscopic nanoparticles, it spins a subway car. A subway car…that will hold you."

On the screen the dot began to spin so fast that it became a singular blur of white light, encompassing the entire loop.

"As any object approaches the speed of light, the phenomenon behind Einstein's Special Theory of Relativity occurs, called time dilation. By harnessing this enigma, Dr. Golden and her team have found a way to cure you and me of all of our diseases. Let me show you."

The film shifted to a homemade style movie with the word "January" at the bottom of the screen.

The camera followed Michel as he walked on a train station-like platform towards a massive three-story tall plexiglass tube that was encircled by a foot-thick copper coil. Resembling a plastic subway tunnel inside of a colossal, elongated Slinky, the circular tube stretched as far behind Michel as the eye could see, with its path curved so slightly that it was imperceptible. Lights from the ceiling gleamed off the copper coiling as the tube stretched into what appeared to be an infinitely long corridor.

As Michel approached the transparent tube, he stood in front of a plexiglass door, and with a slight cough, pushed a button on its console.

With his arms outstretched, Michel dramatically announced to the camera, "I give you, the Ouroboros."

Plastic doors separated with a fantastic hiss of steam, and behind the aperture sat a twelve-passenger subway car that was approximately sixty feet in length. Resembling a large plastic pill, the inside of the coach was spartan, containing only Lucite seats, massive windows, and a rotary calendar on the wall at its front.

On the outside of the shuttle, attached to the rounded front and back ends, were two large metallic cubes that were both approximately the size of an SUV. Their grey color and dull consistency differed dramatically from the reflective qualities of the tunnel's copper alloy and clear plastic.

On the capsule's forward cube, a large "Plus Symbol" was painted on the side, while on the aft, there was an equally sized "Minus Symbol" emblazoned. Hovering several feet from the cylinder's base, the capsule looked as if it floated on an invisible pocket of air.

Charlie and Kerry turned towards each other, unsure of what they were looking at on the screen.

Michel continued, "I am joined today by Dr. Layah Golden, one of the geniuses behind the Ouroboros. Her experience working on particle accelerators was instrumental in our efforts to build what you see before you today."

The camera swung towards Layah who looked noticeably less drained, holding two German shepherd puppies in her arms.

Gilbert inexplicably clapped from his seat and shouted, "That's Layah!"

All eyes in the auditorium turned towards Gilbert in pity as Michel continued on the screen, "She is accompanied by her assistants, Hadron and Cern."

Hearing their names mentioned by Michel caused the dogs to bark, their howls echoing throughout the theater.

"And, of course, our cameraman, a man who spearheaded this project but today is acting as our videographer. A man of many hats, you could say," Michel joked with a wink towards the camera.

"Thank you," the cameraman said.

Michel's face then contorted from delight to consternation as he continued, "But we are not here to celebrate. Not yet. We are here because, as you may know, I was told that I was dying last year. Due to the heavy metal poisoning coursing through my body, it is estimated that I will succumb to my disease within six months. A prognosis like this has traditionally meant an unavoidable death sentence for someone in my position. Until now."

Michel walked over and gently petted both puppies on the head as they squirmed and barked excitedly in Layah's arms. Smiling, he playfully teased the young dogs before rhetorically asking, "So, which one of you will it be?"

Locking eyes with Michel, one puppy panted feverishly, and in that pivotal moment of immense scientific discovery, it was the hand of fate that intervened. Itching behind the German shepherd's ears, Michel grinned and declared, "Very well then…Hadron it is."

Continuing his exposition to the camera, Michel pressed on, "As mankind prepares to embark on the most epic journey in human history, it is man's best friend that will actually be the first to experience the phenomenon of time dilation."

Michel then unclasped a 1980's digital Casio watch from his wrist and nodded towards the cameraman, "Would you be so kind?"

Fumbling slightly as he removed an identical watch from his wrist, the cameraman handed it over to Michel. Fighting to control a cough, Michel held both watches and proceeded to push buttons on them simultaneously. The digital numbers on their dials began to count in synchronicity. Michel explained, "By comparing these two watches, at the end of three months, we will be able to confirm if time dilation has indeed occurred for Hadron inside of the Ouroboros."

Michel then gently took Hadron from Layah's arm and carried him to the subway car. Cern remained behind and began to quietly whimper in distress.

Attaching his watch to Hadron's dog collar, he placed the puppy in front of a water bowl on the floor of the translucent shuttle. Confused, Hadron sniffed the bowl and looked back at Michel as he closed the plexiglass doors between them.

"See you in three months," Michel smiled as he waved goodbye to the German shepherd puppy.

Michel turned and nodded to Layah, who stood next to a control panel. Layah nodded in reply, and pushed a series of buttons on her console, still holding Cern in the cradle of her arm. The subway car began to glide forward silently. Slowly, Hadron was ushered down the plexiglass tube that stretched for miles in the distance.

The camera then swung back to Michel, who stood transfixed as he watched the puppy gain speed and travel out of sight. Captivated momentarily by the magnitude of the occasion, Michel's reverie was quickly broken as he refocused, composing himself.

Slowly turning back towards the camera and addressing his audience, Michel began, "Traveling at the speed of light. Or to be more precise, 186,000 miles *per second*. An unimaginably fast clip that is difficult for the mind to comprehend. At that speed, you could circle the Earth seven times in just one second! In the past, only the creativity of science fiction writers like Isaac

Asimov or Robert Heinlein allowed us to dream of traveling at that rate of speed to far-away stars. But today, their visions are nearly *our* reality."

Behind Michel, a white flash passed inside of the tube so quickly that only a faint outline of the subway car could be seen.

"We do not yet have the technological capacity to propel Hadron at that speed, as the energy needed to move an object of his mass would require more power than is generated by the nuclear fusion of the sun. But we can get close, really close. And really close…is all we need."

Again, the flash zipped past Michel, but only a white blur was discernable this time.

"With a little bit of providence, the Ouroboros will be able to accelerate Hadron to more than 99% of the speed of light. And as he gets closer and closer to that velocity, the effects of time dilation will become more and more pronounced."

Over Michel's shoulder, the subway car behind him was now speeding past so frequently, that its flashes began to resemble a strobe light. With each revolution the shuttle gained speed, accelerating to the point that the intervals between the flashes soon diminished, until they simply became one elongated white mass.

"At ten percent the speed of light, the earliest sign of time dilation begins to occur, and manifests itself as the first color on the visible spectrum. Like light passing and then dispersing through a prism, the concentrated energy used to propel Hadron's capsule focuses on a singular point. Generating electromagnetic waves that produce an array of vibrant hues, the color with the longest wavelength is the first that will appear…red."

Inside the roofline of the thirty-foot-tall tube, a red beam of light began to blaze, enveloping the white that was there only moments before. Soon, the red became fused with an orange tint slowly materializing underneath it.

"Each subsequent color of the spectrum coincides with the magnitude of velocity achieved. Compounded, the entire array of colors will be seen as Hadron reaches 99% of the speed of light."

Behind Michel, a yellow light gradually appeared below the orange, followed by green, then blue, and finally, purple. A rainbow of chromaticity filled the translucent cylinder, the bright palette bathing the platform in vivid color.

"Once the full spectrum of colors is visible, Hadron will have accelerated to the necessary speed for optimal time dilation to occur. Meaning, he will have achieved something that no living creature has ever accomplished before…"

The tube now hummed loudly behind Michel as a rainbow of light burst all around him.

"…time travel."

Michel purposefully turned away from the camera and back towards the plexiglass tube. He gently rested his hand on the enormous cylinder and whispered, "Good luck, boy."

The film dissolved to the same platform, the same colors still beaming from inside the translucent tube. At the bottom of the screen was the word, "April". Nothing was seemingly different about the scene, but it was soon clear that much had changed in the transpiring three months.

Debra pushed Michel in a wheelchair, escorting the ailing entrepreneur to the subway door. Coughing violently, with his eyes sunken and his cheeks withdrawn, Michel appeared to be a shell of the man they had just seen. Clearly fighting for his life, he now only had a few remaining whisps of hair atop his head, while his frame had become alarmingly frail.

Struggling to breathe, Michel addressed the camera, which shook ever so slightly. "Today marks three months since we last said goodbye to Hadron. According to our technicians, the Ouroboros has performed *almost* perfectly. Although the numbers are encouraging, now we must evaluate the most important data point…how our time traveler has fared."

With a nearly full grown Cern waiting dutifully at her side, Layah pushed several buttons on her control panel, and immediately, loud sirens blared, and yellow warning lights flashed throughout the platform. The camera swiveled back towards the Ouroboros, the spectrum of color dissolving in reverse order. First, the purple tint at the bottom began to fade, followed by the blue, and then green just above it.

"Come on…" Michel whispered.

As the rest of the colors gradually began to wane, the flashing white light once again appeared, its intervals becoming elongated as the subway car slowed. Eventually, a faint outline of the shuttle could be seen, and after several more rotations around the loop, the coach finally came to a stop in front of the plexiglass doorway.

Continuing to cough from his wheelchair, Michel shakily extended his arm and pushed a button on the door which swiveled open with a hiss. A blast of steam erupted from underneath the subway car, and as the vapor cleared, Hadron came bouncing through the threshold and ran towards Michel.

With great difficulty, the world's only trillionaire bent over to hug the tiny puppy, who appeared to not have aged a day.

"Welcome home, buddy," Michel exclaimed, fighting to suppress his cough.

No longer able to control his excitement, Cern bound across the platform towards his brother and began to bark wildly as he reached the sibling he hadn't seen in ninety days.

The difference in their sizes was staggering, as Cern was now nearly ten times larger and thirty pounds heavier than Hadron. Although once identical, the puppy that had embarked on the journey now looked like a comically sized runt compared to the twin he had left behind.

Indifferent to the disparity, the two dogs wagged their tails uncontrollably as they playfully touched noses and licked each other's faces.

The cameraman approached Michel and his dogs, pulled at Hadron's collar, and compared the two watches, still counting. The puppy's read two minutes, while Michel's showed more than 131,000.

Fighting to gather breath, Michel looked up at the camera and said, "I'll be damned."

The cameraman replied, "My God, Michel, this means…"

With a gleam in his eyes, Michel said, "It means it works."

The film again dissolved and then refocused on the awaiting capsule with the word "May" at the bottom of the screen, a month after Hadron's return.

Sitting in his wheelchair, wearing a suit that was identical to the one hanging in Charlie's closet, Michel stood with great effort as Debra assisted him to his feet.

Turning towards the cameraman, Michel extended his hand and said with halting breaths, "Goodbye, for now, my friend. I'll see you soon."

Shaking the entrepreneur's hand, the cameraman deadpanned, "Soon for you."

He coughed, chuckling at the inference.

Michel then grew serious, slowly pivoting to face Layah, who stood beside Debra. Michel locked eyes briefly with the woman who had offered him hope and a second chance at life. As if suddenly infused with divine strength, with visible effort, Michel straightened his hunched back and, for an instant, looked like the powerful magnate who had built history's greatest financial empire and saved the world from cataclysmic climate change.

With poise and conviction, Michel's voice no longer waivered as he probed, "Are you sure, Layah? You can still change your mind."

Layah hesitated for a moment, glancing at the camera. After a beat, she turned back to Michel and said with forced conviction, "I am."

Michel nodded, gave Layah a long hug, and then looked directly at her and said, "Thank you, Layah. Thank you for everything."

With a slight twitch visible in her eye, Layah replied, "Thank *you*, Michel."

Michel smiled and hobbled away towards the Ouroboros while Layah walked behind the control panel, ready to enter her commands. As he approached the capsule's doorway, Debra suddenly had a thought and sprang into action.

"Mr. Bouchon! Your medicine!"

Debra quickly ran to the control panel, where she picked up a ceramic turquoise thermos and carried it to Michel, handing him his medication.

"Careful," she cautioned, "It's still piping hot."

Smiling, Michel took the container and a cloud of steam lifted from it as he opened the top to look inside.

Closing the thermos tightly, he paternally rubbed Debra's shoulder, "It sure is. I'll be careful not to spill it."

Michel then slowly turned and stepped aboard the Ouroboros like an astronaut embarking on a space mission.

Standing in the doorway of the shuttle with the turquoise thermos under his arm, he waved towards the camera. With as much strength as he could muster, he uttered the phrase that, up to that moment, everyone had considered synonymous with Layah, "Godspeed, and until next week."

The doors shut tightly, silhouetting Michel's body, and the train slowly departed down the seemingly endless copper coiled tube.

Without warning, Hadron and Cern instantaneously jumped to their feet and sprinted across the platform. Firmly placing both of their front paws up on the plexiglass, they clawed at the doors wildly and howled in anguish as the first flash spun past.

Filming the distraught puppies, an audible weep could be heard off camera. Turning the lens towards the control panel, the cameraman caught Layah in distress, no longer able to maintain her composure. Crying uncontrollably, the quantum physicist covered her face and ran away from her station, overcome with emotion.

The screen at the front of the auditorium then faded to black, and as the lights rose in the amphitheater, all the winners sat stunned in their seats, dumbfounded by what they had just seen.

On stage behind the podium, Layah stood with Hadron and Cern and looked out over the theater.

Wiping away her tears, she steadied herself, turned to the winners, and said, "Let's meet Michel."

CHAPTER 43

Layah left the podium and walked down the stairs of the stage with her dogs. The room fell silent, as the winners sat transfixed, mesmerized by her every move. As she approached the door she had entered through, she realized no one had risen to follow. She paused, and with a wave of her hand, she gestured to the others to follow, saying, "Come. This way."

Charlie and Kerry looked at each other for a moment, and in unison, slowly rose to their feet. "Come on, Auggie, let's go meet the man behind the curtain," Charlie chided.

One by one, the other winners stood and headed towards Layah as she and her four-legged companions waited in front of the doorway.

With great effort, Mustafa wheeled himself down the aisle, muttering a curse with every rotation. "Barbaric," he grumbled.

Once they had gathered together around Layah, she reached for the door handle and then paused, asking, "Ready?"

Frustrated, Chi Kwong lowered his oxygen mask and replied curtly, "Let's go already!"

Smiling, Layah opened the door and led the contingent through.

On the other side of the egress, the winners found themselves standing before an enormous reservoir. The entire body of water - and the stone cave that contained it – was nearly pitch black. The massive cavern, hundreds of football fields in size, was illuminated by only the lights adorning the four-foot-thick humming powerlines running along the walls.

Nearly ten stories high, the basin's volume of liquid was truly colossal, creating a dampness they could all feel the moment they passed through the door.

"The aquifer…" Charlie muttered.

"Yes," Layah replied, "The aquifer."

In the seemingly boundless distance, the winners could see dozens of thirty-foot faintly lit barges crisscrossing the lake, each transporting cargo of various sizes. The vessels were manned by a single Tuvaluan, who navigated the waters as a gondolier, expertly handling the large wooden rudders at the aft end of the craft. Like fireflies weaving through the night, the lamp-lit ships glided silently through the darkness. The only noise echoing throughout the immense grotto came from the humming vibrations from the tapestry of the ever-present power lines.

Fifty feet directly in front of them waited their own barge, flat and rectangular, resembling an ordinary block of wood, softly rocking against the dock as tiny ripples of waves lapped against it.

"I'm not getting on that thing!" Mustafa exclaimed.

"It's perfectly safe, Mr. Farouq, I assure you," Layah soothed.

"No way, not in this contraption." Mustafa whined, pointing at his wheelchair.

"Me either," Oman added, "I can't swim."

Without hesitation, Auggie began to drag himself towards the barge, scraping his feet along the dock as he strained to pull himself forward atop his Lucite crutches. The entire group stood in awe as they watched the young man struggle, unwavering in his courage and determination to do whatever it took to finally be cured.

Reaching the boat with one last effort, Auggie hauled himself on deck, turned around towards the others, and said with a smile, "All aboard."

Kerry glanced at the two men reproachfully and scoffed, "Aye, aye, Captain."

Devlin snickered as he and the others brushed past Mustafa and Oman, following Auggie's lead.

Left by themselves on the dock, Oman and Mustafa exchanged embarrassed glances and quickly joined the others.

The ferryman pushed off from the dock, and the scow began its journey across the lakelet and towards their elusive host. The passengers looked on in awe at the chamber's vastness, with only the slow rhythmic strokes of the rutter through the water punctuating the stillness.

They navigated through the waterway for the next twenty minutes in silence, each winner lost in their own thoughts as they took in their surroundings. Watching the mariners expertly pilot their freight-laden schooners in synchronicity, their movements through the water were like a rehearsed dance routine, choreographed to unheard music.

In the quiet darkness of the hollow, Charlie felt a tranquil stillness - almost, he thought, like the calm before a storm. Or perhaps like a soul being ferried across the River Styx.

This entire experience had been a whirlwind, exposing him to things he never would have believed he would see. From time machines to underground cities, everything Charlie had witnessed so far had been beyond even the most far-fetched of imaginations. And, although what he had been exposed to was truly remarkable, if the last twenty-four hours had taught him anything, it was that no matter what he thought was coming next, it wasn't.

Lost in his own nefarious thoughts, Devlin, too, couldn't help but marvel at what he had observed. But unlike Charlie, he fixated on what he hadn't seen. If Michel Bouchon's film was to be believed, it demonstrated that time travel could indeed be accomplished. And yet, it had not answered the most fundamental question: how doing so would cure these people of their diseases.

Traveling at nearly the speed of light and purging a person of their life-threatening illnesses were two separate enigmas, and Devlin had yet to figure out how they both worked together in tandem. Achieving time dilation, if possible, was undoubtedly a technological breakthrough but not something that that could treat the untreatable.

Layah broke the group's collective contemplation and offered, "Tens of billions."

"I'm sorry?" Shira asked, still spellbound by what she was looking at.

"That's how many gallons it holds. Enough to sustain our drinking water and farming for centuries."

"Absolutely astounding," Shira whispered.

Layah continued, "Not to mention, enough to power the hydro-electrics."

"Hydro-electrics?" Auggie asked.

"Yes, look over there."

Layah pointed across the dimly lit expanse to a dozen towering wheels that spun in sync as water coursed over their wooden blades. Like the paddlewheels of a steamboat, the seventy-foot behemoths churned in sync as their axles spun immense neoprene belts.

"The waterwheels feed the electricity to our living quarters, while the network of tentacle-like cables you see lining these walls all lead to the same place and with the same purpose, to power the Ouroboros."

Staring at the ceiling and walls of the cavern, Auggie asked, "But there are so many. I even saw one in my room."

Layah rested a hand on Auggie's back and said, "Yes Auggie, and they all work together. If just one of those cables failed, it would cause a chain reaction amongst the others and the Ouroboros would no longer be able to function."

Pointing towards the barges on their starboard side that carried large ceramic containers, Layah continued, "It's why you see so many of the Tuvaluans working as diligently as they do. We work as a collective here, with all of our efforts focused on maintaining the facility's upkeep and operation. One severed line could shut the entire Ouroboros down."

Confused, Devlin asked, "And where do the cables get *their* power fr –?"

"We're here!" Layah declared.

The Tuvaluan skipper gently docked against a jetty, tied the boat to a piling, and steadied the vessel for his passengers to disembark. Once the ship was secured, Layah escorted the contingent to a door at the end of the dock that appeared to be encased by the cave's rocky wall.

The group reached the entryway in silent anticipation, and Layah could sense her cohorts' heightened apprehension.

She hesitated for a beat, knowing that they were now just feet away from the moment that would forever change their lives. With a deep breath, Layah resigned herself to take the final step, and slowly turned the handle as she pushed the door inward.

Hadron and Cern excitedly bound through without hesitation, while the winners were momentarily paralyzed by the powerful rainbow of colors that blinded them from the other side. Stunned by the array of light after spending so much time in the darkness of the aquifer, each person instinctively raised their hands to shield their eyes, allowing them time to adjust.

"Jesus!" Ian whined, struggling to cover his face.

One by one the winners' vision slowly began to acclimatize, giving them their first glimpses at what lay beyond the threshold. Carefully lowering their hands from their faces in awed silence, each visitor stared ahead in shock, unable to comprehend the magnitude of what they were looking at.

Noting their disbelief and fondly remembering the first time she had seen it fully operating, Layah smiled and whispered, "Ladies and Gentlemen, boys and girls…the Ouroboros."

CHAPTER 44

The Plexiglass subway tunnel was enormous. In person, the thirty-foot-tall structure dwarfed anything Charlie had envisioned while watching it on the amphitheater's big screen. Just as it had been in the movie, the foot thick coil that wrapped around the tube was also massive, and Charlie soon found himself wondering just how much copper would have been needed to smelt the helix that encircled the Ouroboros' thousand-mile circumference.

Awed by the marvel and its spectral glow, Charlie felt a surreal sense of conflict. Although he stood before mankind's most advanced technological innovation, what mattered most to him wasn't the immense fortune or scientific discovery needed to build such a machine, but the possibility that it could somehow cure the disease ravaging his own body.

"My God…" Oman murmured, mesmerized by the colossus and the rainbow emanating from it.

"It's like nothing I've ever seen," added Shira.

Two Tuvaluan technicians stood at the control panel monitoring their station while Hadron and Cern enthusiastically sniffed at the Lucite door that served as the entrance to the Ouroboros and the capsule inside of it.

The adults stood motionless, mouths slightly agape, but Auggie's inquisitiveness overcame his trepidation. He slowly hobbled toward the towering machine, staring up in amazement at its sheer size. The grand curvature of the tube's siding extended over the boy's head as he propped himself up on his crutches below it.

The copper coil gleamed, reflecting the ceiling's lights. Auggie was unable to resist his curiosity and reached forward to touch the shimmering metal.

"Stop!" Mustafa screamed, "Don't touch that! You might cause some sort of malfunction."

Quickly, Auggie pulled back his hand, afraid that he might have almost done something catastrophic.

Layah approached the boy and rubbed his shoulder, whispering, "It's okay, Auggie. Go ahead. It would take a lot more than that to break the Ouroboros."

Gingerly, Auggie extended his index finger and lightly touched the copper coil.

Immediately, he retracked his hand in shock and exclaimed, "It's cold!"

"Precisely," Layah replied with a smile as she pointed to the tunnel's base. "Sub-zero temperatures beneath the Ouroboros help the superconductors maintain their conductivity, allowing the magnets attached at either end of the capsule to apply the positive and negative charges needed to propel it through the coil."

His interest piqued, Mustafa pried, "Did you say superconductors?"

"Indeed. They allow the shuttle to levitate inside the Ouroboros. Without tires or rails, the shuttle can move frictionlessly, reaching the speeds required for time dilation to occur."

Ian asked skeptically, "I don't understand how the capsule's able to reach those kinds of speeds with those huge magnetic cubes on the front and back ends. From the film, it certainly didn't look very *aerodynamic* to me."

With a smile, Layah offered, "That's because the capsule is inside of a vacuum, Mr. Haynes, so there's no *air* for it to be dynamic against. That's one of the reasons why the shuttle must always be kept pressurized…the inside of the Ouroboros' ring is completely devoid of oxygen."

Still in awe of the rainbow of light that pulsed from within the mammoth tube, Shira said, "Magnets. Superconductors. Propulsion inside of a vacuum. What you've described is like something out of a movie…how is all of this even possible?"

Layah was about to respond, but her smile slowly faded, and her tone became deadly serious. "Perhaps those questions, and many others, would be best answered by our host."

All eyes turned towards Layah as she walked with deliberate purpose to the control panel, positioning herself between the two Tuvaluans manning it. Steadying her breath, Layah began entering a precise sequence of commands into the computer. Her fingers moved with expertise and calm certainty – until they didn't.

She paused, her index finger hovering several inches above the console.

In that critical moment, a flood of conflicting emotions tore through the quantum physicist. Anger flared, hope surged, and fear of the unknown all converged to challenge her resolve. Her adrenaline spiked, and yet, her body refused to respond.

This. Was. It.

Having closely tracked the inputs she had entered, both Tuvaluans exchanged uneasy glances and anxiously awaited her next move.

Her finger floated above the screen, and the excruciating hesitancy loomed for agonizing seconds. One of the Tuvaluans subtly cleared his throat and asked, voice trembling, "Dr. Golden, are you going to –?"

With conviction, Layah pressed a button on the console in front of her and loudly declared, "Initiate."

Sirens and yellow lights began to flash around the platform, and immediately, the ubiquitous humming sound they had heard radiating from the power lines commenced cycling down. From inside the pellucid tube, the rainbow's glow began to dissolve, with purple fading first.

"Look!" Kerry shouted, as she pointed at the fading prism of light.

One by one the rainbow's colors gradually disappeared, until only the red remained visible at the top of the transparent tunnel. It, too, soon waned, and as it did, Hardon and Cern began to forcefully howl in unison, their distressed cries echoing throughout the chamber.

Stepping out from behind the control panel, Layah crossed the platform and watched as the single blur of white light inside of the Ouroboros slowly became a pulsating flash. With each rotation, the flash appeared at longer and longer intervals until, finally, its speed had slowed enough, so that the outline of the capsule could be seen.

Standing several feet behind the two German shepherds sitting at rigid attention in front of the Plexiglass doors, Layah nervously rubbed her hands together, unsure of what to expect next.

The winners congregated as a group off to the side of the platform and beheld the spectacle before them in utter astonishment. Unable to fully comprehend what they were witnessing, they stood silently, holding their collective breaths, each lost in their own thoughts, anxiously awaiting what was about to unfold.

Squinting as hard as he could to get a better look inside the tube, Devlin noticed that his teeth had unconsciously begun to grind. That wasn't a surprise, he told himself, as his patience had worn thin from all of the over-the-top reveals and ambiguous explanations. At this point, whatever came out of that machine was immaterial to the spy, as long as it led to proof of Michel Bouchon's cure and, more importantly, the reason for him being here: Yan's money.

The subway car made one final loop, and gently pulled to a stop directly in front of the Plexiglass doors. The silence on the platform was deafening as all eyes focused on the Ouroboros' entryway and the mystery that lay behind it.

With a loud, sudden hiss, the doors separated, and a tremendous burst of steam was discharged from below the capsule, obstructing the entryway. Hadron and Cern jumped to their feet without hesitation and loped through the threshold, immediately consumed by the thick mist. Excited barks and shrilled yelps echoed from within until suddenly, there was only silence behind the dense cloud of vapor.

An eerie quietness enveloped the platform. Layah's heart raced as she strained her eyes, desperately trying to see through the thick veil of fog. Seconds ticked by, each one stretching into what felt like hours. The silence hung heavy in the air, punctuated only by the faint sound of her own breath, quick and shallow, echoing in her ears

Involuntarily, she whispered, "Michel…?"

Charging back through the steam, Hadron and Cern excitedly romped past Layah across the platform with their tails wagging furiously and their tongues dangling from their mouths. Layah turned back towards the capsule's doorway and stood in shock at the vision she saw before her. Could it be?

In the doorway, shrouded by the vapor, stood the outline of a man whose back-lit silhouette filled the threshold, illuminated by the pod's interior. Light reflected off the condensation, masking any distinctive features of the darkened shape.

Although obscured and perhaps unrecognizable to the others, Layah's eyes widened in excitement. For her, the figure's profile was unmistakable.

It was Michel Bouchon.

As he purposefully walked through the capsule's doorway in the uniform she had last seen him wearing all those years ago, he paused only a few feet before her, like a cosmonaut exiting his spaceship.

With a broad smile on his face and an affectionate gleam in his eye, he whispered, "Layah…"

CHAPTER 45

To Michel, she looked exactly the same. Although the counter inside the capsule confirmed three years had passed, to him, she hadn't aged a day. Her face radiated with the same glow he'd come to know, and he could still feel the halo of palpable energy that had always surrounded her. It was this vitality that had initially caught his attention and, with it, had inspired him to first follow her vision all of those years ago.

She was still the angel he had always known, yet…he knew her well enough to sense an unease flickering behind her eyes.

Unable to contain herself any longer, Layah rushed forward and hugged him with an unintentional ferocity that triggered a bout of spastic coughing from deep within his lungs. As she instinctively pulled away, his fit quickly subsided, and for a moment, the two stood staring, locked in each other's gaze.

Yes, something was definitely wrong.

Regaining his focus, Michel took his eyes off Layah for the first time and glanced over her shoulder. His face quickly hardened as he saw the group of winners standing in awe behind her, gawking at the two of them in bemusement.

Dejectedly, Michel looked back at Layah, and in response to his obvious disappointment, she whispered, "I'm so sorry, Michel…"

As the nauseating reality of their circumstance began to take shape, Michel gathered his composure and mentally prepared himself for the next necessary steps. Although he'd always known it to be a possibility, this was not how things were supposed to have gone.

Slowly, he walked around Layah to face the coterie of onlookers, and, with a forced smile, he spoke to the group for the first time, "Welcome."

Although they all stared silently at him with obvious hope, Michel couldn't help but feel his own sense of melancholy. If these people were here, it could only mean one thing: his lottery protocol had been triggered.

"Damn you, Yan," Michel seethed inside.

Michel scanned the faces of the lottery winners in front of him and wondered which of them was the mole that Yan would have invariably sent. Was it the slick looking businessman with the perfect teeth, or the bulky looking young man with the blonde buzzcut? Either might have fit the bill, but, then again, who was to say it wasn't the gentleman in the wheelchair whose beard reminded him of –.

Suddenly, Michel locked eyes with Devlin, and immediately he knew. *That* was Yan's spy.

His steely gaze and assured stature belied the demeanor of a person who exploited others with their diabolical cunning and devilish charm. Nefarious in nature, he looked like the sort of profiteer who approached Michel from time to time, offering their services should he need to decimate a business rival or exact a personal vendetta.

Although tempting, Michel had always politely declined.

Yan on the other hand had never had the compunction to shy away from devious tactics or unethical behavior. Blackmail, bribes, and informants had always been part of his business' repertoire, a strategy that Michel knew better than anyone had proven quite lucrative over the years. Now, with such a high-profile secret to be uncovered, one that promised a universal panacea, he assumed Yan would have only hired the best in response.

Gauging the adversary before him, Michel gathered this man was it.

As adrenaline began to course through his veins in response to the fox in his henhouse, Michel suddenly began to cough violently and doubled over, falling to his knees. Soothingly rubbing his back, Layah's consoling overtures were ineffective as Michel's hacks became so intense that he fought to catch his breath.

Hadron and Cern nuzzled his ribs to try and help. The two Tuvaluans from the control panel rushed over to aid Michel and assisted him to his feet. With their arms supporting his waist and his draped over their shoulders, without another word, they quickly led their ailing patron away through the aquifer door. In shocked silence, the remaining winners stared as the door closed behind the departing trio.

Unlike the others, Layah was unperturbed by Michel's convulsions, and slowly, she walked onboard the capsule to pick up the turquoise thermos he left inside.

Verbalizing what was on everyone else's mind, Auggie said out loud, "He sure doesn't look cured to me."

Layah walked back onto the platform and opened the thermos. A cloud of steam wafted from within, and sullenly she replied, "He's not. Not yet."

CHAPTER 46

Devlin paced anxiously back and forth in his room, struggling to comprehend what he had just seen. The size, the colors, the concept…Was time travel actually possible? Or, more likely, was it all just a sleight-of-hand parlor trick designed to somehow con these rich saps out of their money?

With a chuckle, Devlin couldn't help but admit to himself that with unlimited funds, he too might have concocted a similarly elaborate scam, albeit one that was a little more plausible.

However, regardless of Michel's intentions or the authenticity of his contraption, Devlin had to give their host credit. Although convincing others to believe a phony narrative was *his* forte, Bouchon's over-the-top theatrics were beginning to sway even him.

Layah had assured the group that Michel would be answering all of the winners' questions later that night at dinner. Yet, one issue continued to race unabated through Devlin's mind: Even if the Ouroboros had indeed worked, why hadn't Michel been cured yet?

If one were to believe that Michel Bouchon's machine could harness the energy of electromagnetism, manipulate the boundaries of time, and distort the visible spectrum, that still didn't explain what any of those things had to do with eradicating the diseases that were coursing through these people's bodies.

Just because a wrench could fix a sink didn't mean it could also cook a souffle.

Devlin collapsed into his chair with a deep sigh of frustration. Begrudgingly, he had to admit that, like the other participants, he still knew remarkably little about the Ouroboros or how it worked. Until Michel revealed the missing pieces of his time-traveling puzzle on his own terms, Devlin would just have to do something that had never come easy for him: remain patient.

Devlin's thoughts spiraled into paranoia as he continued to ruminate on the technological innovations he had witnessed and struggled to tie together their uncommon threads. What if, after hearing Michel's explanations at dinner, his descriptions of how the Ouroboros functioned didn't make sense? What if the cure was some sort of esoteric state of mind like "love", "empathy", or something else equally useless?

Would Yan even pay him?

Forcing himself to snap out of the despair that was threatening to engulf his subconscious, Devlin gathered himself, recalling with relief the proviso he had shared with Yan at their initial meeting: He wasn't a businessman. When discussing the stolen schematics, he had made it clear that he didn't want or need to know the details behind Michel's Photosynthesuit. That same approach now held true for the Ouroboros as well.

Whether Michel's cure came in the form of a time machine, a unicorn, or a flying saucer was immaterial to their arrangement. And if, after hearing the description of the Ouroboros, Yan concluded that Michel Bouchon had lost his mind tilting at windmills, that was for his employer to decide. In the end, the practicality of Michel's device or interpreting its financial applications were not Devlin's responsibility. His responsibility was to simply report back to Yan what he had uncovered.

Clearing his psyche of self-doubt, Devlin analyzed the nuances of his mission. Acquiring any intelligence regarding the Ouroboros and transmitting the details to Yan would prove difficult. Not only were the catacombs crawling with Tuvaluans likely to spot him if he tried to escape, but even if he did manage to evade their attention, he still had no idea where on Earth he even was.

He took a deep breath to steady his nerves. It was time to deploy his operative instincts. He needed to focus on one obstacle, solve it, and move on to the next. Priority one: getting out. Making his way back to Yan was a hurdle he would have to tackle later, but for now, absconding was all that mattered. To do that, though, would require causing a diversion to draw away attention. But how, he wondered. Where?

Devlin closed his eyes to concentrate. His foot once again began to shake from nicotine withdrawals. Twisting his ankle in a circle and stretching it in frustration, Devlin cursed his cravings for not allowing him even a moment of peace to think clearly.

Pulling out the last cigarette from his pocket, he flicked on his lighter, grateful that he still had one stick left. Focusing on the flame in his hand as he raised it towards his mouth, Devlin slowly looked toward the ceiling before lighting the end.

Suddenly struck with an idea, Devlin's finger gently slid off of the butane button, and the flame flickered out. With his foot no longer shaking and his craving now gone, Devlin smiled, knowing exactly where he'd get his diversion.

CHAPTER 47

Michel lay nearly comatose on a gurney in the compound's medical facility, shallow breaths escaping from an oxygen mask strapped to his face. An IV dripped serum into the nearly collapsed veins in his arms. Behind him, machines monitoring his vital signs beeped, indicating his weak heart rate and failing organs. Hadron and Cern sat dutifully at his side, panting in unison.

Layah stood next to Michel, staring at her benefactor's weathered face. Although he looked just as infirm as the day she had said goodbye, it was apparent his situation had deteriorated. His labored breathing emphasized his dire condition and renewed her sense of sympathy for the man whose body was consuming itself.

She delicately brushed the few remaining strands of hair on his head with her fingers, trying not to focus on the cheeks that had nearly withdrawn into his face. Attending to the skeletal figure before her as he wheezed haltingly for breath, Layah found herself wondering, not for the first time, if they had made the right decision.

With a sigh of conviction, she reaffirmed to herself that they had.

As if sensing her resolve, Michel's eyes gingerly began to flutter. Half-open, he peered around the room until his gaze eventually found her. With effort, he managed a faint smile beneath his mask, and in an instant, she could see behind his recessed eyes the impassioned fire that fueled his drive and will to succeed.

His face began to contort, and it soon became evident to Layah that Michel was trying to impart to her something of importance.

Layah lowered Michel's oxygen mask and leaned in close to hear what he had to say. He strained to quietly whisper, "Layah…"

"Yes, Michel? What is it?" she asked breathless, bending in even closer to not miss the critical message he was trying to convey.

Michel murmured, "Now…you almost look as old as me."

Layah couldn't help but jump back in surprise, startling the dogs, laughing and crying simultaneously.

"Impossible!" she teased, fighting to control her emotions.

Michel chuckled with her, triggering another uncontrollable coughing episode. Adjusting a button on his IV, Layah administered a dosage of counteractant that quickly caused Michel's convulsing to subside.

Michel couldn't help but notice the immediate and vast improvement in his condition, and with newfound stamina, said, "Wow, that really helped. Was that the Therma-Adinal?"

Layah shook her head, "No, that medication was replaced a couple of years ago. They have something much stronger now that should help you regain much of your strength."

Amused by the irony of her comment, Michel chuckled and said, "There's something stronger now? Who would have guessed?"

Getting his inference, Layah replied with a bashful smile.

The contentment on Michel's face slowly began to fade as the two locked gazes. His eyes refocused, and his stare became hardened. "I saw him."

"Him?"

"Yan's man."

"Oh, yes. Devlin."

"Devlin…"

Michel turned towards Layah and continued, "Did Yan pay…enough?"

Layah instinctively looked around the empty room to ensure they were alone and replied, "Our forensic accountants think so."

Michel lay back on his pillow and sighed with relief, "Good."

Michel rested in his bed, struggling to expand his lungs with each breath. Layah took his hand in comfort and held it.

Clasped in hers, his hand felt just how she had remembered it all of those years ago. Not the smooth fingers of a coddled paper-pusher but the rough digits of a man who had toiled for years with heavy machinery. The experience and wisdom that had come from his work having forged the thick calluses that endured on his palms. Even though the rest of his body was a shadow of its former self, the strength that emanated from his powerful hands remained.

For a moment, Layah just stared in silence at the man for whom she had devoted years of her life: the man who had occupied her thoughts every waking moment and who held her family's future in the calcified hands she now grasped.

The daunting reality of their circumstances surfaced in her mind. "I just wish…" her voice trailed off.

Michel turned his body towards Layah, "You wish?"

Staring at Michel, she finished, "I just wish it hadn't come to this."

Michel slowly rested his head back on the pillow, gazing toward the ceiling.

In impassioned anguish, he whispered, "Me too."

CHAPTER 48

The remaining ten lottery winners sat around the enormous circular dining table, speculating wildly. As instructed, they donned their "astronaut suits". Two seats remained unoccupied, and the perpetual ambiguity exhibited by their missing co-hosts was not lost on the group.

"I still don't believe it," said Ian, as he bit into a lusciously ripened apple. "This whole thing has got to be some sort of misdirection, like a magician using mirrors or a con man grifting a mark. Traveling at nearly the speed of light? Give me a break. That sort of thing is impossible."

"Are you saying you don't believe what you just saw?" Kerry asked as she sipped tea from a Lucite cup.

With an annoyed snort, Ian replied, "I'm saying, even if I did believe he'd invented a time machine, what good is it if it only goes forward in time? I'm sick, for Christ sakes! I'm not waiting for my oven to preheat."

A grumbling of agreement was interrupted by an outburst from Gilbert, "Yes, forward in time!"

All eyes turned toward Gilbert in pity as Ian chided, "The poor guy doesn't even know he's been scammed."

As the Chosen continued to fervently debate the efficacy of what they had seen over their meal, raising his voice over the prattling chatter, Mustafa argued, "And all I'm saying is that if I'd known I was going to be paying billions of dollars for a metro card, I never would have –"

"It's him!" Auggie shouted, pointing towards the door.

Mustafa's words were cut short as the guests became instantly quiet and turned in unison toward the entryway.

Layah slowly pushed Michel across the expansive room in his wheelchair, her heels echoing along the tile floor. Followed by Hadron and Cern, the Lucite carriage's squeaky wheels reverberated throughout the dining hall. All eyes stared in contemplative silence at the man who ultimately controlled the destinies of their health despite being so ill he was incapable of managing his own mobility.

He arrived at the table, and, with great effort and a heavy sigh, Michel carefully lifted himself out of the chair and onto his seat, endeavoring to join the others for lunch. Layah set aside his wheelchair and gracefully sat down beside her patron. The German shepherds took their places at her feet.

Michel deadpanned, surveying the astonished faces before him, "I imagine you have questions."

Everyone stared speechless at Michel for nearly a minute before Auggie broached the topic on everyone's mind, "How…?"

Michel smiled and finished Auggie's question for him, "How does it work?"

Auggie nodded, as did many of the others.

"Great question, young man," Michel began, "And I'll begin by asking everyone at the table this: Are any of you here hoping to be cured of Polio?"

There was a long silence before Ian forcibly swallowed the pineapple he was chewing and blurted, "Of course not!"

Michel turned towards Ian, "'Of course not?' Why do you say that?"

Growing frustrated, Ian said, "Don't be ridiculous, Mr. Bouchon. Polio was eradicated decades ago. No one is here to be cured of a disease from yesteryear."

Michel smiled, "I imagine you are right, Mr. Haynes. In 1955 a cure *was* discovered, and the scourge of Polio was eradicated forever. But for those living in 1954, Polio was still a deadly and debilitating disease. A menace to be feared and safeguarded against. Was it not?"

Ian looked around the table, incredulous, "I suppose."

Michel continued, "Well, that is exactly why you are here. You all have diseases that just haven't been cured. *Yet.* For all of us at this table, it is 1954."

There was another long silence before Michel turned back towards Ian. "Tell me, Mr. Haynes, I understand you are here to be cured of liver cirrhosis. Is that correct?"

Ian's face reddened as he looked around the room with unease, "Well, I haven't technically disclosed the details of my condition with anyone yet, so I don't think it would be appropriate to discuss the nature of my –."

Michel interrupted, "It's okay Mr. Haynes, Mrs. Golden has debriefed me on all of your afflictions. There's no need to hide behind HIPAA down here, is there?"

Ian looked around the table at the others and said, "I guess…"

Michel continued, "Good. Then, like Shira's Pancreatic Cancer, or Oman's Multiple Sclerosis, *today* liver cirrhosis is a devastating disease, one that ensures an almost certain death sentence. But what about next year? Or in ten years? Or in a hundred years? Or in a thousand years? Do you really think by then that science will not have discovered a cure for all of those diseases?"

Ian shifted uneasily in his seat, "That is quite the presumption."

Michel glanced at Layah and replied, "Is it? With each generation, new medical discoveries are made, and lives are extended. For thousands of years, mankind thought that using leeches could cure unseen illnesses or that drinking liquid mercury would work to fight an infection. Before that, tribal shamans and witch doctors prayed to their ancestors for good health. Today, we know better. And by tomorrow, we will know even more."

Michel paused as he made sure to have the undivided attention of each of the winners, "The Ouroboros was built to take us to that future, where the cures for all of our diseases are already waiting."

Nearly everyone at the table looked at each other in stunned silence as what Michel had just said began to sink in. Only Gilbert, who fiddled with his chopsticks, appeared oblivious to the mind-bending assertion that had just been revealed.

Michel continued, "Which brings us to, 'The How'."

Again, Michel grinned and said, "If you recall, in the film you watched, I mentioned that by traveling at nearly the speed of light, the phenomenon of time dilation would occur. Does that sound familiar?'

Surprisingly, this question drew Gilbert's attention, and the man whose mental faculties had long since left him was quick to chime in, "Time Dilation! I remember that!"

Michel glanced at Gilbert with genuine empathy before continuing, "Yes, Gilbert, time dilation. Once just a theory postulated by Einstein, today we have proven that it indeed can be achieved with the right resources."

In evident frustration, Oman blurted out rudely, "Great, so it can be achieved. What does that mean for *us*?"

As their eyes met, the contentment drained from Michel's face. Instantly, the merchant of death – responsible, directly or indirectly, for the murders of millions – wilted beneath the formidable gaze of the powerful entrepreneur.

Reasserting control of the conversation, Michel continued, "It means that time, for someone traveling at nearly the speed of light, slows when compared to a stationary observer. In our case, those on board the Ouroboros' shuttle would be the travelers, while everyone else on Earth would be the observers."

As he began to grasp the purpose of Michel's invention and the theory behind the magnate's strategy for curing those around the table, Devlin involuntarily asked, "How slow?"

Michel began methodically counting each "Nine" on his fingers as he explained, "At 99.9999999% of the speed of light, every hour on board for us will equal eighty-three days for those who aren't. And as we accelerate faster, that disparity will increase even further. At 99.999999_99_%, each hour will equal twenty-five *years*. And at 99.99999999_99_%, each hour for us will equate to more than twenty-seven *hundred* years for the rest of mankind."

"My God", Charlie murmured, "That means –."

Michel completed Charlie's thought, "It means that once we reach our maximum speed, it will only be a matter of minutes for those of us onboard before the cures for our diseases are discovered by the scientists of tomorrow."

With a desperate look of hope, Kerry asked, "In only a matter of minutes? Will it really happen that quickly?"

With a gleam in his eye and a rediscovered sparkle to his smile that his disease had only recently stolen, Michel replied, "Let me put it this way. We will be traveling so fast that…"

Michel paused as he looked around the table, *"By the time I finish this sentence, three weeks will have passed."*

As Devlin Archer digested what he had just heard, he suddenly realized the futility of every maneuver he had devised. The clandestine drops, false passports, and meticulously chosen safehouses were now worthless.

More importantly, though, so was the money.

He'd never again see the man who had hired him or a dime of the millions he'd been promised.

With his breathing becoming shallow and his pulse quickening, Devlin began to grasp the urgency of his situation. If he didn't escape quickly, he would be trapped in this underground tomb, forced to spend an eternity here with these people.

And most likely, to die with them.

Struggling to formulate a plan, Devlin's mind raced and invariably drifted back to the beginning - the moment when everything had, ironically, been put into *motion.*

Breaking the collective contemplation that permeated the table, Mustafa spoke up, "I apologize, Mr. Bouchon, but as you may know, my family has a long history in the excavating and refining of fossil fuels. Better than most, I understand the energy requirements for such a device to operate as you have proposed. But even if it were possible to propel an object the size of a subway car at the speed you have suggested, the propellant needed would be enormous. Your machine would require hundreds of oilfields' worth of petroleum."

Michel chuckled, "Indeed, Mr. al Farouq, it would…if we were burning oil to power the Ouroboros."

"What? But without oil, how would you possibly generate the necessary power? You'd need something like…like…"

With a wink, Michel finished, "A nuclear power plant complex?"

Mustafa's mouth dropped as he sputtered, "Yes, but there are no *private* nuclear powerplants on Earth."

"No?" Michel smiled.

Probing, Mustafa continued, "Even if there were, keeping cool the number of nuclear reactors needed would require enough water to fill an –."

"Aquifer," Devlin interjected in stunned disbelief.

Michel turned towards Devlin, "Exactly, Mr. Archer. Which fortunately, is something that we have."

Charlie and Kerry exchanged shocked glances.

Michel continued, "The storied 'meltdown' of the Bouchon Nuclear Power Plant Complex was just that, a story. Our power plants remain fully functional, cooled, and located at the very center of the Ouroboros' ring. Their reported radio-active contamination leaks were a ruse designed to give us the privacy and seclusion we'll need in the years to come. And although I lament the method in which we have achieved it, this facility is now, and *must* remain, completely unimpeded.

Furious, Ian exclaimed, "So the massive meltdown every news outlet covered was a hoax, just to keep the outside world away from *this* place?

"Precisely," Michel nodded.

Seething, Ian raged as he slammed his fist down on the table, rattling his empty plate, "Do you know how much money I lost on my investment in Bouchon Industries when "The Meltdown in the Mojave" was announced? It almost ruined me!"

Straight-faced, Michel rebuked, "I think you'll ultimately find yours was money well spent. As was, all of mine."

Incensed and nearly turning blue, Ian rolled his eyes and threw his hands in the air in exasperation, upset with the specious rationale.

As he was about to continue his grousing, a thought suddenly struck him, and Ian involuntarily dropped his chopsticks on to his plate, "Wait a minute, what do you mean 'all of mine'?"

Michel paused as he looked around the table at his guests, "I mean, Mr. Haynes, I spent every penny I had on the Ouroboros."

Unable to comprehend what he was hearing from the world's supposedly wealthiest man, Ian stumbled, "Every penny? Are you saying that building this device caused you to…to go…"

"Yes, Mr. Haynes, to go broke."

With the humming sound no longer radiating from the nuclear reactor's power cables that ran along the dining room's walls, the silence amongst those at the table was deafening.

"Surely you can't be serious, Mr. Bouchon. You're a trillionaire. You spent *everything*?" Mustafa asked, breaking the stillness.

With a wry smile, Michel replied, "*Was* a trillionaire. But as I'm told, I believe Mr. Weaver and Ms. Wilson put it best when they asked: what good is *any* amount of money, if you don't have the time to spend it?"

Charlie and Kerry exchanged knowing glances.

"So yes, Mr. Al Farouq, I put everything I had into the Ouroboros, and because of that, we will have the opportunity to travel into the future…until all of us are cured."

From behind his mask there was an audible choking sound from Chi Kwong. Although he could care less about how much of his *own* money the eccentric inventor had spent, what he had just said did directly affect the Chinese manufacturer.

Lowering his mask, he probed, "'Until all of us are cured'. But there are people here with advanced cancers and neurological disorders. Their cures could take decades to find."

Michel corrected the industrialist, "Or even centuries."

No longer interested in the balance of Michel's bank account and refocusing on his own self-interest, Ian burst out, "But that's not fair! Why do we have to stay onboard until everyone's disease is cured? What if they find a cure for my cirrhosis next week? I'm supposed to waste the next 500 years waiting for science to find a cure for the cop's Parkinson's? No offense, pal."

Charlie locked eyes with the weasel, "None taken."

Patiently, Michel continued, "With our combined masses, the Ouroboros' nuclear power plants are unable produce enough power to start and stop at will. It takes tremendous energy to electrify the copper coils that will propel us and even more to achieve the speed we'll require to maintain maximum time dilation."

"How much more?" Charlie asked.

"Exponentially more. Hadron's trip took a mere fraction of the power *I* needed. Our weight…will require every Gigawatt our complex can produce to gain our initial inertia."

Oman asked, "So, what are you saying?"

Michel became serious, "I'm saying, this is a one-way ticket, until ALL of us are cured."

There was a mutinous grumble around the table until Layah raised her hands to quell the insurrection. "All of you have already accepted that you will never see your friends or family again, and now you know why. Does it really matter if it takes a year, or ten thousand years to be cured? In the end, how you get cured, or *when*, isn't important. It's that you *get* cured."

Layah's explanation calmed the nerves of their guests for a moment as they digested her logic. Although her explanation made sense, each wrestled internally with whether it was "fair."

Michel continued, "As for the copper mines that reportedly 'went dry', and the plastic manufacturing facility that never sold to a single customer…I think now you can all see where those materials really went."

"The coils…and the subway tunnel" Shira mumbled.

Michel continued, "Yes, indeed, Ms. Eisenberg. Every detail has been meticulously planned, and every available resource of mine has been deployed to create and operate the Ouroboros. From the copper coils that will harness centrifugal force, to the plexiglass tube that will house our capsule. From the shuttle's massive magnets, to the superconductors that eliminate friction. And yes, even the nuclear power plants' disinformation campaign and the cloak of secrecy that brought you here. All of it has been designed for a singular purpose: to propel us into the future, unencumbered by anyone from the outside world…today, or tomorrow."

Pointing at Auggie's Lucite crutches, Kerry asked, "The magnets, is that why –."

"Yes, Ms. Wilson, the magnets on each end of the shuttle are why we do not allow any outside metal or electronics in the facility. As we discovered from the tiny battery embedded in Hadron's watch, even the smallest electromagnetic waves can disrupt the capsule's absorption of the nuclear reactors' kinetic energy."

"So the storage room *was* a Faraday Cage", Devlin thought to himself, recalling the boy's crutches and the other metal items that had been kept there.

A silence blanketed the table as the reasoning behind Michel's plan began to register.

Finally, Charlie asked, "You mentioned our weight earlier, Mr. Bouchon. Is that why you're only curing ten of us?"

Michel smiled, "Exactly, Charlie. It's all a matter of mass. We've calculated that the nuclear plants will just barely be able to produce enough energy to propel the train with eleven of us on it. If we could have cured more, we would have."

With a sparkle, Michel continued, "But, only curing a few of us is okay because one day, I believe, everyone will be cured this way."

Chi Kwong scoffed, barely able to pull his oxygen mask down quickly enough to exclaim, "Impossible! There aren't enough nuclear powerplants in the world to cure everyone."

Contemplatively, Michel responded, "That is true, Mr. Kwong. But just as with medicine, in time, technology becomes more advanced."

Michel pointed towards Chi Kwong's oxygen tank, "Wouldn't you agree?"

Stumped, Chi Kwong slowly raised his mask back up to his mouth.

Michel continued, "Take for example, the key fob that unlocks the doors to your car. The technology in that tiny piece of machinery is more advanced than the rockets that sent the first man to the moon. Computers that were once the size of a house were considered all-powerful in their era, but today, the cellphone in your pocket has millions of times more processing power than they had."

The table sat mesmerized by the picture Michel's imagery was painting.

Michel continued, "Technology always becomes faster, smaller, and more powerful. Always. My dream is that one day, machines like the Ouroboros won't have a circumference of a thousand miles but will be miniaturized. Then, it won't just be eleven people that can be cured, but everyone."

Michel turned towards his quantum physicist, "Layah will make sure of that."

Silence engulfed the group. Devlin couldn't help but be impressed. Although he had initially been unconvinced by Michel's presentation, the visionary had since converted him into a believer. Though some might have considered his concepts to be the delusions of a madman, after everything he had witnessed, Devlin now knew not to doubt any idea that Michel could conceive. The man's drive was obviously relentless.

Devlin smiled as it suddenly occurred to him that if Michel had indeed spent his entire fortune, him employer was, by default, the world's wealthiest man. Offhandedly, Devlin wondered if Yan concerned himself with such ostentatious titles and dismissed the thought quickly. With so much money already, why would the Chinese magnate even care about such a meaningless title?

The details gleaned at this meal were fascinating. The fortune they were worth suddenly burning a hole in his pocket. All he had to do now was find a way back to Yan with what he had uncovered and collect the massive payday he had been promised. Doing so, though, would require formulating an escape plan and implementing his diversion sooner than he had initially intended.

Undeterred, Devlin began to mentally prepare. He was ready to begin.

As if reading the mole's thoughts, Michel slowly rose to his feet and declared, "We leave tonight."

CHAPTER 49

Devlin paced his room, ruminating on all that he had just learned. He recalled the conversation with Yan by his pool and couldn't help but agree with his employer's assessment all those months ago: Michel was truly a visionary. Curing the diseases of today by traveling to tomorrow was an astounding stroke of brilliance and, from what he'd seen, one that just might work.

For them.

Spending centuries spinning in a circle while they waited for scientific breakthroughs might solve the others' problems, but for Devlin, it led to just one: not getting paid. If he didn't find a way out of here by this evening, he'd sit with the rest of them as they spun into oblivion. He needed to figure out a way to escape, and he needed to do it now.

But escape to where? They had all been brought here under a veil of obscurity. Their airplane windows were shrouded, and their communications devices confiscated. Days in the air meant they could be on any continent...or beneath any sea. Having arrived under the cover of darkness, Devlin couldn't be sure if they were submerged below an oil derrick in the middle of the ocean or on top of a snow-covered mountain in the heart of the Andes. Would escaping one untenable situation just lead to another?

Devlin fought to quell the scream rising inside him, steadying his breath and loosening his joints - a technique honed through countless interactions with Jorge. Screaming was a temperament he had forsworn long ago, and he wasn't about to restart now.

Finding calm as he closed his eyes, Devlin rested his hands on the edge of the sink, and mentally arranged the few pieces he'd deciphered of Michel Bouchon's puzzle. Arriving at the facility by helicopter, the swirling sand had stung his eyes. That meant they were most likely in a desert, didn't it?

Splashing water on his face from the sink's nozzle in an attempt to focus, Devlin racked his brain for more clues until he suddenly noticed the running water drained clockwise. It wasn't much, but circling in that direction meant they were likely in the Northern Hemisphere.

Now, he was getting somewhere!

With just these two pieces of information to work with, he cerebrally narrowed down the options and began talking through the possibilities.

"A desert…in the Northern Hemisphere…Perhaps the Sahara, or the Arabian, or -"

Abruptly, Devlin's eyes shot open with a start as he recalled a comment from the sleazy finance guy at lunch; *The Meltdown in the Mojave.*

Was it possible that's where they were, or was the story about the nuclear complex's mishap just another feint by Michel?

Even if they were in the Mojave Desert, how would he possibly cross it once he managed to escape this sarcophagus? With no food or water and only the jumpsuit on his back, heat exhaustion would undoubtedly cripple him while he endured the elements outside. No – limited resources and minimal shelter in such an unforgiving environment would only lead to one outcome: death within hours.

Devlin's thoughts began to race again, struggling to conceive of a plan through the barren wasteland. Without transportation, it simply wouldn't be possible.

His mind operating at peak efficiency, Devlin's mouth subconsciously dropped as a thought occurred, and a way to cross the desert's mighty expanse became clear: the electric car that was sitting in the hangar! Fully charged, vehicles like those could travel for hundreds of miles, which would be more than enough to reach civilization from anywhere in the Mojave.

With a triumphant smile and pat on his own back, Devlin couldn't help but congratulate himself. He had not only uncovered their location but also devised a clever plan to escape.

His excitement, however, was short lived. Solving this conundrum just led to another. Although he'd boosted countless cars in the past, breaking into this one would prove to be a problem. There had been nothing in the facility that he could use to break the car's glass window, which was crucial if he were to hotwire it after accessing the onboard computer. He'd need something hard or metal to crack the window, but everything in the facility had been made of Lucite.

If only he had a…

As if struck by a bolt of lightning, Devlin had an idea so brilliant that he shook with epinephrine. Without further hesitation, Devlin pocketed Rami's knife and headed straight for the storage room.

CHAPTER 50

As Gilbert rested his head, his mind drifted from one thought to another, recalling so many of the wonderful things he had seen in his life, places he had visited, and colleagues he had worked with. With a smile, he fondly reminisced about the street mimes he had seen and the pointy structure he had visited while vacationing in Paris as a child. *What was the name of that building again?* He couldn't think of it now, but he was sure it would come to him eventually.

He murmured as he recalled some of the people he had met throughout the years and the love they had always shown him. They had made life worth living and driven his passion for his work. The co-workers he had encountered during his career had always been so kind and caring to him, often marking the brightest moments of his days. He could see their faces now, but he couldn't quite place their names even as he strained to think of them. There had been that one peer with the glasses who had always made him laugh named Carl. *Was* it Carl? Or the employer who had always treated him like an equal. Michael was his name, wasn't it? Gilbert didn't think Michael was right, but it had been something like that.

His thoughts wandered as he visualized the days he'd spent studying at the universities and the accomplishments he had achieved there. He recalled he'd earned one degree from that place in England, but at the moment, he couldn't recollect exactly where. Its campus had been beautiful though, and he wondered if he would ever go back. He thought the dissertation for his second Ph.D. had made the news, but now he couldn't quite be sure why or where that had been either. Boston sounded familiar, but then again, that might have been where he'd received one of his master's degrees.

It was so frustrating not being able to recall the details of his life, especially when he had built his entire career and legacy on the strength of his intelligence. He had given lectures around the world and written books on topics that had transformed industries, but now, he could not even remember their titles. Something about energy he thought, or was it physics?

As his mind drifted, he took solace in the presence of his family. It was comforting to know he had them to lean on as he had grown older. Like his daughter. Ah, yes, his wonderful daughter. He had seen her recently, hadn't he? Although he couldn't quite place her name at the moment, he did recall that she had a beautiful smile. Such a beautiful smile. The kind that filled a room and turned heads when she entered it.

Almost like her mother's.

Yes! Her mother…his wife! He had an incredible wife. A beautiful, intelligent guardian angel. She had been his best friend and his most loyal protector. The one who had looked out for him and always made sure he was safe. What was her name?

Gilbert's body tightened in his struggle to concentrate. He forced himself with every fiber of his being to remember. Surely, he could recall the love of his life! What was *her* name?

Suddenly, it came to him, and with a smile, Gilbert remembered the woman who had made his life worth living.

His wife's name…was Layah.

***

With his head lying in her lap, Layah stroked Gilbert's hair. As he had for so many years, he twitched and trembled as he dozed, often with a smile on his face. Countless times she had wondered what he thought about and if he remembered the times they had spent together. Did he recall how they'd met in graduate school? How they'd fallen in love? Or how, brimming with youth and optimism, they'd moved to Lausanne, Switzerland, to work on the Large Hadron Collider together all of those years ago?

She hoped so. The two of them had been the foundational blocks of its creation, and Gilbert's brilliance had been the catalyst behind most of its record-breaking achievements. His tireless work, unbridled genius, and ceaseless obsession for scientific discovery had ultimately built history's most technologically advanced machine. A maverick of innovation, Gilbert's drive had propelled mankind further and faster than anyone before him.

She remembered.

But she also remembered the day he had been diagnosed. She remembered his strength in the doctor's office and the subsequent months she had spent crying until her eyes had become numb. He repeatedly reassured her that everything would be okay, but she had done the research and understood they would soon be facing the inevitable. His disease was degenerative, and over time would only get worse. The man she had fallen in love with, spent her life with, and cared more for than herself, would soon be gone.

Worst of all, she knew.

She knew that one day, in the not-so-distant future, his mind would be diminished and his faculties eroded. She would be mourning her husband's death...even while he was still alive.

Remarkably, soon after Gilbert's diagnosis, she had first read about the health challenge facing the world's wealthiest and most famous man. He, too, was afflicted with an incurable disease that left no hope of survival. Destined to slowly fade away until there was nothing recognizably left of the great innovator that once was, the comparisons between the two intellects' circumstances were striking.

At that moment, she had resolved to do what needed to be done: implore the help of Michel Bouchon.

Combining his nearly limitless financial resources with their theories, Layah knew their vision had the potential to become a reality. It would cost Michel his entire fortune, and necessitate a timeline that was preposterously accelerated, but it *could* work.

Together, the three of them could save both men's lives.

Michel had immediately been receptive to the idea. He understood her proposed concept and put his full monetary backing into her project. The costs had been staggering, more than she could have ever conceived, but Michel had never once balked at the price tag or the methodology with which she implemented her strategy. Perhaps he had understood the societal benefit of their invention, or he, too, saw the Ouroboros as his only hope for survival. Either way, he wrote the checks without hesitation, the totals of which soon ballooned and completely depleted his largesse.

The design, logistics, and scale of the Ouroboros were unprecedented, and there were many days Layah had found herself on the verge of giving up. But each time she looked into Gilbert's slowly dulling eyes, she'd seen glimpses of the man she had fallen in love with decades ago and knew she could not stop.

Even if she'd wanted to.

Gilbert had helped as much as he could, of course, for as long as he was able, but soon, it became apparent that his cognitive decline had left him with little to offer. Relegated to the sidelines, he eventually transitioned from overseeing the project as its chief architect to serving the role of lovable mascot. Filming Hadron and Michel as they embarked on their initial trips had become emblematic of his fading involvement and a reminder of his disease's relentless progress.

Now, as he lay in her lap, she wondered if she'd done the right thing. Had it been ethical to rig the lottery so that Gilbert was the first to win? Or to have enticed a bidding war by letting it be known that fifty million dollars had been "offered" for his spot? She understood the intricacies of Michel's plan, and the rationale, but that didn't mean she felt clean while facilitating it.

What she felt most of all was guilt.

Guilt that she had allowed Gilbert to stay with her for as long as she had, knowing that his condition was deteriorating each day. Michel pleaded with her to allow Gilbert to join him, but she had refused, knowing that they would never see each other again once he left aboard the Ouroboros.

Yes, he would be cured in the future and perhaps better off there, too, but a future with Gilbert healthy meant a present without him here, with her.

Had she been selfish? Undoubtedly. And each time Gilbert struggled with a simple task or lost a piece of the brilliance he once had, the guilt of her self-serving actions stung her a little more. But she had overseen the creation of the Ouroboros, envisioned its potential from the beginning, and had found a way to fund its construction – hadn't she earned the right to spend as much time as she possibly could with her husband?

In the end, she had decided that he would remain behind with her, for as long as his mind and body allowed. She had accepted that, one day, his deteriorating condition would force her to halt the Ouroboros, add him as a passenger, and finally confront the one thing she had been avoiding from the very beginning: saying goodbye.

The nature of his disease was inescapable. His symptoms would reach a point where the only compassionate course of action would be to let him go. But until then, she had planned to make the most of the only commodity they had together, which, ironically, she couldn't replace - time.

Now, the love of her life was being taken from her prematurely by the very same man who had stolen the Photosynthesuit's schematics. His actions alone had triggered the events that led to this evening's inevitability, and inside Layah raged, knowing Devlin had ensured that after tonight, she would never see her husband again.

He had taken the one thing that meant the most to her in this world, and as she lightly stroked Gilbert's hair with her fingertips, she vowed to return the favor.

CHAPTER 51

Devlin dismounted his "borrowed" Invisi and glanced up and down the long, brightly lit corridor, ensuring the coast was clear before he entered the storage room. Having accessed it undetected, he bee-lined for Mustafa's gasoline-powered wheelchair, still sitting in the corner of the room. Now, just inches from his grasp, Devlin's excitement convinced him its powerful two-stroke engine shimmered underneath the ceiling's lights.

With precision, Devlin removed Rami's Kirpan knife from his pant pocket and began unfastening the casing screws around the engine compartment. With only the very tip of the knife to act as a screwdriver, the process of removing each screw was painstakingly slow. Blood dripped from his nicked fingers, sweat stung his eyes, yet Devlin fought the urge to give up.

Devlin found resilience in returning to familiar patterns. He controlled his breathing, steadied his nerves, and, with focused persistence, eventually removed the screws and the engine's metal casing. Inside the engine compartment, Devlin found exactly what he was looking for. He cut several wires and removed multiple hoses, gaining access to the interior workings of the cylinder head.

With the engine's internal combustion exposed, Devlin used his knife for one final undertaking as he roughly dislodged one of the motor's ceramic sparkplugs.

He let out a grunt of triumph, cradled the treasure in his palm, and growled, "Bingo."

Devlin exhaled a cleansing breath, releasing the tension of the task. He carefully placed the sparkplug on the ground and steadied his shaking foot. He crushed it under his shoe with as much force as he could muster, shattering the engine component into several pieces. Picking up the fragments, commonly known as "Ninja Rocks" in the smash-and-grab community, he held them in his hand and smiled.

Years ago, while breaking into secured buildings around the globe, he had discovered that these tiny ceramic pieces worked as a better tool for removing windows than glass cutters or explosives. They were small, portable, and, best of all, made little to no noise. Once thrown against a typical pane of glass, they shattered it immediately, making them a favorite of car thieves worldwide.

If getting away from this facility by the electric car meant first gaining entry to its interior, these pebble sized granules would be the perfect instrument to do the trick.

Devlin dropped the sparkplug pieces into his astronaut suit pocket and rolled Mustafa's wheelchair to the center of the room. He climbed onto the machine, precariously balancing on its armrests and removed the last cigarette from its box.

He stared at it momentarily, ignited the end, took a deep drag, and blissfully exhaled the smoke. He appreciated the nicotine and its effects on his nerves. Devlin took one last drag and placed the lit cigarette in the sprinkler head hanging from the center of the ceiling. As the end of the butt continued to burn bright orange, Devlin quickly jumped down from the wheelchair, pushed it back into the corner, and headed for the storage room door.

As he reached for the handle, Devlin glanced back over his shoulder, quietly admiring his own ingenuity. A fire alarm in a place like this would be the perfect diversion to draw the entire facility's attention. With everyone indisposed and distracted by the alert, he would have the opportunity and time needed to escape.

Getting back to Yan and his payday were now just moments away.

As he turned back to head out, Charlie's electric toothbrush caught his eye. Devlin instinctively couldn't help but think to himself, "I wonder…"

Shutting the door firmly behind him, Devlin quickly jumped into the waiting Invisi, cognizant that the cigarette's burning embers made time of the essence. It would only be a matter of seconds now before all hell broke loose.

Aboard the transport and about to pedal away, once again he couldn't help but feel as though he were being watched. The sense was much stronger this time, too, and as he swiveled his head around swiftly to try and catch his pursuer, Devlin was relieved, and unnerved, that he didn't see a soul in either direction. His survival skills had taught him to trust his gut over the years, and now it screamed a warning that something wasn't right.

There were only moments left before the sprinkler system was triggered, though. Devlin did not have the time to individually inspect the rows of doors that lined the long hallway or second guess what his eyes were telling him. Chalking up his nerves to exhaustion and paranoia, Devlin refocused and began to pedal down the brightly lit, white hallway and toward the lone elevator that led to the surface.

As the operative rounded the corner, Gatlin slowly emerged from behind a door down the hall and sauntered towards the storage room, curious to see what the imposter was up to. Now that Devlin knew precisely what the Ouroboros was and the principle behind its cure, Gatlin assumed the spy would do whatever it took to get that information back to Yan.

But how?

Inside, Gatlin took stock of the room's surroundings, and immediately noticed Mustafa's wheelchair had been tampered with.

Unsure of the intent behind its dismantling, Gatlin asked himself, "What the hell were you up to?"

His senses answered for him. Almost instantly, Gatlin's nose wrinkled as he intuitively sniffed the air. Glancing towards the ceiling, he noticed the source of the smell, spotting the brightly lit cigarette just as the facility's alarm began to blare and water poured from the sprinkler's head.

Drenched in a cascade of water, Gatlin slowly bent over and picked up the soaked cigarette butt as a veritable river washed it against his feet.

Examining the soggy stub between his fingers, Gatlin smiled and thought, "Clever, Mr. Archer. But you aren't going anywhere."

239

CHAPTER 52

Michel sat at the desk in his room, hand-writing detailed instructions for Layah to deliver to Art Decker. Hadron and Cern lay at his feet. It wasn't the first time he'd put pencil to paper for her, having done the same thing with the announcement regarding his lottery. Then, like now, she had been briefed to implement his course of action "only if necessary."

Then, like now, it was.

Unlike the accommodations for his guests, Michel's living quarters were spacious and inviting. Though spartan, the walls were painted with warm hues that mirrored the setting of the sun, while plush rugs lined the otherwise barren floor of his temporary residence.

Of course, without the comforts of electronic devices like a television, computer, or phone, it didn't feel like "home." Then again, he wondered to himself, what did?

He hadn't lived in one place for longer than a school year since he was a child, as his family had moved from city to city due to the nature of his father's job. Having been born in Quebec and emigrating to the United States at the age of nine, Michel struggled not only with the challenges of learning a new language and culture but also with the merciless teasing inflicted by his American classmates because of his first name.

Their taunts had marred Michel's sleepless nights while their actions had tormented his angst riddled days. Each new school looked different on the outside, but all held the same relentless terrors waiting within their walls.

In time, Michel had learned to stick to himself at each unfamiliar institution and ignore the jeers from his contemporaries. By his senior year of high school, he had transferred to eight different schools in eight years and found his best and most loyal friends lay between the pages of books where he spent most of his time. Books never insulted his fading accent or mocked the pronunciation of his name, but they had led to new worlds and an insatiable desire to change his own.

Before he graduated from college, Michel had already become a self-made millionaire when a venture capital firm bought the desalination device he created in his dorm room. However, watching them corrupt his invention into a poorly executed money grab had soured Michel on the experience, and he had vowed to never sell out or compromise again.

He dropped out of school soon after and went on to build three successful business ventures that later generated the capital to fund his greatest invention up to that point: The Everwake pill. Changing the world, it turned out, had been easy. Saving it, he would soon discover, would prove much more difficult.

Now, as he sat beneath the oversized Ouroboros painting above his desk, he took a break from outlining Layah's instructions. His eyes returned to the captivating image, staring at the serpent in wonderous admiration.

The ancient Egyptians saw the enigma of a snake eating its own tail as a depiction of "renewal." The Greek alchemists believed it represented the concept of eternity. The Ouroboros had inspired Michel, just as it had inspired some of history's most advanced civilizations. With a few thousand miles and even more years separating their societies, cultures like the Norse, Hindu, Mithraism, and Mesoamerican had all worshipped the symbol, for whom they had attributed the concepts of infinity, rebirth, and ever-lasting life.

In a way, Michel's invention ensured they had all been right.

Michel recalled the ingenuity cland Machiavellianism it had taken to safeguard the implementation of such a concept. For the Ouroboros to work, it had meant that under no circumstances could it be disturbed. Insulating themselves from society topside meant that plagues, civil unrest, or even wars on the surface had to be protected against thousands of feet below.

With unlimited food, water, and energy available, he hoped he'd found a way to shield everyone here from the potential threats looming above.

The threat of curiosity was perhaps the most likely and dangerous threat to the Ouroboros' success. A student of history, he had learned from the ancient Egyptians that the impenetrability of the world's most impressive man-made structures was only as strong as the deterrents that kept prying eyes away.

Unlike the Pharaohs of epochs past, who had planted deadly booby traps to protect their most treasured possessions, Michel hadn't had the stomach for such curbs. Instead, he chose the illusion of fictitious danger. Publicizing the story of a nuclear meltdown had undoubtedly tarnished his legacy, but the perceived threat of fatal radiation exposure had ensured that their whereabouts would remain undisturbed.

For millennia, if need be.

Millennia. It had seemed that long ago when Layah had first approached him with her idea for the Ouroboros. She had been passionate, driven, and unfortunately, just as motivated as he was to make it work. The timeline of Gilbert's terminal condition, though slightly extended compared to his own, was still an inevitability. He and Layah were similar in that nothing would stop her from ensuring her vision became a reality.

The Ouroboros was their only hope.

Michel shook his head, cursing himself for needing the Ouroboros in the first place. His stubbornness had led to his illness, as he had insisted on overseeing, and in many instances leading, the team of engineers who had built The Orbital Solar Shade. With climate change accelerating and few options available, he had spent all of his waking hours on site, ensuring the satellite was built as quickly and efficiently as possible.

Sure, one of the reasons he had put so much time into its construction was the remorse he felt, but how could he not? His Everwake pill had eliminated sleep, leading to leaps in technological innovations, creative brilliance, and more time for families to spend with their loved ones. And yet, as a consequence of those extra eight hours, he had directly contributed to increased pollution, accelerated sea level rise, and impending disaster for mankind.

No, he had convinced himself, he had to oversee every aspect of the OSS – it was *his* responsibility.

In the end, of course, months of working directly with the mercury lining the massive Solar Shade led to toxic heavy metal exposure and, ultimately, an all-but- certain demise.

Or at least that's what they had thought. Layah's brilliance and his trillion-dollar investment had miraculously secured a future free from disease. Building the machine had required every penny of his fortune, but that mattered little to Michel. Liquidating his entire net worth had been the choice that was right for him, and, with it, a future that promised a healthy tomorrow.

That was, until yesterday.

His thoughts returned to the man attempting to steal that future from him. Michel cursed Yan under his breath for forcing him to initiate the lottery. Reminding himself why he had implemented it in the first place, Michel recalled the unmitigated disaster of trying to prevent his rival from reproducing his revolutionary idea the first time.

Nearly an impossibility to stop in overseas courts, Michel had watched in horror as Yan had infringed on his earlier invention. Replicating the Everwake Pill and then skirting the legal consequences, Yan's inferior generic version had left thousands dead across the globe and millions more struggling with its life-long physical afflictions.

As a result, Michel had promised himself to do whatever it took to prevent the theft of one of his ideas from ever happening again.

Now, with the stolen Photosynthesuit schematics firmly in his adversary's hands, Michel had been left with no other alternative. If he hoped to protect his idea, restore his legacy, and ensure that a safely produced version was released to the public, there was only one option left that he could employ.

So, he had.

Michel's reverie was suddenly broken by the deafening fire alarm sounding throughout the facility.

Calming Hadron and Cern as they jumped to attention at his feet, only one word came to Michel's mind, "Devlin…"

CHAPTER 53

The elevator doors opened, revealing the enormous hangar atop Michel Bouchon's facility. Devlin surveyed the empty depot and sighed wit relief. He felt his tension begin to melt, and its disappearance alerted him to the burden he had struggled to carry since his arrival. No longer trapped underground, the subconscious claustrophobia vacated his body with every breath, and for a moment, he enjoyed the same exaltation he'd experienced that night he had escaped from his Panamanian prison.

On his way up, he had heard the sirens below and had briefly wondered if they would trigger an automatic recall of his carriage. Like elevators in high rises, fire suppression systems often override direct inputs from inside and return the cab back to the ground floor. But security protocols here were non-existent, and his journey to freedom remained unimpeded.

Despite their lax security, Devlin knew time was short. Someone would notice if he were unaccounted for, even for a brief period, and the search for his whereabouts would immediately begin. Getting caught before he'd reached Yan with his intel wasn't an option, and Devlin quickly began scouring his surroundings, looking for his planned mode of escape.

His chariot to freedom sat at its charging station. Devlin sprinted across the empty hangar, his feet echoing off the walls with every bounding stride, arriving at the electric car slightly out of breath. He quickly reached into his pocket and pulled out one of the tiny sparkplug pieces to throw at the driver's side window.

His arm cocked back, he was struck by a random thought. Was it possible? Slowly gripping the driver's side door handle, Devlin was almost relieved to find this door locked. Glad that he hadn't wasted his time and effort preparing for this potential obstacle, he once again took aim and threw the shard at the window with all his force.

The window shattered. Devlin reached his arm through the hollowed-out pane, pulled the car door handle, and opened it from the inside.

He brushed the glass shards from the seat onto the floor. Devlin squatted behind the steering wheel and quickly began to pry open the console with Rami's knife. Having hotwired hundreds of cars over the decades, he was familiar with this one's electronic control unit and knew it would be a matter of moments before he heard the engine engage.

Devlin began to score a series of wires inside the car's mainframe before splicing them together, allowing the ignition system to be configured for a manual start. After ripping out the underside of the dashboard and linking several couplings together, Devlin let out a sigh of relief as he bracketed the final connection.

With a bit of flare and a sense for the dramatic, Devlin smiled as he reached over to push the "Start" button and said aloud, "Let's get the hell out of here."

The button depressed with a "click" - but to Devlin's surprise, the engine didn't engage. Pushing it several more times and getting the same result, the spy sat dumbstruck, doublechecking his connections while tinkering with the unresponsive dashboard.

"What the hell?"

Devlin meticulously assessed his handiwork, but suddenly caught his breath, noticing the display on the car's console. Horrified by the image that he saw, a red battery indicator light blinked "0%", and Devlin quickly realized that although the car was parked at the charging station, it hadn't been charged.

"For Christ sakes!" Devlin shouted as he jumped out of the vehicle.

Searching for the power cord, he found it unplugged and hanging limply from a receptacle attached to the wall. Devlin cursed the idiots who had forgotten to charge the car and wondered how someone could be so willfully stupid.

With a grunt of frustration, he extended the cord from its mount and then plugged it into the automobile's power outlet. Scurrying back to the driver's side, he examined the dashboard's readout and suppressed his urge to scream as the message on the display read: "12 hours until fully charged."

That was far too long.

If Michel was truthful, they would be leaving on the Ouroboros that evening, hurtling at nearly the speed of light toward a future that was bereft of diseases for the others and generational wealth for him.

Panicked, Devlin began mental gymnastics as he tried to convince himself they weren't where he'd suspected. Was it possible they were actually near civilization? Had all of this been some sort of elaborate ruse after all?

For the first time in his life, Devlin hoped he wasn't right.

He pushed the button on the remote control affixed to the car's sun visor. At the hangar's far end, the large metal doors slowly began to open, and a dim light illuminated the floor. Filled with hope bordering on delusion, Devlin quickly walked to the hangar door's massive archway and stepped through, heading to the top of the ramp.

Devlin instinctively squinted in the dwindling daylight as he reached the peak of the egress and got his first look at his surroundings. With the sun gently setting on the Western horizon in the distance, Devlin could see that, unfortunately, he *had* been right.

They were indeed in the middle of an enormously vast desert, presumably the Mojave, without a single person, building, or sign of life to be seen in any direction. Only the expansive rolling sand dunes, punctuated occasionally by the passing of a lone tumbleweed, could be seen from where he stood.

By Michel's design, they were completely isolated.

Trying to escape on foot would not only be reckless but undoubtedly suicidal. Taking his chances without transportation meant he would either end up freezing to death during the frigid night or, if he somehow survived, roasting alive during the sweltering day.

Outside in the fresh air, Devlin never felt more trapped than he did now.

In a daze, filled with confusion and despondency, Devlin stumbled back down the ramp and into the hangar. He couldn't help but second guess the decisions he'd made to put himself in this position. How could he have let things get like this? Why had so many things gone wrong? What options did he have?

The futility of his predicament began to settle, but Devlin couldn't help but continue to troubleshoot. His location was too remote to make it anywhere safely without a fully charged car. And without the time for the automobile to charge, the vehicle was essentially useless.

"If only I had more time…"

And there it was. The smile spreading across his face mirrored the idea spreading through his mind.

He knew exactly where he could get more time.

CHAPTER 54

A Tuvaluan mopped the water lining the storage room floor. Devlin approached the doorway and innocently asked, "What a mess. What happened?"

The man paused his work and turned towards Devlin, "The fire sprinkler accidentally discharged. Pretty strange, actually. We've never had something like that happen before."

Feigning concern, Devlin replied, "Jeez, that's terrible."

Pointing at Mustafa's wheelchair, he continued, "Well, I sure hope that wasn't damaged with all the water."

The Tuvaluan turned to look at what Devlin pointed to, and the double agent adroitly palmed Charlie's toothbrush from the contraband rack, slipping it into his pocket.

With a genuine smile, the Tuvaluan turned to face Devlin and said, "I'm not sure, but hopefully, it won't matter. If all goes well, he'll never have to use it again."

With a twinkle in his blue eyes and a smile that had charmed some of the world's most powerful leaders, Devlin nodded in agreement, "Let's hope!"

Devlin left the storage room and made his way to Chi Kwong's quarters. He rehearsed the lie he would tell to get the man out of his room. Devlin was well practiced in the art of the con, confident he could convince the cripple that an issue required his immediate attention elsewhere. Once out of the way, Devlin would have the privacy he'd need to implement his plan.

Glancing both ways to ensure he was alone, Devlin gingerly knocked on Chi Kwong's door. After a moment of waiting and rehearsing his lines, Devlin's skin began to crawl as alarm bells sounded from within his subconscious.

"Christ," Devlin squirmed, looking over his shoulder for the invisible boogeyman who wouldn't leave him alone. This search was just as unfruitful as the rest. The hallway remained empty and silent, reinforcing Devlin's self-doubt that his mind continued to play tricks on him. Maybe he just needed a cigarette.

Devlin turned his attention back to Chi Kwong's room and knocked again. After a moment without an answer, Devlin tried the door, found it unlocked, and slowly pushed it open.

"Mr. Kwong?"

The inside of the room was configured exactly like Devlin's, but to his surprise, Chi Kwong was nowhere to be found. Perhaps he'd fled during the fire alarm or went to the lounge for one last drink? Regardless of the reason for his absence, Devlin couldn't help but give a sigh of relief at his good fortune.

Turning his attention to the numerous ceramic oxygen tanks that Chi Kwong had stored in his room, he rubbed his hands together, murmuring in anticipation, "Let's do this."

Nearly a dozen eight-pound containers lined one side of the room, and Devlin assumed the man wouldn't miss one since he'd invariably not be allowed to take all of them with him where they were going.

Devlin chose a tank and began to remove the strap from its casing, carefully detaching it from its holster. He was nearly finished when he heard a familiar squeaking from the hallway.

On the other side of the door, Devlin could hear the distinctive sound of Chi Kwong's Lucite oxygen tank cart being dragged as he pulled it behind him. Turning towards the door, Devlin's heart raced, realizing he was utterly exposed with his hand caught firmly in the cookie jar.

He hid behind the door with lightning reflexes and stealthily pulled out Rami's Kirpan knife.

Ready to pounce and take the man's life, Devlin silently cursed at how things were rapidly devolving. With no other alternatives, he was faced with an untenable situation. Either kill the convalescent about to walk through that door or spend the next several millennia trapped hundreds of feet underground.

The choice was easy for Devlin; if need be, he'd figure out a way to dispose of the old man's body later. Sinking it in the aquifer was the obvious solution, and while they spent hours searching for the guy, he'd have the time he'd need for the car to fully charge.

Devlin congratulated himself once again for having intuitively found a way out of a seemingly no-win situation.

The door slowly opened. Devlin steadied the knife, raising it above his head, and firmly gripped the blade to easily slit the man's throat as he passed through the threshold.

Ready to descend in one swift motion, Devlin suddenly heard another man's voice from the other side of the door. It sounded like one of the Tuvaluans.

"Mr. Kwong?" the voice asked.

"Yes? What is it?" Chi Kwong asked gruffly.

"Would you mind coming with me, sir?"

"Come with you? Why?"

"We have some questions for you regarding the fire alarm from earlier. This way, sir, if you wouldn't mind."

"You can't be serious," Chi Kwong accused, annoyed at the inconvenience.

"Please, Mr. Kwong, it will only take a moment," Gatlin insisted.

Exasperated, Chi Kwong angrily pulled the door shut and slowly followed Gatlin down the hallway with his squeaking cart in tow.

Watching the door close, Devlin involuntarily sighed as he lowered his arm and pocketed his weapon.

Still on edge, Devlin smiled to himself. Chi Kwong had no idea just how lucky he'd been. Without knowing it, the unseen Tuvaluan had inadvertently saved his life.

Devlin got back to work and couldn't help but find amusement in the irony of their exchange. The Tuvaluan's request had been the exact lie *he* had intended to use to draw the old man away from his room.

The coincidence was almost uncanny.

CHAPTER 55

Charlie paused outside of Kerry's room, ready to escort her to the Ouroboros' platform. They were leaving in less than an hour, and he hoped she would summon the inner strength he had come to rely on – because his was quickly beginning to fade.

Were they really about to do this? What had he been thinking? What if, after everything they had been through, it didn't work?

Charlie looked down at his hand and noticed it had begun shaking more than usual. It wasn't his Parkinson's, he quickly realized, but his weary nerves. Although he'd faced dangerous criminals and survived high-speed car chases, this kind of anxiety was completely different. The adrenaline coursing through his veins reminded him of energy he'd often seen in fentanyl addicts and heroin junkies. He hadn't liked seeing the effect that sort of agitation had on them then, and he certainly didn't like what it was doing to him now.

Charlie clenched his fist, took a deep breath, and strengthened his resolve. He knew if anyone would have the courage to face the unknown, it was her. She'd shown poise in moments of doubt, and mettle when his had faltered. She had been his rock, and he hoped, would be again.

Composing himself, Charlie knocked on Kerry's door and entered when she called out, "Come in."

Charlie was surprised to find Kerry slouched at her desk, her eyes bloodshot and filled with tears. She sniffled and wiped them away with her sleeve as he approached and squatted next to her.

"What's the matter?" he asked, his voice low and full of concern. "I thought for sure you'd be excited."

Embarrassed to be seen in her current condition, Kerry glanced around the room and said, "It's nothing. I'm fine. Just a little, well –."

Sensing her unease, Charlie reassured her, "Come on, what is it? You can tell me."

With fresh tears streaming down her flushed cheeks, she confided, "I'm just so scared, Charlie. Nothing will be the same when we finally stop…spinning. I just can't…I can't even wrap my head around it."

"What do you mean?"

"I mean…the future? What will that even look like? How long will we be in that thing? I just…"

Kerry began to sob, burying her head in her hands. Charlie rubbed her shoulder gently, giving her time to release the emotions that had long been welling up inside. Although equally anxious, Charlie fought to control his own fears and hide the unease that bubbled within him as well.

After a moment, Kerry continued, "And what about all of my friends? I'll never see them again. Can I really do that to them?"

Charlie tenderly put his arm around her shoulder and whispered, "Your friends would want you to live, Kerry, more than anything. They'd understand because that is what's best for *you*."

Kerry's sobs slowly abated, and Charlie continued, "As for the future, I guess we'll see. Flying cars? Little green men? Who knows?"

Kerry smiled and looked up at Charlie, "As long as you're there," she whispered, hugging him with genuine affection.

As they slowly pulled apart from their embrace, their eyes met, and they kissed with a passion both thought they had lost long ago.

CHAPTER 56

Alone in his room, with only minutes left before their departure, Devlin sawed furiously at the casing of the batteries he had removed from Charlie's electric toothbrush using the Kirpan. Just as he'd hoped, they were lithium. With a little elbow grease, he was confident he could remove their protective casing and access the lithium sheets wrapped inside.

Smiling to himself, Devlin saw the finish line ahead - having sourced everything he would need to sabotage the Ouroboros.

Devlin's resolve surged. With sweat cascading down his brow and blisters forming on his fingers, he sawed even faster.

CHAPTER 57

Facing each other in his office, neither Michel nor Layah knew exactly what to say. Everything they had worked so hard for was now mere moments away, and yet, a feeling of despondency pervaded the room. The upcoming launch of the Ouroboros not only meant never seeing each other again, but for Layah, it meant never seeing her husband as well.

Layah gazed past Michel's shoulder at the Ouroboros painting on his wall, her expression heavy with sorrow. It had represented so much hope when she had envisioned its creation, but now, it only embodied pain. Although the symbol depicted a snake eating itself from the outside, it was her insides that now felt like they were devouring her.

She forced herself to remember that although this evening's sendoff might not be what was best for her, it *was* what was best for Gilbert.

More than anything, she wanted to join the others and travel into the future with her husband by her side. There, they would be able to enjoy the rest of their lives in perfect health, spending their remaining years not in the frustration of dementia's challenges, but in the bliss that came from a disease-free life.

In the end, however, she had been left with only a Hobson's Choice: fulfill her obligations to Michel and her husband in the present or selfishly join them on their journey to the future, leaving all their fates to chance. The decision hadn't been easy, but it had been right.

She would stay and finish what she had started.

After a moment, Layah asked Michel, "You'll take care of him, when you get there, won't you?"

Michel nodded and whispered, "Of course."

A long silence followed between them. The sort of silence that feels natural when two people are close friends, and comfortable enough not to need small talk.

Lost in their thoughts, Layah noticed the papers Michel held in his hand and asked, "Are those them?"

Taking a final look at his handwritten instructions for Art Decker, Michel offered them to Layah and said, "They are. You still know what to do with these, and the account?"

Scanning the details she would be sharing with the newscaster who had unwittingly become their mouthpiece and recalling the password to Michel's investment account, she acknowledged her final role in her benefactor's concerto, replying, "I do."

After a moment, she searched Michel's eyes and continued, "You once asked me if I was sure about what I was doing, and offered that if I wanted to, I could still change my mind. Are YOU sure this time?"

With a heavy sigh of despair, Michel answered woefully, "It's the only way."

Gatlin suddenly burst through the door, breathless, shattering their moment of quiet. "It's Devlin."

"Now what?" Layah asked, exasperated.

"The car up top, it's been tampered with. One of the windows was smashed in, and it looks like he tried to hotwire its ignition system."

Layah turned towards Michel, "Just as you'd anticipated."

Michel questioned Gatlin, "But we left it uncharged, correct? So he's still here?"

Gatlin nodded and said, "Exactly. Without the car, there was no way for him to escape. But…"

"Yes?" Michel prodded.

"I know his type, Mr. Bouchon. He won't give up that easily."

Layah looked back at Michel and said, "Agreed. He'll try something else for sure."

With a despondent sigh, Michel said to Gatlin, "Okay, then go keep an eye on him. And make sure we know exactly what he's up to."

As Gatlin quickly sprinted away, Michel could see a genuine fear in Layah's eyes. This man had tried to take everything from her, and she knew better than anyone exactly what a miscreant like Devlin Archer was capable of.

Taking the physicist's trembling hand to reassure her, he consoled, "Don't worry, Layah. Once we get him on the Ouroboros…there's nothing he can do."

CHAPTER 58

With their scheduled embarkation only minutes away, Devlin's senses sharpened as his nerves frayed. There was little room for error now, and he knew that meant that he'd only have one shot at putting his plan into place.

Quickly, he gathered the pliable lithium sheets extracted from the batteries, crushed them into a silver ball, and stuffed the metal sphere into his pocket. Carrying a water bottle, Chi Kwong's oxygen tank, and Hadron's water bowl under his arm, he stealthily peered out of his room's front door to ensure the hallway was clear. As he did, he caught a glimpse of Charlie and Kerry pedaling away on their Invisi, presumably to the rendezvous point where he and the rest of the winners were supposed to meet.

Adrenaline coursed through Devlin's body. He exited his room and headed for Charlie's now empty one next door. This was the most perilous moment yet – when discovery was most likely. Although only a few feet from his own room, he was now out in the open with contraband clearly in his possession. If he were to get caught now, he would undoubtedly be exposed as the turncoat that he was.

Quickly able to slip inside the cop's room undetected, Devlin smirked at the irony that it would initially be someone in law enforcement who they blamed for what was about to happen, not him. By the time they figured out the stooge wasn't involved, he would be hundreds of miles away and, with luck, aboard one of Yan's private jets with a cocktail in his hand.

The massive power lines that had snaked through their rooms no longer hummed with the energy that fed from the nuclear reactors. It had been that way since Michel's grand entrance from the Ouroboros' capsule. After shutting down, they remained inert, which was a vital aspect to the success of

Devlin's plan. Once all the passengers boarded the shuttle and the nuclear complex restarted, vibrations would ensure that his ploy would work.

Standing atop Charlie's desk, Devlin gingerly rested Chi Kwong's oxygen canister on the four-foot-thick powerline, laying it flat against the wall to which the cable was attached. Adjacent to the canister's nozzle, he poured water from the bottle into the dog's bowl, filling it nearly to the brim.

With a deep breath, Devlin steadied himself, knowing that the next task was, without question, the most dangerous. As a consequence, his hand shook involuntarily. Devlin reached into his pocket and pulled out the lithium ball, delicately holding it between his thumb and index finger. Resting the orb on the edge of the dog's water dish, he suddenly pulled it back in terror as he could feel the nerves in his fingers begin to tremble uncontrollably.

"Jesus!" Devlin hissed to himself, fully aware that he had been only millimeters away from setting off a massive fireball directly in front of his face, "Get yourself together."

Devlin closed his eyes and controlled his breathing in order to steady his nicotine-starved nerves. Soon, Devlin was able to focus and methodically concentrate on the task in front of him.

With measured breaths, he slowly placed the lithium ball on the lip of the water bowl which rested against the wall. Careful to delicately balance it on the edge, Devlin envisioned that the powerline would vibrate as the Ouroboros' nuclear reactors restarted. This resonance would undoubtedly cause the lithium ball to fall into the water bowl, trigger an explosive chemical reaction that would detonate the oxygen tank that lay right next to it.

Cognizant of how little time remained before they were slated to leave, Devlin meticulously opened the valve and listened as highly purified oxygen hissed from the tank. At this rate, it would be empty in about an hour – just enough time for his improvised device to trigger a powerful explosion.

Devlin smirked, satisfied that his improvised device would ultimately sabotage the Ouroboros. He recalled Layah's words on their ride across the aquifer. Just one downed power line was enough to force the Ouroboros to shut down and become inoperable. Repairing the damaged cable would almost certainly take days, more than enough time needed for the electric car in the topside hangar to charge.

Escape was nearly in his grasp!

With his booby trap now primed, Devlin carefully climbed down from the desk, straightened his jump suit, and covertly exited Charlie's room. Glancing in either direction to remain undetected, he methodically shut the door and then sprinted down the hallway towards the meeting point where the winners had been instructed to gather. With only seconds remaining, he raced with everything he had, desperate to rejoin the others before anyone grew suspicious.

Running hard himself, Gatlin arrived just in time to see Devlin round the corner at the far end of the corridor. Watching the mole speed away, Gatlin fought to regain his breath and desperately searched for a sign of what the mischievous recreant had been up to.

With no obvious clues to follow and the launch time now only moments away, a sense of panic began to wash over the hardened Tuvaluan.

Whatever Devlin had been up to, it hadn't been good.

CHAPTER 59

On the platform in front of the Ouroboros, the winners gathered together, ready to travel to a future that promised a life free of disease. Wearing their jumpsuits, they chatted nervously as they anxiously waited for their host to arrive.

"Where is he?" Oman Disden asked out loud, eager to get going.

"Exactly what I was thinking," added Chi Kwong.

More eager to depart than anyone else, Devlin fidgeted nervously, knowing that with each passing minute, the oxygen tank in Charlie's room became more and more depleted.

"Come on…" Devlin whispered to himself.

Standing next to Gilbert, Layah covertly grabbed his hand, squeezing it affectionately while the others groused.

"Are you ready, my love?" she whispered into Gilbert's ear, trying to catch his distracted attention.

Gilbert's eyes were glossy and unfocused as they had been for years. Once filled with assuredness and charm, now they only emanated emptiness and confusion. They were the eyes of a child who was amazed by things they had never seen or experiences they had never before felt.

Except Gilbert *had* seen, done, and experienced more than almost any person ever born. His scientific accomplishments had eclipsed some of the generational icons in his field and garnered him immeasurable esteem from countless contemporaries. And yet, even though he had achieved feats that most could only dream of, his disease had turned his life into one never-ending state of dream-like bemusement.

He absently looked around the platform. His gaze drifted to the three-story-tall plastic tunnel in front of him, which caused him to declare to no-one in particular, "I know this place."

Layah squeezed his hand tighter as tears began to stream down her cheeks, the overwhelming guilt of having allowed him to deteriorate this far consuming every fiber of her being.

She slowly raised her hand, tenderly touched his face, and whispered, "Forgive me..."

On the far side of the group, Charlie rubbed Kerry's shoulder in a comforting manner and lightheartedly quipped, "Next stop, the future."

Kerry smiled and touched Charlie's hand. Her warmth felt reassuring to Charlie, and for the first time in nearly a year, his hand no longer shook. Staring into her eyes, he couldn't help but wonder if this was exactly the future he was looking forward to. One filled with a steady hand and someone to hold it.

Dragging his legs behind him, Auggie hobbled forward on his crutches to Charlie and Kerry and asked, "Can I sit with you when we go? I...I've never..."

Sensing his unease, Charlie asked, "What is it, bud?"

Embarrassed, Auggie said bashfully, "It's just...I've never been on a train before."

Kerry smiled at the young boy and said, "Of course, you can sit with us Auggie. We wouldn't want it any other way."

Auggie grinned up at the two of them, and for a moment, Charlie felt something he hadn't felt in a long time – as though he were surrounded by a family.

Lost in his own thoughts, Devlin's agitation continued to grow with each passing moment as their host's presence remained elusive. Where the hell was he? What was taking so long? Had he found the makeshift device?

Examining the faces of the other winners on the platform, Devlin was unable to detect a hint of suspicion and had to remind himself to stop being so paranoid. These people were rubes without a clue as to who he really was or the explosive he had put in place.

Especially the biggest fool of them all, Devlin thought with a smile: Michel Bouchon.

Soon, everything he had worked for and spent his entire fortune building would be in the hands of Yan Huen. Having extracted the former trillionaire's most prized intellectual property once before, Devlin relished the certainty that he was now only moments away from doing it again.

Fleetingly, Devlin wondered what the Chinese magnate would do with the Ouroboros' details once he had delivered them to him. Certainly, his employer would find a way to monetize it or extract its technology for his own profit. Regardless of what he wound up doing, Devlin was confident that from the few interactions they'd had, at the very least, Yan would find a way to take credit for Bouchon's groundbreaking innovation and claim it as his own.

As he pondered Yan's next move, Devlin remembered that he simply didn't care how his benefactor ultimately used the information he had gleaned. Whatever the tycoon decided to do with the intelligence he provided was his concern. While he was plotting to take credit for revolutionizing the world, Devlin would be too busy spending his generationally-sized paycheck and enjoying the rest of his life.

Of course, all of that depended upon one tiny detail: Michel Bouchon showing up!

The group began to grow more and more restless. Mustafa whined to Layah above the grumblings of the others, "Isn't he supposed to be here by now, Dr. Golden?"

Ian Haynes sarcastically piled on, "Yeah, I thought if anyone would be on *time*, it would be him."

Raising her hands to placate the agitated group, Layah replied, "Please, everyone, be patient. I'm sure he –."

At that moment, all eyes turned as the aquifer's door opened, and Michel Bouchon hobbled through.

"Finally…" Devlin seethed under his breath.

As he ploddingly approached the assembled gathering on the platform, he took a moment to compose himself and proclaimed magnanimously, "Ladies. Gentlemen. I apologize for the delay; I was just taking care of some last-minute loose ends. Is everyone ready?"

Shira Eisenberg cynically replied for the group, "Those of us still here were ready yesterday, Mr. Bouchon."

Michel smiled and said, "Yes, of course. Very well then, my fellow travelers, if you will all follow me, let us begin our journey aboard the Ouroboros. Our cures await!"

With laboring strides, Michel walked towards the open doors of the Ouroboros' capsule, and, one by one, the winners followed his lead across its threshold.

Watching each of them step aboard as she stood at the control panel, Layah's body ached as her soul screamed in agony. Happy that Gilbert would soon be cured, she also knew their departure meant she was now only moments away from never seeing her husband again.

If only she could reach him and make him understand the finality of what was about to happen…

With the rest of the other winners inside the shuttle, Gilbert was the last passenger to join them, and as he delicately stepped inside the capsule, he slowly turned to look back across the platform at Layah.

Staring directly at her, she was shocked to see that his eyes were clear, alert, and focused for the first time in years.

Stunned by his apparent lucidity, she whispered, "Gilbert…"

As the plexiglass doors closed, he gently raised his hand and mouthed, "Goodbye, Layah."

With tears streaming down her face, Layah raised her hand as well…and then slowly lowered it to press the button on the console in front of her that read, "Engage."

CHAPTER 60

After boarding the sixty-foot-long shuttle, the passengers' weight caused the train car to bob gently inside the Ouroboros' pressurized ring. The capsule's interior was well lit, with seating accommodations divided into three rows of four seats each, two paired on either side of a seven-foot-wide aisle. The spacing was well appointed, with plenty of room for the travelers.

Like everything else in the facility, all was made of Lucite, except for the sides which were blanketed by massive glass windows. Although both the forward and aft of the carriage were comprised of bare white walls to which the large cube-shaped magnets were affixed on the outside, at the interior's front was a mechanical rotary calendar that rested inside its own Faraday Cage.

Facing the passengers, it displayed the "day", "month", and "year."

As the train began to move, Devlin watched as Mustafa rolled himself to an empty space in the front of the tram while *he* strategically took a seat at the back. Unsure exactly how a sudden decrease in power from his explosion would affect the train's momentum, he adjusted himself in his seat, prepared for the car to lurch.

Or, God forbid, crash.

The capsule's speed increased as the remaining winners settled into their seats. Michel Bouchon stood at the front of the car, ready to address his guests. Sitting next to Auggie and across the aisle from Charlie, Kerry held the young boy's hand as he stared nervously out the window. Within a few moments, the train picked up even more velocity, and although initially they could see the platform every few seconds as they passed, it soon was only a blur.

Breaking the stunned silence, Michel addressed the group, "Let me be the first to welcome you, my friends, aboard the Ouroboros. We are officially underway, and although our epic journey will ultimately lead us back to the very place where it began, it won't be the distance traveled that will mark this trip…but the time. Within a few moments, we will reach relativistic speed – the point at which time dilation begins. Time for us will become slower, while it will, *relatively* speaking, become faster for everyone outside. The first indicator of this will be when the red hue becomes visible. Does everyone remember that from before?"

All of the passengers nodded their heads.

"Good, because that will be our first sign that the Ouroboros is working. And as we gain more and more speed, the rest of the colors of the rainbow will slowly begin to appear, until the entire spectrum becomes visible, at which point we'll be traveling so fast that –."

Auggie offered, "We'll be time traveling."

"Exactly, Auggie. We'll be traveling at 99.999999999% the speed of light, where every few seconds inside this capsule will equal days, and months out there. Do you see this counter above my head?"

Everyone raised their gaze towards the mechanical device Michel was alluding to.

"This calendar will tell us how long we have traveled and the date when all of our cures are eventually found. When that time comes, the Ouroboros will finally be stopped."

All eyes looked at the calendar and its copper wheels, each wondering exactly when that would be. A hundred years? A thousand years? More?

"Are you sure it even works?" Chi Kwong asked impatiently. "You said we'd be cured in a matter of minutes, and the date on that thing hasn't even moved yet."

Michel spread his arms and pointed throughout the cabin, "Look around you, Mr. Kwong. The number of people on board and our combined masses is significantly greater than when it was just me sitting in your chair. The power needed to propel this much weight is tremendous and, therefore, requires considerably more time."

Holding court, Michel continued, eager to describe the nuances of his technological marvel. "In essence, the currents coursing through the Ouroboros' copper solenoid generate electromagnetic induction from its rotation. This process, in turn, harnesses the immense G-forces produced by centrifugal acceleration and captures the very energy that would otherwise tear this capsule apart. You see, according to Lenz's law -"

In his seat, Devlin had already tuned Michel out as his palms began to sweat in anticipation.

Any moment now, the powerline's vibration would trigger the bomb he'd put in place, leading to this monstrosity shutting down. As these Pollyannas struggled for days to piece together what had happened, he'd make his way to the surface above. From there, he figured it might be a one- or two-hundred-mile drive in the electric car to some sort of civilization, but with a full battery, he'd easily make it.

Once there, of course, he wasn't exactly sure how he'd get back to Yan, but he would find a way. He always did. If that meant hurting a few innocent people as he commandeered transportation, so be it. He'd done it countless times in the past and was ready to do it again.

Nothing would stop him now.

After reveling in his own cunning, a thought suddenly occurred to Devlin. Speaking of stopping, why hadn't the train stopped yet? They were going fast now. So fast, in fact, that he couldn't discern anything outside the glass windows. The power lines certainly would have begun to vibrate at this speed, wouldn't they? And yet, the light outside of his window was beginning to turn a light shade of crimson, almost as if…

"Wouldn't you agree, Mr. Archer?" Michel asked from the front of the train car.

Startled, Devlin snapped out of his contemplative thoughts, "What's that?"

"I said, wouldn't you agree that time is worth money?"

Bewildered that he was being addressed directly, Devlin replied, "Sure."

Michel reached into his pocket, pulled out a silver ball, and lifted it up, clearly showing it to Devlin. It was the orb of lithium battery sheets he had planted in the cop's room – the trigger for his homemade bomb.

"So would I, Mr. Archer. I'd say it's worth exactly seventy-two billion dollars."

The interior of the shuttle slowly began to turn scarlet, as the light from the outside fully transmuted from white to red, illuminating the large bay windows.

Devlin stared in shock at the ball in Michel's hand, but it was Ian who spoke first, "Seventy-two billion dollars? What is that supposed to mean?"

"It means that that's how much *Yan Huen's* blind trust paid for his spot in my lottery, which he then gave to his operative here. Isn't that right, Mr. Archer?"

Devlin couldn't breathe. His ears rang and his mind raced, trying to interpret what was happening. As if under a microscope, the other passengers turned in unison to look at the former undercover agent. Unperturbed by their judgmental glares, Devlin kept his piercing blue eyes focused on Michel.

Although he didn't run in the same circles as most of the others onboard, even Charlie recognized the name and asked, "Yan Huen, the billionaire?"

Michel nodded, "For the time being."

Ian stumbled, "My God. For Yan to come up with that kind of money, he would have had to leverage himself to the hilt. If word got out to the media that he'd spent *that* much money for the last spot..."

"It already did, the moment we left..." Michel pointed to the counter above his head, and with a loud audible "CLICK", the dial that denoted the date flipped to the next day.

"...yesterday. Layah made sure of that."

The red in the cabin radiated in every direction and was slowly accompanied by an orange hue leaching in below it.

Flabbergasted, Ian continued, "But…but that kind of news would cause a run on his company's stock. He'll be ruined."

With his eyes still locked on Devlin's, Michel said, "Exactly."

Although Devlin hadn't felt it initially, from his perspective, the train car traveling in an enormous circle at thousands of miles per second was only now beginning to spin. Dizziness and flaccidity washed over his body as his reality sank in.

Michel continued, "You see, Mr. Archer, we have been ahead of you and Mr. Huen from the very beginning. The fifty million dollars offered for Gilbert's spot? *We* divulged that information, sparking a bidding war and ensuring that the final spot sold for billions. The leaked identities of the other winners? That was our doing – carefully orchestrated to focus worldwide attention onto the blind trust when Yan was eventually exposed. And as for the "failed" assassination attempt on Umberto? It provided the perfect cover to impose anonymity over the lottery and control just how much Yan would ultimately pay."

Devlin's fists began to ball up, his fight or flight instinct overtaking his body. As the capsule became flooded with red and orange light, in the deafening silence between the two men, only the calendar's loud "CLICK" behind Michel was heard.

Michel continued, "As for the seventy-two billion Yan *did* pay…it was Bouchon Industries who held that last spot. So in the end, he paid it…to me."

All became clear, and shocked, Devlin couldn't help but murmur, "You?"

"Yes, Mr. Archer, me."

The others on board stared at Devlin and, he presumed, wondered how he would react. A flood of responses ran through his mind, but he realized there was nothing he could say. Worse than being uncovered, however, was the fact that he was trapped. Michel had obviously waited until he was onboard before exposing him, knowing there was nothing he could do and nowhere he could run. He was stuck spinning into the future with these infirm people aboard a speeding train without an emergency brake.

Claustrophobia returned, tightening its grip on Devlin as the capsule's walls seemed to close in around him. Addled and desperate to flee, he barely registered the yellow hue bleeding into the existing spectrum, casting an uneasy glow across the interior. Behind Michel, the days of the calendar began to "CLICK" with even more frequency, as every few seconds, the sound would reverberate within the stillness of the cabin.

"Of course, none of this would have happened if Yan hadn't stolen the schematics for my Photosynthesuit in the first place. Without the protection of patent laws or international courts willing to enforce them, we had no other way to stop him from stealing my idea once again. His track record of cutting corners with his generic version of the Everwake pill and his blatant disregard for human life left us with little choice. Bankrupting his empire was the only way to prevent him from potentially killing millions."

The horrifying truth began to wash over Devlin in waves of panic-stricken horror. Having always been able to find a way to escape, he was now wholly unfamiliar with the bleak reality he was facing: he'd been caught.

With boundless adrenaline coursing through his veins and his desperation to escape overwhelming his better judgement, Devlin leapt to his feet and grabbed Kerry around the neck. Pulling out the Kirpan from his jumpsuit pocket, with deadly precision, he held it to her throat as Shira screamed in terror.

Pressing the knife to Kerry's jugular as he held her tightly against his body, Devlin shouted, "I know you've got a way to stop this thing, Bouchon! Do it now, or I'll kill her!"

Charlie's body intuitively became taut as his eyes furiously bulged and his legs coiled in reflex.

Michel raised his hands defensively and calmly replied, "I don't, Devlin. As I said before, this is a one-way trip." He then pointed towards the calendar, "For all of us."

Devlin had been distracted by his own thoughts from the moment he had taken his seat and had not paid attention to the spinning timetable at the front of the capsule. Staring at it in stunned disbelief, the days on the calendar "CLICKED" with increasing speed until the sound it made mimicked that of a baseball card attached to the frame of a child's bike. Unlike a bike, however, each click did not represent the rotation of a spoke but the rotation of the planet.

Unable to fully comprehend the speed with which the days were flying past, Devlin mumbled to himself as the shuttle's interior began to add the color green to its palette, "My God…"

Charlie made eye contact with Kerry while Devlin was distracted, looking imperceptibly toward the floor. Catching his inference, she quickly fell to her knees, leaving Devlin standing in the middle of the aisle, clutching only her wig in his hand.

In shock, Devlin stared at the blonde hairpiece and muttered, "What the f –."

Charlie instantly sprung to his feet and lunged at Devlin, tackling the spy and knocking the Kirpan out of his grip. Rolling on top of each other in the aisle, the two trained brawlers exchanged brutal punches, pummeling faces and cracking ribs. As they swapped one vicious blow after another, blood began to seep from a cut above Charlie's eye while bile rose in Devlin's throat.

The two men grappled on the floor for nearly a minute until Charlie delivered one final, powerful strike to the operative's exposed kidney. Staggering to his feet as he wiped the blood out of his eye, he backed away and left Devlin in a crumbled ball near the rear of the car.

With space now between them, Charlie quickly snatched the Kirpan from the floor as the rest of the passengers gathered behind him for protection. Shakily holding the knife in front of him, Charlie kept the sleeper agent at bay as Devlin slowly rose to his feet and spit out a tooth.

"Give it up, Devlin. Enough of this." Charlie wheezed.

Unwilling to concede, Devlin frantically searched the inside of the capsule, hoping to devise one last desperate means of escape. Despondent, he could see nothing around him he could use as a weapon, just more of the same sterile material he'd been surrounded by for the last 48 hours. If he never again saw another piece of Lucite, glass, or –.

A sly smile spread across Devlin's face as he was suddenly struck by an idea.

Watching the madman's body confidently relax in front of him, Charlie could see the same maniacal look develop in Devlin's cold-blue eyes that he had often seen when interacting with cornered criminals on the streets.

This wasn't good.

Hoping to convince himself as much as his adversary, Charlie declared, "Devlin, it's over."

With the sneer of a deranged lunatic, Devlin hissed, "Never."

Without hesitation, the mole quickly reached into his uniform's pocket and pulled out several pieces of broken sparkplug.

Having arrested countless "smash and grab" thieves throughout the years with the same "tool", Charlie's eyes flared in horrifying realization as he shouted, "NO!"

With one fluid motion, Devlin flung the ceramic pieces as hard as he could toward the train car window, and as they struck it, the three-inch thick glass slowly began to crack in a spiderweb pattern.

Watching the large pane fissure from the impact as the jagged clefts spread, Ian shouted, "You fool! You'll depressurize the cabin and kill us all!"

As air loudly began to rush out of the shuttle, whose interior now included a shade of blue, Charlie intuitively turned towards Kerry to ensure she was safe.

Facing her directly, he shouted over the almost deafening roar of the wind, "KERRY! ARE YOU O –."

Suddenly, Devlin jumped forward and tackled Charlie, knocking them both to the ground again. Grabbing his arm, Devlin slammed Charlie's Parkinson's weakened hand against one of the passenger seats, the impact causing him to drop the knife onto the floor.

Both men scrambled to pick up the weapon, each trying to jockey for position. They exchanged blow after savage blow, until Devlin swung his elbow into Charlie's jaw, knocking him to the precipice of unconsciousness.

Sensing his moment, Devlin straddled Charlie's prone body, squeezing his neck with all of his remaining strength. As the life quickly faded out of his foe, Devlin was unsure if the cop's face was turning purple from the strength of his grip or the color now emanating outside of the failing window.

"Die!" Devlin seethed.

No longer able to feel his limbs as numbness set in, Charlie's eyes rolled to the back of his head, and though the entire capsule was bathed in the full spectrum of the rainbow, the colors around him began to fade to black.

Struggling to inhale what little air remained, Devlin's resolve to choke the last ounce of life from his rival remained unshaken – until, suddenly, an excruciating pain erupted from his back. Instinctively, his spine arched, his eyes bulged, and he howled in agony.

His demonic gaze quickly became unfocused as his pupils dilated, and slowly, he loosened his grip around Charlie's neck.

Choking as he struggled for breath, Charlie watched in shock as the man who, only moments earlier, had held his life in his hands now, inexplicably, crumpled face-first onto the floor beside him.

Standing above both men, Kerry's trembling hands clutched the bloody Kirpan, the weight of Devlin's toppled body dislodging it from his back. As a hurricane-force wind rushed past her, she locked eyes with Charlie while her uniform whipped in the gale.

Terrified and gasping for breath, she slowly let the dagger slip from her fingers onto the capsule's floor. Her legs wobbled and her eyes fluttered as she implored, "Charlie, I can't feel my…"

The air pressure continued to plummet inside the cabin, the loss of oxygen sapping Kerry's strength and forcing her knees to buckle. Unable to maintain her balance or consciousness, she collapsed, her face resting on Charlie's chest.

Struggling to lift his head, Charlie felt a wave of helplessness wash over him as he took in the sight of the other passengers sprawled across the cabin floor, having already succumbed to hypoxia.

The deafening roar of leaking oxygen, and the kaleidoscope of colors that now enveloped the shuttle's interior, barely registered with Charlie as he fought to retain consciousness. Unable to move, his eyes flickered, mesmerized by the relentless "CLICKING" of the calendar.

As the days spun in a blur, the months quickly followed suit, and as the overwhelming heaviness of his eyelids forced his eyes to close for good, the first year on the counter turned with a resounding "CLICK."

CHAPTER 61

No longer moving and now eerily quiet, the train car sat in near total darkness, the only light inside from a flickering bulb above the calendar. Charlie's watery eyes began to flutter as he slowly regained consciousness, but the dimness of the shuttle and his blurred vision made it nearly impossible for him to see.

Kerry lay unconscious atop his chest, her breaths shallow. Charlie struggled to lift his head and distinguish the counter's date at the far end of the craft. His body shook from the progression of his disease, and his eyes failed to adjust to the opaqueness.

Incredibly, he was alive, and yet he had no idea *when* they were.

He gingerly tried to gather himself, until out of the corner of his eye, he caught a glimpse of movement on the outside of the shuttle's window. Faint artificial lights slowly approached the cabin, and his body instinctively became paralyzed with fear.

Pausing briefly in front of the capsule's entrance, the doors to the train car slowly opened with a hiss, and a pair of floating black probes glided inside through the expelled steam.

Scanning the bodies on the floor with reddish lasers and emitting high-pitched beeps, the orbs hovered over the prone passengers like pool ball-sized vultures examining rotting carcasses. Emotionless and robotic, the devices lingered above each traveler as they appeared to search for signs of life.

After several moments, a muffled voice resonated from one of the probes and declared, "Vital signs are weak, but stable. Can anyone hear me?"

The only person yet conscious, Charlie lifted his shaking hand to attract the probes' attention. Sensing his movement, the two spheres quickly converged on his position and began scanning his body with their crimson-colored rays.

"We have movement," one of the probes announced, "Weaver, Charles."

Throughout the cabin, moans began to weakly emanate from several other passengers, and the voice from the orb ordered, "We have additional activity. Dispense adrenaline vapor."

Still hovering above the prostrate travelers, the spheres slowly began crisscrossing from one end of the capsule to the other, expelling a mist from their chassis that blanketed the dazed voyagers below. The steam jolted many of the sleeping passengers awake, and as they slowly began to regain consciousness, the probes stealthily floated out through the shuttle's open door.

For what felt like an eternity to Charlie, the cabin's interior remained completely silent, occasionally punctuated by a feeble cough or groan. The stillness was broken, however, as a being wearing a futuristic alloy suit strode through the cabin door. Pausing momentarily, it slowly and methodically swiveled its head, examining the prone passengers at its feet. Charlie and others who had regained consciousness remained motionless, stunned as they stared in shock at the alien figure before them.

Bulky yet somehow malleable, the suit was unlike anything Charlie had ever seen, with glowing green sensors that covered its body. As the creature took stock of its surroundings, he strained to get a better look but could only make out its silhouette. With two arms and two legs, it looked humanoid. And yet, with a dimly lit glass face-shield that obscured its appearance, he could not be sure.

As it drew closer, his body reflexively tensed in defense, until the being leaned down within a few inches from his face.

Getting a closer look, his eyes adjusted in the darkness and Charlie whispered, "It's…

"A Photosynthesuit," Michel finished meekly from the far side of the car.

Suddenly, two German shepherds bound through the cabin door towards Michel and excitedly began licking and nuzzling his face.

Michel stammered in delighted shock, "Hadron! Cern!"

The figure beside Charlie then began slowly lifting its face shield, revealing a familiar visage: Layah's.

Appearing only marginally older to Charlie, she smiled and radiated unconditional warmth.

As Hadron and Cern continued to enthusiastically lick Michel, Layah turned to her benefactor and said, "Welcome back, Michel. Again."

Trying to respond but unable as he laughed uncontrollably, Michel rolled around on the floor with his two friends as they playfully bounced on his body and nudged his hands for attention.

Satisfied that Michel was unharmed, Layah began to take stock of the cabin and immediately noticed Devlin lying in a pool of his own blood.

Lifting her arm, Layah worriedly spoke into her wrist device and instructed, "Bring in the *trauma-bots*. We have injuries."

Now frightened and concerned for who else might be injured, she swiftly searched the rest of the capsule until she spotted the man she had waited so many years to see. Barely conscious, Layah quickly bent down next to Gilbert and gently cradled his head in her hands.

With his eyes gradually adjusting to the dimness, after a moment, he slowly recognized who was comforting him and whispered, "Layah…where…?"

Overcome with emotion, Layah began to cry uncontrollably. Rocking her husband's head in her arms, she kissed him deeply and said soothingly, stroking his cheek, "It's okay, my love. You're home."

Still lying limp on his chest, her breaths shallow, Charlie gingerly caressed Kerry's smooth head. After a moment, his touch stirred her, and her eyes fluttered open. Struggling to focus, she slowly took in her surroundings before her gaze finally found Charlie's.

Taking her hand, Charlie reassured her, "We're here."

CHAPTER 62

The rhythmic crash of the ocean waves and the gentle breeze ruffling the silk curtains awoke Charlie from his deep sleep. The sunlight shone through the opened accordion doors, and he could smell the sea air as it wafted into the bedroom. Engulfed in plush pillows, his bed was opulent, with sheets so soft he could barely feel their touch.

Charlie lifted his head slightly. His eyes still glazed; he looked past the foot of his bed through the open doors and could see the turquoise ocean lapping a white sandy beach that was dotted with swaying palm trees. The water was a color he had only imagined in his dreams, and for a moment, Charlie wondered if he had died aboard the Ouroboros and had somehow wound up in heaven.

Wasn't this the Utopia he had always wished for?

That thought was reinforced as he slowly turned his head and saw a stunning vision standing beside him.

With long auburn hair and a radiating smile whose warmth was only matched by the tropical temperature outside, Kerry whispered, "Welcome to Tuvalu, Charlie."

Staring up at her in disbelief, Charlie struggled to grasp the transformation before him. No longer emaciated and gaunt, Kerry's eyes beamed with strength while her rejuvenated figure exuded unbridled vitality.

Self-conscious about her change in hair color, Kerry lightly brushed her chestnut locks with her fingers and demurred, "Do you like it?"

Still in shock, Charlie murmured, "It's perfect."

The two locked eyes for several moments before Kerry broke the trance, "There's someone else here who wants to see you too." Charlie glanced around the room as Kerry called towards the entryway, "He's awake!"

The bedroom door quickly burst open, and Auggie sprinted across the room, hugging Charlie around the neck with all his strength.

"Auggie!" Charlie exclaimed, as he stared in disbelief at the young man's unencumbered legs, "You're…"

"Cured," Auggie finished. "Most of us are. Even you!"

Charlie glanced at Kerry as she smiled and nodded, "It's true."

Stunned, Charlie slowly withdrew his arms from beneath his blankets, stretching them out in front of him. Taken aback, he stared in disbelief as they remained steady, no longer shaking.

"But how is that even possi –?"

"Modern medicine my boy," Michel Bouchon said as he bounded through the door with a veritable twinkle in his eye, "Modern medicine."

With both Hadron and Cern following closely behind him, Michel looked unrecognizable, his gait now powerful and his body's posture emanating vigor. His once greyish-blonde hair now returned, full and healthy, and the labored breaths that had defined his former frailty were gone. With his cheeks flush and no longer sunken, the entrepreneur embodied the picture of perfect health.

Charlie smiled as Michel joined Kerry and Auggie at his bedside while the German shepherds nudged at his hand.

"Of course," Michel began, "Your Parkinson's took a little longer to cure than some of the other ailments, such as Auggie's, but that's to be expected when restructuring the entire sequence of a human's DNA."

Charlie let out a sigh of relief as Michel's assurance confirmed that he was no longer afflicted, and once again, he noticed a twinkle in the man's eye.

However, Charlie's euphoria quickly dissipated as he impulsively glanced around the room, and a nauseating thought overwhelmed him, "Wait, what did you mean by 'a little longer'? What year is it?"

"Layah stopped us after only four years!" Auggie exclaimed.

Bewildered, Charlie looked at Kerry, "What? How is that even possible? They cured your cancer in just four years?"

Smiling, Michel said, "Actually, as Umberto will attest, it only took a few months to cure *all* cancers after we left. Thanks to the Photosynthesuits of course."

"Photosynthesuits?"

Charlie was sure he saw a sparkle in Michel's eye *this* time.

"Yes, like the one Layah was wearing when she rescued us. That version was one of the original iterations, which, I must admit, were quite bulky and cumbersome. But you've been gone for two years since our return, Charlie, and a lot can happen in that amount of time these days."

Michel gingerly touched his eye with his forefinger and held up a contact lens so that Charlie could see it, "Today, *this* is the Photosynthesuit!"

Awestruck, Charlie asked, "A contact lens?"

"Precisely. An innovative leap for an invention that freed all of us from the constraints of food. Much like the Everwake pill eliminated the need for sleep, today, we no longer have to eat."

Incredulous and unsure if he'd fully awoken, Charlie asked, "Am I missing something, Mr. Bouchon? How did not eating cure something like Kerry's cancer or my Parkinson's?"

Michel smiled as he wandered around the room, eager to explain, "When mankind evolved from a hunter-gatherer society to an agrarian one, it no longer had to spend the majority of its days struggling to find food. With the advent of farming came more free time, and those extra hours each day led to monumental societal advances in things like reading, writing and the creation of cities. Almost instantly, people's lives improved, and in much the same way, the Photosynthesuit has had a similar effect on us."

Michel returned to Charlie's bedside and continued, "Without the need to eat, humanity has used that extra time, money, and resources to improve every facet of our lives. Improvements, such as finding cures for diseases…and reimagining the Ouroboros."

"Reimagining?" Charlie began, "So when you said I was gone for two years after we were rescued, you meant –."

"I meant you've been gone for two years as far as the rest of us are concerned, but for you, it's been less than a few minutes. You've been time traveling since the day Layah first awoke us."

Confused, Charlie pressed, "Time traveling? So, I was placed back into the Ouroboros until a cure for Parkinson's could be found? But I thought you said your machine couldn't be restarted after it had been stopped?"

"The original couldn't, but you weren't placed into *the* Ouroboros…you were placed into *an* Ouroboros."

Stunned, Charlie asked, "So…there's more than one?"

Michel gave a chuckle and replied, "Technology has advanced, Charlie, and much like the modernization of computers, today's Ouroboros isn't nearly as big, but it is infinitely more powerful. For Oman, Ian, and so many others whose diseases have yet to be cured, they have their own Ouroboros, spinning inside until their individual panaceas are found."

"Unbelievable," Charlie murmured.

"In the end, we didn't have to wait until a cure for all diseases was invented; we just had to wait until the next version of the Ouroboros was."

Astonished by the man's genius, Charlie stared at Michel in awe, until a worrisome thought occurred, "And Devlin, what about him?"

"Oh, Mr. Archer? Yes, well, let's just say you won't be seeing him for quite some…time."

Michel gingerly placed a hand on Charlie's shoulder, "Rest assured, Charlie, you no longer have to worry about Devlin, your disease, or anything else ever again."

Unsure how to interpret Michel's affirmation, Charlie asked, "What do you mean?"

"I mean, I want you to be my guest, for as long as you like. Anything you've ever wanted is yours; any place you want to live, you can. What's mine is yours. You risked your life for ours, Charlie, and it's my small way of saying, 'Thank you.'"

Charlie smiled until he suddenly had a mischievous thought, "And what if I have expensive tastes, Mr. Bouchon? It sounded like you spent all of your money building the Ouroboros. Isn't it true that you're no longer a trillionaire?"

With a hearty laugh and a genuine sparkle in his eye this time, Michel replied, "You're right, Charlie, I'm not a trillionaire. But just before Layah exposed Yan's blind trust, she made sure to short-sell his stock with the seventy-two billion dollars he paid me, so today… I'm now a *multi*-trillionaire."

Shocked, Charlie asked, "So, you're even wealthier than you were before?"

"I suppose," Michel began, as he locked eyes with Kerry, "but as someone I know once said, 'What's the point of all of that money, if you don't have the time or loved ones to share it with?'"

Smiling at the inference, Charlie slowly pulled back his bed sheets and rested his feet on the lavishly tiled floor, flexing his toes. Gingerly swinging an arm around Auggie's shoulder and another around Kerry's waist, he carefully rose from his bed and hobbled to the sunlit balcony that overlooked the crystal blue water below.

Standing beside Kerry and Auggie as the warm breeze kissed their faces, Charlie absorbed the magnificence in front of him and couldn't help but marvel at how much his life had changed in such a short period of time. The overwhelming depression that had engulfed each day and his fear of a life potentially cut short no longer consumed him. Now, he only felt the kindness and compassion of those around him and the optimism that comes from the hope of a promising future.

Glancing back at the bed, Charlie squeezed Kerry and Auggie a little tighter, realizing - for the first time - that he was looking forward to taking one of Michel Bouchon's pills, and never sleeping again.

Sensing Charlie's contentment as he watched his three guests embrace and take in the splendor before them, Michel walked towards the bedroom's doorway with Hadron and Cern in tow, before slowly turning around and offering, "But Charlie, don't forget what happened to the man who suddenly got everything he always wanted."

Bewildered, Charlie asked, "What happened?"

With a wry smile, Michel replied, "He lived happily ever after."

The End

EPILOGUE

Devlin's lethargy began to fade as he groggily came to. To his surprise, he found himself being pushed in a rickety wheelchair down a long, sterile hallway. The squeaking of rubber tires and the harsh brightness of the corridor jolted his senses, forcing him to regain his bearings.

Noticing him awaken, Gatlin chided, "Glad you could join us, Mr. Archer. You've been unconscious for quite some time, but it looks like your surgery was a success. You'll be happy to know that you should make a full recovery from your injury."

Devlin shook his head, disoriented, but quickly realized his arms and legs were strapped to the wheelchair, immobile and restricting his movements. Struggling against the restraints, he found his efforts frustratingly futile.

Incensed, he blurted, "What…what's going on here? Where the hell am I?"

Gatlin smiled as he continued to push the spy down the expansive hallway, "Not to worry, Mr. Archer, you're in your new home."

A chill ran down Delvin's spine. His palms began to sweat as memories of his dark days in the Panamanian jail crept back from the recesses of his mind. Gatlin's words echoed in his ears, hauntingly reminiscent of what his captors once said.

No…not again.

Despite the anxiety welling inside him, he fought to maintain his composure, and like he had so many times before, Devlin stifled the overwhelming urge to scream.

"Like a prisoner?" Devlin asked, his voice low, a mix of dread and disbelief.

"Of course not, Mr. Archer," Gatlin said, his tone dripping with faux sympathy. "Like a guest."

Self-assured, Devlin's confidence snapped back, "A 'guest'? Please. Yan is bound to come looking for me. I'm much too valuable of an asset for him to lose."

Feigning genuine concern, Gatlin furrowed his brow. "Yan? I don't recall a…ah, yes, Mr. Huen."

He let the name linger before continuing.

"Well, Mr. Archer, you may be disappointed to learn that once the media caught wind of just how much money he'd spent on your spot, a run on his company's stock ensued. As a result, its price collapsed and, unfortunately, Mr. Huen was left penniless."

"Penniless?" Devlin mumbled in stunned disbelief, "Impossible…"

Panic surged through Devlin as the realization hit – if Gatlin was telling the truth, the money he'd been promised was gone. The ninety-nine million dollars he was still owed would no longer be waiting for him, and if Yan were truly bankrupt, he might never be able to collect.

Surely, though, Devlin reassured himself, Yan must have stashed away *some* money that he could still tap into. An emergency fund of some kind. Yes, together, they would figure out an arrangement that, although not exactly like the one they had initially agreed upon, could work if they just –.

Gatlin continued, interrupting Devlin's internal delusions, "Yes, penniless, Mr. Archer. And I'm afraid to say, as a consequence, poor Mr. Huen committed suicide some years ago."

The weight of this revelation washed over Devlin, leaving him stunned. Struggling to process the magnitude of what he had just heard, his vision blurred, and his mind raced to comprehend the seemingly impossible truth.

Savoring Devlin's profound shock at this news, Gatlin let his words hang in the air, heavy and suffocating. He slowly bent down behind him, his voice a cold whisper of finality, "So, you see, Mr. Archer…there is no one coming to look for you."

Silence followed.

The faint squeak of the wheelchair's tires were the only sounds that accompanied the spy's tortured thoughts as the two men approached a colossal set of doors, with Gatlin forcibly pushing Devlin through.

As they entered a massive warehouse, Devlin was stunned by the sight before him. Countless containers, each one the size of an above-ground pool, stretched across the cavernous space as far as his azure eyes could see. A distinctive hum resonated from every one, like a mechanized orchestra performing its own symphony.

The circular containers resembled giant tuna cans, neatly stacked atop one another by scores of colossal robotic arms that moved at a frenetic pace.

The whirl of activity was hypnotic, almost dizzying. Devlin's senses were overwhelmed by the noise, the movement, and the sheer scale of the operation before him. It was like nothing he had ever seen – an industrial beehive of staggering proportions, each arm moving with flawless precision.

Still reeling from disbelief, Devlin's gaze slowly settled on two figures standing on either side of a similar container, strategically placed directly before him. His thoughts spun as he was unsure if he recognized the pair.

Was it possible?

"Thank you, Gatlin," Gilbert said, his voice steady and his eyes sharp.

"My *pleasure*," the stoic Tuvaluan replied, a coy smile spreading across his face as he turned, leaving the physicists with their prize.

To Devlin's utter shock, Gilbert was reborn. The frail, sickly man once consumed by cognitive decline, had vanished. In his place stood a figure brimming with vitality. The debilitating disease that had once ravaged the scientific genius was nowhere to be found.

Gilbert now looked like the visionary he had once been — poised, confident, and strong.

Turning his attention to Devlin, Gilbert slowly opened the door to the circular container, his voice clear and powerful as he said, "Welcome, Mr. Archer. We've been expecting you."

Devlin, still dumbfounded, fought to find the words, "Gilbert? You look...You sound...What is all of this?"

Gilbert purposefully approached Devlin and rested his now sturdy hand on the operative's shoulder, "This is the newest version of the Ouroboros, Mr. Archer. Small enough and powerful enough to send a single person into the future."

As Devlin processed this concept, Layah silently stepped behind him and took hold of the wheelchair's push handles.

"Today," Gilbert continued, "that single person...is you."

With a sly wink, Gilbert nodded to Layah. As she pushed Devlin toward the diminutive Ouroboros, an instinctive surge of adrenaline shot through the spy, sparking a desperate struggle against his restraints. Powerless to escape, he watched in agonizing slow-motion as she placed him inside.

Closing the capsule's door with deliberate resolve, Layah ignored the widening terror in Devlin's piercing blue eyes as he pleaded, "Layah! I'm begging you! Don't!"

With a look of reproach, Layah gently leaned in behind Devlin's ear, her voice low and unwavering, meant only for him to hear.

"You tried to take my husband from me, Mr. Archer..."

"No! Please!"

"Godspeed, and until next...*eon*."

Shutting the door tightly, Layah turned a knob on the outside of the container, setting the year to "1,000,000 A.D". In an instant, a massive robotic arm descended from the rafters, its powerful claws deftly gripping the miniaturized time machine.

Wrapping their arms around one another, the architects of the Ouroboros watched the container whisk away down an aisle lined with countless others.

As they turned to leave, the corridor behind them echoed with the terrified screams of Devlin Archer.

www.ingramcontent.com/pod-product-compliance
Lightning Source LLC
Chambersburg PA
CBHW020403110726

47899CB00006B/1832